Red Zone Realizations

EMILY REX

Published by Park Lane, LLC

First US Edition: November 2025

Paperback ISBN: 979-8-9987408-0-0

Cover: Ink and Laurel

Editor: Elaine York

To everyone out there staying true to themselves regardless of what society says.

Prologue

AUDREY

SIX MONTHS AGO

I read somewhere that you can bounce back from anything in a relationship except disgust. Once you're disgusted by your partner, there is no coming back from that. It's the end of the road.

I discovered that truth tonight at our engagement party. I'd gone into the kitchen to grab more chips to put out for the dip when I overheard Hunter, my fiancé, talking to his mom.

"We'll probably wait a few years to start trying for kids," he told her.

"Well, don't wait too long. Time goes faster than you think. You'll blink and the next thing you know, you'll be thirty," his mom replied.

"I don't intend to wait that long. Audrey talks a big game, but I think she'll have changed her mind before we're thirty. When all our friends are slowing down, she'll see that this is what life is meant to be about—our purpose." He paused. "No one has their mind made up for that long. We all change as we grow older, it's inevitable."

I heard his mother's earrings, always oversized, jingle as she shook her head at him. "I'm not sure you know that girl as well as you think you do. She isn't uninterested in children because that's what everyone expects of her. She truly feels that way in her heart—that children aren't in either of your future."

"That's why she says she doesn't want kids, but would she be willing to stand on those same principles if it meant losing me? Us? Family?" he said, gesturing at the party going on around us.

I'd reeled back as if I had been slapped and was unable to listen to his drivel any longer. I could feel the acid welling up into my throat, and it only took me a split second to realize what that was.

Disgust.

Absolute repulsion.

I knew in an instant that what he said about losing him over my long-held beliefs was true because yes, I could—and would—walk away from our relationship without blinking an eye. Somehow, I kept it together until we got home, but I couldn't fathom going to bed and lying next to this man for even one moment longer.

———

A few hours later, long after this sham of an engagement party ended, I set my marquise engagement ring on the kitchen table in front of Hunter. It makes a quick click as it lands. I stare at it like it's a snake in the grass ready to strike. Then my gaze travels to the man in the chair across from me.

The man who had slipped that ring on my finger a year ago. He had looked so handsome down on one knee in the restaurant we had our first date. His brown eyes were confident but questioning. His soft brown hair had been freshly cut and perfectly styled. Looking at him now, though, I don't see any of that man in him anymore. It's like I had imagined him.

"I can't do this."

"Do what, Audrey?" Hunter's voice is low, like he knows exactly what I'm talking about.

"Be with you anymore," I say under my breath.

Hunter runs his hands over his face as if tired by my dramatics. "What is this really about?"

I gather all the courage I've ever had to speak my truth. "You know I don't want kids."

"I know you say that." He pauses. "I didn't think you meant it."

"You never thought to ask me? Instead, you tell your mom you know me better than I know myself?"

"Eventually you'll change your mind. Every woman does. We're young right now."

"I won't, though."

"You can't possibly know that now." At the very least, he's consistent in his messaging.

"You know what? You're right. We are too young." I cross my arms over my chest, the weight comforting. "Too young to get married."

He stands, leaning over the table. "You don't mean that."

My throat is too constricted with emotion to talk, so instead, I nod. He drops back in the chair, all the fight gone out of him. Silence falls between us. There's nothing left to say. I can't magically become who he wants me to be. I won't. Kids are the one thing in my world that has no compromise. You can't have half of a kid.

He's unknowingly hit me where it hurts the most. He can't understand how much I want to want what everyone else seems to know intuitively. When I was made, there was a piece of me missing. I have never had the desire for children. I've never had baby fever. I see moms smiling, holding their baby, looking like the entire world is in their arms, and I feel... nothing. Happy for them, of course, but there's no tug in my gut, no swelling of my heart. Just stillness. Now, I've come to understand that the stillness differentiates me. It makes me part of the other. I will never willingly feel that way again.

I walk down the hallway, the click of my kitten heels resounding against the hardwood, as I enter our bedroom to pack a bag. Panties, bras, pajamas, shorts, and T-shirts. The rest I can come get later, right now I'd do anything to get out of this apartment. To stop feeling the weight of this failed engagement hanging in the air like smoke after fireworks.

On my way out of our apartment, I walk right by Hunter. Still where I left him at the kitchen table, staring at the glint coming off my ring. I expected he would have more to say. He sure had an awful lot to say to his mother tonight about what I do and do not want, but he remains silent as I turn the door handle to leave. The silence from him isn't surprising considering the bomb I just dropped, but it's certainly deafening as I close one chapter in my life.

I pull out my phone and dial Nicole's number. She answers in two rings.

"I'm coming over. I'll be there in ten."

I don't remember any of the drive to Nicole's, but I've done it so many times I could probably do it with my eyes closed.

They may as well be. My memories with Hunter roll in my mind's eye like a film.

Nicole wraps me in her arms when I arrive. Tears sting my eyes. "It's over," I whisper.

She holds me tight. "It's going to be all right."

She lets me go and I place my duffle on her couch. We sit close. "What happened? Do you want to talk about it?"

"You've known me since elementary school."

She nods. "I was there through your whole tomboy phase. When you refused to wear anything pink."

"Thank God that was a phase, but..." My breath hitches. "My not wanting kids wasn't. That's something I'm dead set on, Nicole."

"I know." She has never once judged me. Not when I told her the first time that I thought I might not want kids, even though we used to discuss name ideas. Not when I left the Catholic faith we had been raised in together.

"Apparently, Hunter didn't." I sniff a laugh, but it sounds liquid in my throat. "He thought I would change my mind. I overheard him telling his mom tonight."

"Why didn't you come find me at the party and tell me?"

My cheeks are hot, burning with second-hand embarrassment. "And ruin my engagement party in front of everyone? Be the hysterical crying bride?" I shake my head. "No way."

"Well, you're here now. We don't have to handle everything tonight. You can stay here as long as you need." I hug her, fully wrapping my arms around her. I smell her floral shampoo and feel the comfort that only a childhood friend can bring you.

She tucks me under her arm, leading me toward her bed.

Since elementary school, we've never slept in separate beds during sleepovers. We always shared her bed. Tonight is no different. Having the weight and warmth of her next to me helps keep me calm as the reality of what I'd done crashes around me. My heartbeat plays an erratic tune, and I take deep breaths to try and slow it. I pull out my phone, and open the notes app to start a list:

1. Get the rest of my stuff.

2 Find a place to live.

3. Swear off men.

4. Buy a vibrator.

At the ripe old age of twenty-nine, I'm going to have to start over.

Having the steps laid out in order makes the lizard part of my brain happy. Nothing is impossible when broken down into attainable steps. At least that's what I tell myself as I review the list and listen to Nicole's gentle breathing as she sleeps. The heaviness of the argument and the exhaustion from socializing are apparently too much for me to fight. What I assume would be a fitful night of regret and tangled emotions that prevent me from falling asleep turns into the opposite and I am somehow able to find sleep. Maybe this is my subconscious telling me I'd made the right choice to leave?

————

In the morning, I check my phone and wake up to twenty texts. Some from Hunter, others from my family. None are supportive. The top one from my sister, Sarah, simply reads, *What did you do?!* I knew Hunter was up my family's ass, but I didn't think he would immediately run to them and expose his belly like a scared puppy.

I guess it's time to face the music.

But at least this time, the tune and the lyrics will be completely my own.

Chapter One

AUDREY

MAY

I check my phone. Four forty-five. I'm sitting in the drive-thru line at the bank on a busy Thursday afternoon, depositing a check for my family's business, Space City Auto. I barely made it to the bank before they closed after stuffing a PB&J in my mouth. I spent the morning babysitting my nephew Mikey for my younger sister Sarah. She had a doctor's appointment to get to, so I took Mikey to the park. It's been a very long day—hell, a very long week—and I didn't even have time for a proper lunch. At this point, I might not make it to yoga class on time.

I still have to respond to Polly, my client who's waiting on a contract from a sponsor, and make a short form video for my social media management business, but I also have errands to run for my mother, this bank deposit being one of them.

The teller asks me to put the check in the tube after I tell her I just need to deposit it. This has been my job every week since coming home from college. You'd think that my brother,

Lane, would be doing errands like this, since he'll eventually take over the auto parts store, but no.

I bid Melinda, the teller, goodbye as I pull away. Big Power Yoga isn't far, and if I hurry, I'll be able to get my regular spot.

Thankfully, I get every green light and make it in record time. When I pull open the door, I'm hit with the familiar fragrance of frankincense. Joe is the Thursday evening teacher, and a big fan of incense. The best way to tell a great yoga teacher from a mediocre one is how wild their instructions get. A good yoga teacher might tell you to "breathe into your ribs," but an amazing one (the Joe kind) will tell you to "breathe the earth below into your toes and feel the vibrations releasing from your fingertips as you stretch them out and away from each other."

That's the very definition of digging into your soul and finding inner peace.

As I approach the desk, the warmth of the studio envelops me like a hug. Hot yoga is its own special kind of masochism, but one of which I am a dedicated patron. After years of coming to this same studio three days a week, it feels a little like coming home. Or, at the very least, what I imagine it must have been like on those old TV shows like *Cheers*, walking into the same townie bar every Friday night. I walk up to the front desk where Gigi is checking people in. Her long, dark hair hangs loose down her back and a smile blooms across her face when she sees me approaching, my hands full. Water bottle, keys, phone, mat, towel… all balancing precariously.

"Hey, Audrey! How are you today?"

"I'm good," I reply.

She nods. "Okay, you're all checked in. Enjoy your class."

The five-fifteen class is always upstairs, so I head up the rounded staircase to the second floor and over to the cubes. I set my mat down so I can unload everything else from my arms and get my shoes tucked away in the cubby. I unceremoniously hike my leggings up one more time, then shoulder my mat, grab my other stuff, and head toward the door of the yoga room. I grab my usual rectangle on the floor. It's almost like a lingering habit from college—where you sat on the first day became *your* seat all semester.

After unrolling my mat, I settle in to do a few stretches while waiting for class to start. I take this time to let the heat of the room warm my muscles. Working on taking my focus off the day and my never-ending to-do list.

I'm casually glancing around the room while stretching my left arm over my chest, telling myself I'm not looking for anyone in particular... but I am.

I'm looking for Hot Yoga Guy.

I cross my legs on my mat and listen as Joe talks to us before class starts. He has dark, shaggy hair. He's not the type of person you'd look at and think he's an experienced yoga teacher, but when he strikes a firefly pose and he's got both his legs off the ground, you'll be convinced. You can tell he's been a yoga teacher for a long time. I feel the whoosh of cooler air run over my shoulders as the door behind me opens and someone walks in and down the row. Out of the corner of my eye, I catch a glimpse of athletic leggings.

The sexiest thing a man can wear is those tights under athletic shorts. It's the male equivalent of just hinting at what could be underneath. *Man cleavage.* A couple of the dudes here wear them, but I only have eyes for this one.

He lays his mat down at the back of the class, as per usual. He always practices against the back wall. Just like I always sit by the door. I silently think that he did the same thing in college, like me. Waiting for the class to start, I find myself wondering what he's like in real life. Is he a coffee drinker? Does he have the gene that makes cilantro taste like soap? What does he do for work?

He's in amazing shape. The muscles on his arms and calves are defined. It hits you immediately when you see him. After his muscles, his green eyes are what stand out the most. Not emerald or forest, but more like a proud pine. One that stands high above the other trees. They're surrounded by dark lashes that would make most women jealous. His hair is so dark brown it's almost black, and the same color of heavy but neatly kept brows makes his green eyes pop even more.

I'm jolted out of my gawking when Joe starts class. His voice is soothing as he instructs us to move into child's pose. We flow in unison for the next twenty-five minutes. The air in the room is humid, a balmy ninety-five degrees compared to the May breeze outside. Despite the sweet distraction of the man behind me, I find myself lost in the flow, feeling only my inhales and exhales as the tension leaves my body. I feel my feet planted on the mat and the sweat dripping long rivers down my face. It's a pleasant, satisfying kind of exhaustion. The practice is meant to make you struggle, meant to break you apart until you're just a body on the earth taking in oxygen.

"On your breath in, face the right side of the room. Lift your chest toward the ceiling, and on an exhale, bend forward for a wide-legged forward fold," Joe instructs the room.

I'm an avid yogi, but I'm still human, and I cannot help that my eyes wander.

I'm immediately glancing around the room looking to see who will move upside down into a headstand. There's a couple in the front row who's here all the time, and I know they will find their headstand with ease. They're both ripped. I have no idea what else they do besides this, but I wouldn't be surprised if it's CrossFit.

My eyes land (naturally) on Hot Yoga Guy. He's currently hanging out in his forward fold with his black-clad booty toward me. He straightens up for just a second to readjust his feet and sinks deeper into his fold. I catch the sight of a bead of sweat dripping down the strong arm closest to me. It continues down his forearm, sliding over delicious bands of blood vessels. Here I am, in a wide-legged forward fold on a Thursday evening in May, ogling a perfect man with a perfect ass, whom I have never spoken a single word to.

I'm hopeless.

I follow the line of his arm to his hands which he gently rests on the floor next to his foot. For the first time, I notice an angry red scar along his ankle. It looks fresh, the skin still shiny. I wonder again who this man is outside of Big Power Yoga.

"The light in me sees and celebrates the exact same light in you. Namaste." Joe bows his head, ending the class.

With my hands held to my third eye center I bow in return. "Namaste."

I clap along when the rest of the room does. We don't always clap, it really depends on the vibe. I usually just go along with what everyone else decides to do. The feeling of the room is tired but lighthearted. People are greeting their neighbors and making small talk. I scoot off my mat so I can roll it up and put its strap on it, giggling in my head at my own words—*Ha. Strap on.* I pick up all my yoga shit and walk out of the room to retrieve my shoes and belt bag.

As I'm digging in my cube, I overhear Joe talking to a student. "How's the ankle feeling, Noah?" His voice has a very distinct lilt to it that's easy to recognize.

A deeper voice replies, "Good, thanks. I think the balancing poses are really building the strength back in it."

My ears perk up.

Oh my God. Was that Hot Yoga Guy?

Noah.

"I'm so glad you were able to spend some of your recovery time with us."

It's everything I can do right now to keep my eyes fixated on my bag like it could sprout legs and walk off when all I want to do is stare at him. The back of my neck prickles like someone is looking at me. I turn just barely to peek over my shoulder to find Noah looking right at me. I quickly turn back to my bag and shove everything in it. I've got to get out of here.

"It's way more fun than the team training room. They're always forcing me into the cold tub." He chuffs a laugh. "I think I'm going to be back to one hundred percent for training camp."

I can hear the smile in his words even though I can't see it.

Team? Training room? Who is this guy? I figured he was just another finance bro with a penchant for a good sweat. He's ripped, but lots of students here participate in other harder workouts and do yoga on their rest days. Not that I'd ever admit it out loud, but these classes *are* my hard days.

I turn and head toward the door, sneaking one last glance at him. His familiar form graces my eyes. His eyes flick to me again and I duck from his gaze. He's definitely taller than my dad, who is over six feet. Strong, so it makes sense that he spends some time in a training room. We've spoken nary a word, besides polite greetings and "excuse me" when we're in each other's way, but I always catch him looking at me. I must perpetually have a piece of food stuck in my teeth from lunch or something. Otherwise, I don't know what he could be looking at. Now that I know his name, I'm pretty positive that he doesn't know mine. But it sounds like he won't be back for a while, however long this training camp is he referred to?

Not that it matters because six months ago I swore off men anyway.

Then why have I been coming to this class for months... and quietly watching out for Noah every week?

Chapter Two

NOAH

Audrey walks by me on her way out the door looking deliciously ruffled, her brown ponytail all messed up from savasana. Lying on her back must pull some of the hair loose from its hold. She's got that matching legging set I love on today—the black camo one. It matches the brand on her mat. Whenever I catch her looking at me, I try to make eye contact, try to show her that I'm open to saying hi. Gigi greeted her by name once, that's the only reason I know it.

I thank Joe for a great class and head to the cubes to get my stuff. Sweat drips down my forehead and I errantly wipe it with my towel. I'm feeling looser now than I was this morning. Who says football players can't be flexible? Hopefully that's something Coach can see when I return for preseason training camp next week.

My mind drifts to the last football season. It's the last game before playoffs and we aren't in the mix, once again. We had to fight hard, reaching for those precious postseason games, but we came up empty. Talk about adding insult to injury.

The stadium is loud with opposing fans. A rematch with our rivals, the Miami Hammerheads, who beat the shit out of us in the beginning of the season. I have hope that our next matchup will end with us victorious because it's extremely hard to beat a team twice in the NFL. We're only down by six and on our last offensive drive. I jog into the huddle, ready to hear the play Colin calls.

"Forty-two, on three, on three!" he yells.

We all clap in unison and step up to the line of scrimmage. Careful not to be too close or too far. I watch as Colin sees the defense shift to adjust to us. "Kill-kill, kill-kill!"

He didn't like the defense he saw so he shot the previous play. He thinks something else will be better, and as a team we have to trust our quarterback.

"BLUE FORTY-TWO!" He stomps his right foot, calling me in motion. I take off from my spot to the right of Wyatt, our defensive tackle, running behind Colin. Moving from my blocking slot to my receiving spot for this new play, as tight ends often do. As I swipe past him, he yells, "Hut!"

The ball is snapped. I take off straight through a narrow seam in the defensive line. My defenseman is trailing me, trying to keep a hand on me. I'm going as far as I can as fast as I run directly toward the end zone.

I turn to look back at Colin. His eyes meet mine and I can see him ready to launch it. He drops back as the pocket starts to collapse around him and blasts it. I track it with my eyes as I run the slant toward the end zone. The ball is a little high, so I jump, hands ready to contest for the football. It hits my gloves as gravity brings me back down. The safety had time to catch up while I was waiting for the ball to stop careening through the air. We tangle in midair as he tries to get a hand in to break up the play. There's nothing I can do to keep myself from falling awkwardly. A defenseless receiver.

I land on my right foot first and the pain is instant.

The play over.

My season ended there. I've been clawing my way back ever since. Surgery, recovery, months of physical therapy. I was bored and restless not being able to move like I did before. The stillness of injury is uncomfortable when you're used to the level of movement of a professional athlete. When the trainer suggested yoga, I was desperate for anything that would allow me some physical freedom. I discussed it with my therapist, a little gun-shy to get back out there. She encouraged it because yoga has so many mental health benefits.

Needless to say, I loved it.

At first I looked forward to coming to yoga because it let me stretch my tight body, and allowed me to get out of my own head for sixty minutes. It only took about three classes for me to notice Audrey. At first it was just the way her yoga pants hugged her curves, but as time went on, I noticed how she greeted every employee with a genuine smile. How she knew all of them by name. It's been six long months of wanting to introduce myself to her, but she's always so focused when she gets here, clearly on a mission to get in a good workout, that I didn't want to disturb her. I hate when someone walks up to me as I get ready for a weight set and tries to start a conversation, and just because this is a yoga studio and not the Hurricanes' weight room doesn't mean she doesn't have that same right.

So even though sometimes it physically hurts me, I keep my mouth shut and my hellos to myself.

Chapter Three

AUDREY

I'm sitting in the left-hand turn lane on my way home from class. I switch on my blinker as I wait to cross over Waugh Bridge. In two hours, two-hundred-fifty-thousand bats will emerge from under the bridge and fly off into the night in search of food. Almost every night a small crowd gathers to watch. I see an older man out of the corner of my eye. Houston has seven-million people in its metro area, so it's not unusual to see unhoused people near the highways. This gentleman has a beard, jeans, and is in a wheelchair. I undo my center console to dig around for random protein bars I keep in there.

I come up short on food, and when I glance back up to see if the light has turned green, I see a familiar face approaching the man. Holy crap. With seven-million people, what are the chances of me being at this light, at this exact moment, when I just left that tall drink of water at yoga?

Hot Yoga Guy, whom I now know is Noah.

They shake hands and Noah sits on the concrete barrier next to him. They make small talk. *Oh my God. He's hot, athletic, and a humanitarian?* They're obviously familiar with each other, judging by the ease of Noah's posture.

Noah must live close enough to walk to class. I could never do that. I'm so exhausted by the end I can barely get myself in my car. Does he live really that close? Or is he trying to erase his carbon footprint by walking as much as he can?

As I'm taking him in, my phone rings through my speakers. I click the answer button on the dash.

"This is Audrey."

"It's Shelby. I'm calling to see if you had a chance to respond to my email from this morning?" I have to refrain from rolling my eyes. That email barely hit my inbox before noon today, but of course it was *this morning*.

"I did. I'm still waiting to hear back from the brand about the payment details of the sponsorship. You told me your financial expectations, and I intend to have them met." She already knows this because we discussed it two weeks ago. The sound of my professional voice grates in my ears.

"I can't wait to see what they say."

I want to say, *obviously*, but instead I say, "That's great! Thanks so much for your patience. I'll chat with you later." I click the end button before she can ask more questions.

When I started my own social media management firm, I thought filling this niche would be easy. My shiny business degree would say I'm qualified, but they don't teach entrepreneurship at Houston University. Marketing, taxes, fees, all that you have to learn on your own. And I'm proud of myself for doing it. When I called off my engagement to Hunter, it was easy to throw myself into my work even more. A business owner's to-do list is never complete, but now that I've had all this extra time on my hands, I've been even more focused.

I pull into my driveway, and I know that I have work to do, but I can't help that my mind drifts back to Hot Yoga Guy. Noah... That's a great name for him. Google tells me it means "rest" and "repose." I can see that. He has a calmness about him, a sure-footedness. Maybe that's because I've only ever seen him at yoga. He's obviously some kind of athlete. I would never have considered a pro athlete to be so... salt of the earth. Maybe he's in a minor league? That's entirely possible. Houston is full of sports teams.

The second I step foot in my house I'm on my phone pulling up Google. I type *Noah professional athlete Houston* in the search bar. I hesitate before I hit search. Is this stalker behavior? Or am I simply fulfilling my natural curiosity? I decide it's completely natural to wonder and hit the search button.

The first two results are for a guy named Noah who currently runs track at the university downtown, so that's not him. The next one down is a player page for the Hurricanes, Houston's NFL team. I click the link and I'm looking at Noah's headshot. He looks almost the same as he did in yoga today; his hair is just a bit longer in the photo. He's number forty-nine, tight end. It has a bunch of stats listed, but I don't know what any of them mean. That doesn't matter. It's enough that I've confirmed my suspicions and hushed my curiosity.

I leave that there for tonight. Or I try anyway, but when I finally collapse into bed, I lay there for hours staring at the ceiling, thinking about Noah, about what life as an NFL player might be like and what brings him to a tiny yoga studio in the Heights.

Chapter Four

NOAH

JULY

How a team performs in the red zone will make or break them. It's where the biggest decisions and the biggest mistakes are made. Slinging it from the twenty-yard line of your opponent's end zone is either high scoring or high turnover. You can walk away with a touchdown or screw it up and give the other team a safety. That's why we practice red zone drills—specific plays to manage our time starting off at the twenty-yard line.

Under a partly cloudy sky we walk through shoot routes with the corner over the top. I run a deep out route, and we practice them against different possible zone defenses.

Wyatt saunters over to me. "We look good this season."

I nod as I watch Wyatt, our defensive lineman, slide through the cracks in the defensive line and run into the end zone. "I agree. Wouldn't it be crazy to win big in your first season here?" I look over to him, using my hand to shield the sun from my eyes, but he doesn't meet my gaze. He just stands, hands on his hips, looking out at the other men on the field. There's a reservation to his face that I don't understand. He just came from Green Bay on a trade, and I feel like the team has been welcoming, but I get a sense that this team wasn't what he wanted. Like he's making the best of the hand of cards he's been dealt. After our field time, Jaden lets loose a huge belch as we get dressed in the locker room.

Man, it's good to be back.

Sixty-five men are here fighting for a spot on the fifty-three-man roster. Not me, thank God. I'm in the last year of my rookie contract. Every time it's a crazy three weeks. The most recent memories I have of the Houston Hurricanes' facilities aren't great. They mostly involved ice baths and physical therapy. A long summer of workouts with Colin, our quarterback and my best friend, have kept me in shape, but not game ready.

I stack my binders one on top of the other and shove them in my backpack. I'll organize them later. I'm running late as it is.

On my way out of the building, I walk under the Hurricane chandelier. Ninety-four, long glass poles hang from the tall ceiling over the main entrance. Each pole represents a season of the Hurricanes, the year detailed on the bottom. They're color coded to the outcome of each season. White for a winning season, navy for a losing season, and red for a Super Bowl year. In nearly a century of football, only one red pole hangs.

I intend to change that this year. We're ready.

I normally take my time leaving, stopping to chat with coaches and teammates, but I've got to get across town to catch one last yoga class before football is in full swing—before my contract says I can't.

My regular attire is workout gear, so no need to change. I

pull into the parking lot of Big Power Yoga and fling my door open. I grab my mat, towel, and water, and jog toward the door. I push through with my shoulder, my mind solely on making it up the stairs in time.

Putting one foot through the door, I hear a surprised *oomph*, followed by the sound of the door hitting something. Full contact is kind of my deal, but this isn't good. I glance up, an apology on the tip of my tongue, and I'm shocked.

Staring back at me, pain etched on her face, is Audrey.

And she has her hands over her nose. She looks up at me and my heart sinks in my chest. Her beautiful brown eyes are wide with shock, and I feel like the world's biggest asshole.

"Oh my God! I'm so sorry! Are you okay?" I put my hands on her shoulders in an attempt to steady her. I realize this is kind of intimate for two people who simply exist around each other, but never speak. I'm afraid she's going to cry or hit me back. "I was in a rush, and I wasn't paying attention!"

"It's not that bad." She touches gingerly around her nose. "It doesn't feel broken."

"You should still go to urgent care and have them look at it. I could take you if you need a ride?"

"I'm good," she says but her eyes are watering. She takes her hand away from her face for a second and small drops of blood splatter on her palms. "But there is one teensy problem."

I'm hovering. I'm totally hovering, but I can't help it. My body is coiled with tension and ready to jump into action for whatever she needs. Anything to assuage this guilt building in my chest. "What?" My eyes are solely focused on her. I notice her gaze is a little hazy, like she can't fully see me standing in front of her. I put my hands under her elbows for support.

"Blood makes me pass out." And then she's gone.

Unconscious.

I knocked her out.

Well, *I* didn't. The blood did. But I caused the blood! This normally poised woman is in a heap in my arms, and I hover, knees bent, above the floor. Bearing her weight, I move my legs out from under me and sit on my butt. I do my best not to jostle her, fearing I'll make things worse. Her head is in my lap, and though everyone is buzzing around me, I can't help but take in the delicate details of her face. Tousled brown hair, still damp with sweat. The gentle slope of her nose. Even the bow of her upper lip isn't sharp. It's delicate. And looking at it this close, like a true creep, I wonder how it tastes. A little line of blood trickles out of her nose.

"I need a napkin or a tissue," I call to anyone who is listening. I don't mean to bark orders but there's an unconscious woman in my arms. A yoga teacher rushes over with a tissue and a pamphlet that details all the different ways to purchase classes and fans her with it.

I wait one second.

Two.

Three.

Finally, her eyes flutter.

I breathe a sigh of relief. I had no idea I was literally frozen in place waiting for her to come back. To look up at me with her brown eyes, which are the softest color rather than rich like chocolate. "Audrey, can you hear me?" Something like *mmmurrmmm* comes out of her mouth. "I'll take that as a yes."

I hold the tissues to her face. Thankfully, the blood has already stopped.

"We're going to sit you on the bench," I tell her as I place my other hand under her knees and lift her into my arms. She's so light even though she's leaning her full weight into me. Curling up against me like she can't help curving into my chest. When she's safely deposited on the bench and has a cup of cool water in her hands to sip on, I slide in next to her. Her delicate pink lips touch the cup as she tips a little sip of water into her mouth. "I'm so sorry. I can't believe I did that. I was in a rush. I wasn't looking where I was going."

"I'm fine," she says, but her laugh is breathless, and she squeezes her eyes shut as another wave of dizziness hits her. I move to kneel in front of her, worried she'll go out again and tumble forward.

"Let me make it up to you. Please. Anything you want. Coffee? Do you drink coffee? Of course you do, everyone does." I pause and think. "Is this worth more than coffee? Dinner?" I'm frantically trying to come up with a fair way to make this up to her. If she doesn't accept me—I mean my apology—I'll be condemned to live with this horrible feeling for the rest of my life.

"It's really not necessary. That could have been anyone." But it happened to her.

"You'll make me feel so much better if you let me do this for you. Really, you'd be helping me."

She looks around us; there's at least five people standing in a tight circle seeing what all the commotion is about. She looks back at me, this time her eyes are guarded again. "I promise, it's okay."

My brain is mush and I'm scrambling for something—anything to make this better. "Please just take my number. If you do go to the doctor, send me the bill. I want to pay for it. It's all my fault."

"You really don't have to—"

"Please," I beg. And she must read something on my face that says I'm sincere because she holds her phone out to me and I quickly put my number in and save it. She looks at the new contact and then looks back at me like she's trying to match the name to the face. I realize that while I've been flirting with her from afar, we've never been formally introduced. I hold my hand out for her to shake. "Noah Fox."

A shy smile splits her lips even though she does her best to tame it, but she takes my hand anyway. Her palm is a little sweaty, but I would never hold it against her. "Audrey Dupree. Nice to finally meet you."

Chapter Five

AUDREY

After getting out of the shower, I lean close to the mirror and check on my poor nose. I touch it lightly on each side and on the bridge. It's a bit tender, but it's definitely not broken. I might have to call Chelsea, the client I was supposed to have dinner with tomorrow night, and tell her that I have to cancel since my face might be black and blue.

Nicole will be here any minute for our weekly *Survivor* episode. She works Wednesday nights so we're streaming it tonight. I've been dodging spoilers online all week. I'm hoping they bring back the auction this season, and tonight might be the night. I want to see someone spend all their money on a giant fish eyeball—and actually eat it.

A key sounds in the door and I know it's her. She has my only spare.

"I've got boxed wine and the Whirley Pop Popcorn Maker!" she announces as she lets herself in. What started as an excuse to see each other on a school night in high school continued over video chat when we went to different colleges.

It has reemerged as my favorite night of the week now that we both live in the city.

Nicole sets her offerings down to take off her boots.

"Bless you. I've been swamped with work. Who would have thought working for influencers was so stressful?"

"Literally everyone."

I point at her with one finger. "You're right." I giggle. "I just thought I could win them over with my Type-A personality or beat them into submission with it."

"You catch more flies with honey than vinegar, Audrey," she scolds teasingly.

When Nicole and I first met in kindergarten, I didn't fully appreciate her friendship because she was so mature for her age. I mean, she organized her nail polishes in rainbow order. She hates ketchup and mint. She has an obsession with trashy dark romances. And I don't know what I would do without her.

Nicole and I move easily around one another, a dance that we've fine-tuned over the years. First at our parents' houses, making her mom's signature sugar cookies, the Christmas tree all lit up behind us. Then at each other's first apartments when we went to separate colleges. We'd take turns driving the hour to visit one another and hang out. We always run our errands together, too. Target, HomeGoods, Trader Joe's—the holy trinity of a girls' day.

I groan. "I need this night so bad, you have no idea."

"Tough day?" she asks.

"Hot Yoga Guy hit me in the face with a door today."

She slams the boxed wine down on the countertop. "What? When did this happen?"

"Literally like two hours ago. I went to an earlier class so we could do *Survivor* tonight instead of Friday and he was coming in for his regular class as I was leaving and he just wham"—I smack one hand into the other—"got me with the door."

"Are you okay?"

"My nose is fine." I wave her off, but she is a nurse, so she comes closer to me and holds my face still so she can look at it. When she's satisfied, she lets me continue, turning back to getting the popcorn ready on the stove. "He felt so bad though. He tried to get me to go with him to urgent care, which I said no to. Then he tried to get me to let him take me to dinner as an apology, which I also said no to."

Nicole whips her head back around. "Hot Yoga Guy asked you out and you said no?"

"His name is Noah, we really should start calling him that."

"Audrey, why would you say no when a perfectly handsome and concerned man asks you out?"

I frown at her. "You know I'm not ready."

She dumps the popcorn and butter from the ready-made bag into the Whirly Pop. "Maybe this is a sign that you should try and get back out there."

"Getting assaulted by a door is a *sign*?" The turning of the kernels is so loud I almost have to yell to be heard over them.

"No. *He* is the sign. Don't be so quick to say no. At the moment, maybe it seemed like a bad idea since you were in pain, but you're fine now. It's time to think about the future again."

"It's too soon."

"It's just a first date. If you see even one red flag you can block his number and move on, but I don't think you will."

I set the huge bowl I got for our popcorn next to her. "I'll think about it. I have his number so if I decide I want to get ahold of him I can."

She dumps the steaming popcorn into our individual bowls. "That's all I'm asking for. Let's catch up on *Survivor* and you can figure it out later."

I move to the fridge to get the fresh veggies out for the girls. "I'm going to grab Dolly and Reba so they can hang out and eat."

Nicole takes two wine glasses, the popcorn bowl, and the green leaf lettuce to the living room while I go to the built-in where I keep the guinea pigs in a huge cage. Dolly is a mix of white and yellow, whereas Reba is a black and red tortoiseshell color. They squeak happily when I undo the latch because they know exactly what time it is.

I hold them both against my chest and bring them to the couch where they have a designated cushion covered in an old bath towel. This is special for *Survivor* nights; they normally eat in their cage. I hated coming home to my empty apartment, but I didn't have time to walk a dog. Guinea pigs are great because you don't have to take them out to potty, their little noises add ambiance to any home, they're very trusting once they know you, and they're perfectly content to just sit and eat. Much like Nicole and me.

Sitting with my fur babies and my best friend, watching a lawyer choke down a fish eyeball on TV, I can't help the worry in the back of my mind about my promise to Nicole. As much as I hate to admit it, she's probably right. It's time for me to get back out there.

It's late when Nicole leaves and I finally crash into bed. I look at the new contact in my phone again. At the very least, I should let him know that I'm not hurt.

I click his name and open a message.

> Hey, Noah, this is Audrey. I just wanted to text you to let you know that I'm fine. No worries!

But I have many worries. I worry that I'm permanently fucked up from my relationship with Hunter. I'm worried I'm unlovable because of my distaste for having kids. I'm worried that there's no man out there who is good with living a life with just me, and I worry that I'm not enough to fill someone's life without the happiness people say comes with having children. How could I be a stand-in for all of that when I'm just me?

Noah's little dots appear immediately.

NOAH

> Hey! Happy to hear from you, but so sorry again about busting you in the face...

I stare at his words on my screen and think back to how safe I felt in his arms today. Like he was going to make sure everything was okay before letting me out of his sight. The concern on his face was obviously as painful for him as my bruised nose was for me. There was desperation in his voice, like he wouldn't be able to sleep tonight if he couldn't fix it for me. If there was any man in the world who would make my first time getting back out there comfortable, it would be Noah. And what kind of person would I be to not let him rid himself of this guilt?

> It's totally okay. Definitely not broken.

> But I was wondering if dinner is still on the table? I kind of freaked out at the studio, but now that I think about it, it sounds fun.

I'm so glad you're taking me up on that! I really feel like I owe you for this.

Not that that's the only reason I want to go. I want to take you to dinner no matter what.

Fuck I'm screwing this up, aren't I?
Ignore me.

What day is best for you? This Friday is good for me, and I know just the place.

He's a multi-texter. I like that.

Friday is good for me, just let me know where and when.

The Lush on San Felipe Street at seven.

Oh, so he's that kind of guy. He just makes decisions and tells me when to be ready. I can be into that.

There. It's done. No backing out now. Well, I could, but then I would feel like a dick. He's given me no reason to believe that at the very least this will be a fun dinner between friends, and at its best it will be proof to myself that I'm not afraid to put myself out there again.

What's that old saying? Something about well-behaved women rarely making history.

Guess it's time for me to write my own history now.

Chapter Six

NOAH

I slide the sweaty Hurricanes athletic shirt over my head and throw it in the team hamper.

Team workouts went well today, but my ass has been thoroughly kicked. I flex my ankle, testing how it feels. It definitely has its strength back, thanks to months of balancing poses. The ability to stay on your feet, moving forward, is important for a tight end, and balance plays a key part in that.

I catch a flash of red in my peripheral vision as Mack approaches his locker. As the only redhead on the team, he's hard to miss. "So, where are you taking her?" he asks.

"You know where," I reply tersely. Everyone knows I have a preference. Pia is a family friend and is the head chef at The Lush. When she called me, terrified that the rapidly rising rent prices might put the restaurant out of business, I knew I had to step in—hell, I *wanted* to step in. Buying the entire commercial strip was an investment, anyway.

Mack puts his hands up in surrender. "Just asking. I didn't know if this was that serious, considering you've barely spoken to her."

"It could be," I say, more nonchalantly than I feel. "Even if it wasn't, the Atlantic cod in miso butter sauce is unmatched."

"You do you, man."

The restaurant scene in Houston is amazing. Our huge melting pot means you can get any cuisine here and it will be good. But The Lush is my favorite restaurant in the city. It's a known haunt of mine. Besides the amazing chef, the staff is incredible, and the ambiance can't be beat. I take my mom there occasionally, but a lot of times I go by myself just to enjoy the food, which is beyond anything I can whip up for myself. I'm no slouch in the kitchen, but I don't have a culinary palette. Taking Audrey there is a no brainer. She would get a better idea of who I am there than she would at any chain restaurant. That's really what I want most from this night.

I heft my backpack onto one shoulder and turn to head out toward the parking lot. "I'll see y'all later."

My phone rings on my way to my car and I grimace when I see it's my dad calling. Thank God for my mother. She kept my feet firmly planted on the ground and was always there to balance my dad out. Reminding me that football isn't everything. The man I am on the field was definitely shaped by my father, but the man I am off the field was molded by my mom. It feels silly to complain about this now that I've made it to the NFL, since he was right about the extra effort it took.

I answer stiffly, wondering if I would get the *coach* version of him, or my actual father. "What's up, Dad?"

"Just checking in on how the first couple days back are going." His way of passive aggressively asking why I wasn't still in the weight room.

"They're good. We worked out as a team today."

I braced myself for another one of his NFL stories.

"There's nothing like a team gym. I had my best workouts

with the Outlaws. All of us are there together, on the same page, striving to get better."

I want to roll my eyes. Dad never hesitates to remind me what it was like during his glory days with Dallas. It's as if he thinks because of his experience, he doesn't have to be an actual dad. Instead, our entire relationship has revolved around football, and that's where our connection ends.

"That's what it felt like today, but it's hard when the roster is still getting finalized." I keep my tone neutral, not letting my annoyance creep into my voice. "I really like some of the new guys, but there's a chance they won't be here in a couple weeks."

"Don't worry about anyone but yourself. This season is about making sure you aren't one of them next year." This is a classic Dad line of conversation. I've heard it a hundred times. Next, he'll tell me to not let anything distract me. "Keep your head on straight. Blinders on. There's work to be done. You had plenty of time to play this summer."

"I was injured," I remind him.

"Yeah, yeah. Don't forget your goals, your legacy." *His* legacy is undoubtedly what he wanted to say.

"I won't, Dad," I assure him, knowing that earning his approval was the best way to keep our relationship status quo.

"Call me after practice next week and tell me how everyone looks. Remember, no distractions."

"I will," I promise.

I hang up, knowing he'd be disappointed to hear that in a couple hours I'll be on my way to meet Audrey.

Who is most definitely a distraction.

Chapter Seven

AUDREY

I don't know why I'm trying so hard.

I spent an hour and a half showering, shaving, exfoliating, and moisturizing. For a man I don't intend to be charmed by? I must have had a slight freak out because I briefly considered getting a Brazilian wax—which I've never done before in my life. It seemed like poor timing to start now. That's the only reason I didn't make an appointment at Pretty Kitty down the street.

Maybe I'm just nervous about going out to dinner with a man I'm attracted to. Six months ago, I was happily engaged. I was picking wedding colors and thinking about cake flavors. In one day, it all came crashing down and, at some level, I'm preparing myself for this to be the same. It was easier to distract myself with all kinds of beauty treatments than to sit and wonder what it will be like. How rusty will I be? How will he behave? Will he flirt? Will we get dessert? Will we—

SEE?! This is what I'm talking about. I have time to spare, and I need to find something to tidy if it's going to be like this all evening.

I hear Nicole's keys in the door and mumble "Thank God" under my breath. She's here to save me from myself. I meet her at the door to help her carry everything. She's weighed down with all her beauty shit and is here under the guise of helping me do my hair and makeup, but really, she's here to keep me sane.

"Where are we doing this?"

I look around, trying to think which room has the best lighting. "Maybe my bathroom with the big mirror?"

"Great, I'll go put everything down in there."

"I'll get the girls." Guinea pigs love having a chance to stretch their legs. I try to keep them out of their cage as much as possible when I'm home, and it's easy to let them out in the main bathroom while I shower. They love the humidity since they're from a tropical country and often reward me with their happiest tea kettle whistles.

Nicole brings a kitchen chair for me to sit on and I shut the door behind me and put the girls on the floor. They scatter to explore.

I plop into the chair and Nicole asks, "What are we going for today?"

"Can you do that nice beach wave?" Nicole's hair is the thickest I've ever seen. It never ends. Her ponytails are the size of a golf ball when it's all tied up. Mine is more like a marble. So I'm hoping beach waves will make it look fuller.

"And makeup?"

"Normal but more, you know what I mean?" I want to look like myself. Like I didn't try too hard, but also better than the near-death version he sees at Big.

"Gotcha."

We fall into the comfortable silence that only comes with two decades of friendship. While she works, I let the feel of her fingers in my hair distract and relax me. She's methodical in her movements, just like she approaches life. A perfectionist at heart, I know she won't stop until she's happy. Her standard has always been higher than mine.

I'm surprised she's done when she tells me to flip so she can spray the curls one more time. She runs her fingers through them, strong from many years of playing piano as a young girl. I guess it's been a while now, but when we were kids, she was good. I distinctly remember a Taylor Swift piano music song book.

She finally speaks when she moves in front of me to start on my makeup. "How do you feel?"

"More confident now that you're here to turn me from pumpkin to princess."

She laughs her wind chime laugh. "You've never been a pumpkin in your life."

"Not even in high school when I had a full set of braces that they took off, realized my teeth were still messed up, and then had to be put back on?" I counter.

"Even then. It was well worth it for your beautiful smile!"

"That is one of my favorite parts about me."

She nods. "We'll do a gloss to frame your smile with kissable lips."

"There will be no kissing."

"Uh-huh."

"None."

"Sureee." She draws out the end. "I'm not trying to push you into the arms of the first man who pays you any attention. But Audrey, you need to get back out there."

"I am. Literally tonight."

"And if things go well?"

I hesitate.

Nicole speaks into the silence. "I just want you to have an open mind. I don't think it needs to be said, but I'm going to say it." She puts down the wet makeup sponge and takes my hands in hers. "Noah is not Hunter." I nod even though my nose is stinging. Obviously, Noah is not Hunter, but aren't all men kind of the same on the deepest level? Doesn't society allow them to be that way? My emotions are bubbling under the surface. Thankfully, Nicole doesn't push me anymore. She just picks up the pink sponge and goes back to work.

An hour later, I have mismatched shoes on. "The heels are hot, but the sandals are much more comfortable."

Nicole eyes my outfit. "You can get away with a more casual shoe if you want to wear a dress, but if you want to wear these jeans and the silk top, you should wear the heels to dress them up a little." Who am I to argue with that? Noah is plenty tall. Not that I'm short. I think I'm exactly average for a woman.

Some final touches with earrings, rings, and perfume are all I need.

Nicole hands me the tiny clutch she picked out and wraps me in a hug. "If nothing else, have fun and eat some good food."

"I love you."

"Love you. And call me later. I want to hear everything." She turns to collect her already packed things and leaves.

I check the time on my phone: 6:20. I'm trying to be relaxed, but my jiggling knee is giving me away. I'm strung up like a high wire.

This is just an apology dinner. No expectations. No strings.

Noah might be a delicious mountain of a man, but that doesn't mean anything to me.

I do what I always do to keep myself focused and on track: write a list.

I open a new note on my phone which I title "Reasons I Don't Need a Man:"

1. They lie.

2. I'm too busy.

3. They all want to be dads. (And will lie about it. See reason one.)

I check the time again and see if I have a text. The time is inching toward 6:30 at a snail's pace. A *drunk* snail's pace. He's not even going in a straight line, poor snail.

Finally, finally, it's time to leave. I grab my small purse and keys and head out the door. My Uber waits for me in the cracked concrete driveway, and I'm met with the delicious smell of fried chicken being blown my way from the restaurant across the street.

I arrive five minutes early, which is right on time, and allow the valet to open my door.

"Audrey," a voice calls from behind me and I turn toward it.

My jaw drops when I take Noah in.

He looks so different in casual clothes. Until now I've only ever seen him in gym clothes—those devastating man tights he wears. I thought those would be the death of me, but Noah in a hunter green Henley just about wipes my brain of all intelligent thought. If I die right now, it's because he looks so good I forgot to breathe. He takes long strides toward me, eating up the concrete between us. I momentarily panic. Are we on hugging terms? What if he kisses the back of my hand? Is that gross or romantic? It would definitely give me a sense of what this night is. If he shakes my hand I may die from embarrassment on the spot.

I'm more than a little relieved when he pulls me into a hug that's surprisingly gentle for his size.

He holds his hand out for mine. "Are you hungry?"

A smirk splits my face. "Starving, actually."

The list. The list. The list.

Don't be so easily charmed, Audrey.

"This is my favorite restaurant." He guides me through the dark glass front doors hand in hand.

Inside is full of murmuring undertones. Even at seven-thirty, they have the lights turned down, enhancing the beautiful candlelight coming from each table. The smells of fresh-baked bread and searing steak mingling. "It's beautiful."

Noah speaks to the maître d'. "Fox, for two at seven-thirty."

They look down at their tablet before saying, "Ah yes. Mr. Noah, your regular table is ready." They walk around the hostess stand and we follow.

His regular table? How many women has he brought here?

I slip into the chair Noah pulls out for me. The table has two small votive candles, and a single white rose in a demure vase. The white tablecloth is perfectly ironed, and a small basket of warm bread is already waiting for us. I pull my napkin into my lap and pick up the menu. It's got a bit of everything on it. A chicken breast, of course, but steak and various seafood offerings as well. Movement catches my eye, and I glance up as our waiter approaches.

"Good evening, Mr. Noah. So glad to have you tonight."

Noah smiles and greets him. "Matt, so good to see you! Been a couple weeks." Matt is average height with sandy hair and blue eyes. I've never seen anyone greet a server like this. He really must come here all the time. Or maybe he's this friendly with everyone? That would explain his insistence in taking me out to dinner.

"It has. We've updated the wine list since you were here last. I'll bring Jacque over to discuss that with you shortly." With a nod, he moves to the next table. I turn toward Noah, my mind whirring with the new light I'm seeing him in tonight. I know so little about him, but I plan on changing that right now.

To satisfy my curiosity, of course. No other reason.

"So, you come here often?" I ask.

Could I embarrass myself any worse? Be any more cliché?

"I come here for all my special occasions." He wraps a hand around his water glass, letting that tidbit of information soak between us. "My mom's best friend's daughter is the head chef. I do my best to fill the tables and get my friends to write five-star reviews."

I tip my head. "I'll be sure to write one." There's a pause. Both of us are looking at the wine list, although I already know I'm going to let Noah decide.

"Smack women in the face with doors regularly?"

His eyes widen in surprise, but he quickly recovers when he sees the smirk splayed across my face.

"I don't make a habit of it, no."

"And that's what you consider a special occasion?" I tease.

"My special occasions involve people I know—friends, family, but some include those I want to get to know better." He looks at me as he says the words "get to know better" and every lady part I own starts to tingle.

Holding my breath, I lean my elbows on the table and rest my chin on top. I don't trust myself to respond, so I change the subject. "So, how long have you been doing yoga?"

"Six months, maybe? I've been battling an injury, and yoga

has been helping me get my strength back. Now that I have a yoga practice, though, I won't be quitting."

He turns my question back on me. "How long have *you* been doing yoga?"

"It's been part of my routine for a couple years, but lately I've been using it to keep busy after a bad breakup. I miss it when I don't go."

"I'm sorry about your breakup. Were you together long?" He pauses. "You don't have to answer that. It's none of my business."

"No, it's okay. Like I said, it's been about six months. We'd been together for years, but engaged for one." I definitely didn't want to have this conversation tonight, but I don't see any reason to outright lie to a man who has been nothing but polite and kind to me.

"Why did you split up? If you don't mind me asking."

"We had irrevocable differences." It's not the whole story, but it's the truth. Tonight we're just getting to know each other; there's no reason for me to bring out my crazy parade. I probably shouldn't change the subject again, but I do.

"How did you get hurt?" I should also feel guilty about asking leading questions when I already know the answer, but I don't. I want him to tell me in his own words.

"Playing football."

"So, you know a lot about romancing women then?"

He chokes on his sip of water but recovers quickly. "I can see how you would think that, but I'm not a player—well, I'm a player in the literal sense, but not with women."

I lean back, a small smile playing on my lips. "Noted." That went better than I expected.

Something spurs him to continue. "Football has been my

whole life. I walked onto my college team freshman year and battled my way into a starting position. After my college career was over, I went into the draft, and here I am. Tight end for the Houston Hurricanes. It's been a roller coaster. We've been in a rebuilding season. Every year we get better, but sometimes disappointment comes with the territory. I was injured trying to catch a deep shot. I broke my ankle and ended up with the whole nine. Surgery, crutches, then walking boots, physical therapy. All of it."

"Wow, I had no idea."

"Not a football fan?"

"I just like for both teams to have fun." I smirk. He guffaws.

"So, what are you into?" His eyes are alight, interested.

"In reference to what? TV? Hobbies? Kinks?" I mock him indignantly. "I'm not sure that's dinner conversation."

He shrugs but I catch a playful glimmer in his eye. "It can be, if you want." I can feel the pink rising in my cheeks.

I didn't expect to be so unwillingly charmed by this man. I clear my throat, trying desperately to dissipate the blush on my cheeks. "Yoga, obviously. For work, I'm a social media manager for influencers. Well, I own my own firm, so really, I'm accounting, marketing… A jack of all trades."

"Would I know anyone you represent?"

"Probably not. Right now, I'm mostly in the beauty influencer space."

"Have you seen the girl who went viral for painting her face like a different fish every week?"

I lean forward, shocked. "You know Tanya?"

He chuffs. "I think that hit everyone's For You page."

"She's really nice. Values my opinion. Takes my advice."

"She didn't let the fame get to her head?"

"Not at all. She's just the same at one-million followers as she was at one hundred." I consider him. "Seems like you didn't let fame go to your head either."

"What do you mean?" He wipes a hand over his mouth, his eyes shifted down. We're both leaning over the table as if drawn together.

"You're a professional football player. I've seen *Friday Night Lights*. Aren't you supposed to be all baby mama drama and testosterone?" I'm being serious, but a smile cracks across his face.

"That's a TV drama about high school kids. I wouldn't exactly call it a source of truth."

"That's all I know." I shrug. "'Texas forever' and all that."

We're interrupted by the sommelier approaching the table with a bottle of wine. As he presents the wine to Noah, I relax back in my chair.

My head was full of folly, but reality is settling my imagination. After the sommelier pours my glass, I pick it up and tip it so it just barely touches my lips to taste. Noah watches me carefully, like he's trying not to miss any details.

"Do you like the wine?"

"It's great." I'm not usually a wine drinker, but when presented to me, I try to be a good sport.

Noah tilts his head to the side. "When's the last time someone took you out?"

Holy shit, can he read the nerves behind my eyes?

"It's been a while. Not because there weren't any opportunities, because there were." There's fake sternness in my voice. "I'm my own boss so when I don't work, I don't make money." Sure, it's been a while, but I'm not about to admit exactly why right here at this dinner table. It's the twenty-first century, we don't need men to be sexually satisfied. That's why we invented vibrators. Something that I've become highly appreciative of in the last six months.

A banked fire roars behind his eyes. "So, I've already met your high standards?"

"I thought this was an apology, not a date."

"Why can't it be both?"

I lower my eyes to get away from the heat in his. I scan the menu one more time, confirming my already decided order. I'm going to get the steak, of course. I took a door to the face for this meal. He could have broken my nose! And he's asking lots of questions; that costs extra.

Noah looks like he's about to say something else, probably about why I didn't answer his question, but I'm saved by the waiter. "Are you ready to order?" Matt asks.

Noah's eyes are on me when he says, "I know what I want."

Okay, maybe not saved.

It's hard to take my attention off him. The hard plane of his jaw line and the darkness of his green eyes—the kind you can get lost in.

Realizing how far I was leaning toward him, I sit up straight.

The list. The list. The list.

I read off the menu to him. "I'll have a side Caesar salad and the fourteen-ounce ribeye."

"And how would you like that cooked?"

"Medium rare." He nods, turning to Noah.

I can see Noah considering me. Everyone tries to tell you that a filet is the best cut of steak, but they're wrong. I've always found them dry and underwhelming. A ribeye—with its melt in your mouth marbling—is the perfect steak. I won't be denied the enjoyment of a good piece of meat because I should be ordering a female-sized dinner. I got a salad too. *It's called balance.*

Chapter Eight

NOAH

I've died and gone to heaven.

That ribeye is definitely going to be as big as her face. I've treated myself to it after a hard practice once or twice.

What an amazing woman.

She knows what she wants, and she's going to get it.

"What are your teammates like?" she asks, taking a sip of her water.

"Well, Wyatt is our new defensive lineman. This is his first season here. He played for Green Bay during his rookie years. He's from Wisconsin, very much a Midwesterner. Jaden is from Louisiana originally, so he's dealing with the heat much better than Wyatt. He's also been here a few years, about as long as me. Colin is my best friend on the team. He and his college sweetheart got married last year. Mack is our team class clown. I don't think the man has ever been embarrassed in his life. He just wants to have a good time. Nice to have someone who's a glass half full kind of guy. I think that's my main group. The ones I see outside of the required organized team activities."

"They sound like a fun bunch."

"It's kind of a circus, but in a fun way." I butter another piece of fresh-baked bread. I shouldn't fill up on this stuff, but I can't resist. "What about you?"

"My work team is just me. But in regular life it's me and my childhood best friend Nicole. We've known each other since kindergarten. We went to different colleges, but never lost touch. It's so nice to live close to her again. She's a nurse, so she works holidays and weekends. Hard to get together, but we make it work by DVRing *Survivor* and saving it to watch together."

"It's nice to be so close to a friend again. What about your family? Do they live here?"

She looks down at the butter on her knife as she spreads it slowly on her bread. "They do. They run Space City Auto, the car shops. We have a… strained relationship. There are things in life they thought I would do, but I took a different path."

"Like what?"

"Like not joining the family business in preparation to take it over one day. My brother, Lane, is going to, though, so I don't know what the big deal is."

"That's it?" Her eyes go back to her bread plate.

"Among other things, yeah." I'm going to ask more questions, but she doesn't let me get a word in edgewise.

"What about your folks?" she asks.

It's my turn to fiddle with the napkin on my lap. "My dad was a pro football player as well; now he coaches a local team. We also had a strained relationship, but it got better when I went into the league. It's what he always wanted for me. My mom and I are really close. She's responsible for me not becoming an overly macho, testosterone alpha. She's also responsible for all my southern gentleman manners."

Audrey laughs at this and it's the sound of bells ringing just for me. "I like her already."

Our food comes and I struggle to hold conversation because my focus is on every bite that passes through those lips. When another bite of soft bread touches her tongue, little noises of appreciation escape her mouth and go straight through me, rewiring my brain. I will never come to this restaurant again without replaying this meal in my head. I give myself a mental shake as Audrey talks animatedly about her guinea pigs, Reba and Dolly. "They sound super cute. I've never held a guinea pig before. We didn't really have pets growing up."

"It takes them a second to warm up, but I'll let you feed them, and they'll be your best friends." A smile spreads across my face. She's already planning on seeing me again.

I insist we order dessert, just to keep the night going. "The crème brûlée here is amazing. We have to get that."

When the custard comes, I let her crack the torched sugar. I'm barely hanging on by a thread as I watch her slowly put the silver spoon in her mouth. Her eyes close in ecstasy as she savors the sweet cream flavor, and I feel her little noise of delight all the way to my toes.

The conversation so far has been meandering and comfortable. Like we are getting to know each other, but also like I've always known her. I can feel the familiarity in my chest and absentmindedly put a hand there to settle the feeling. I've never been a guy to get so deep so quickly. I'm a professional football player, for fuck's sake. If I fell for every girl who gave me a lick of attention, I'd have been married and divorced ten times by now. She didn't even flinch when I told her about my NFL career. It seems to have no effect on her whatsoever, which is nice. I guess that comes with the territory of managing the mildly famous influencers.

I tear my eyes away from Audrey's radiance for a millisecond to catch sight of the chef coming toward us. Pia likes to come out and greet my guests and get their honest opinion of the food since I can't be impartial. She's my age, cheeks pinked from the heat of the kitchen, and her hair is tucked under her toque.

I look back at Audrey. "Excuse me." I push my chair back and put my napkin on the table so I can hug Pia. Audrey catches the familiarity and rises as well.

I step back from Pia and gesture toward Audrey. "Pia, this is Audrey. Audrey, this is Pia. The head chef here at The Lush."

Pia's eyes cut teasingly to Noah. "Also his neighbor growing up. Our moms are best friends."

"So he told me. It's very nice to meet you," Audrey says as they shake hands. "I loved the food."

"I'm so glad you enjoyed yourselves! I like to see for myself. Noah's already given us a five-star review on every existing platform, so now I have to rely on his friends."

"I'll be sure to write one," Audrey says.

Pia turns back to me. "It was so good to see you, Noah. Good luck this season. I know it will be a winning one!"

I embrace her again. "Don't work too hard back there." She struts back to the kitchen, waving me off, and checking on various tables as she goes.

I turn back to Audrey. "Are you ready to go?"

"Let me just run to the ladies' room real quick."

Audrey stands and grabs her shiny black purse from the table and weaves through the room toward the back.

While she's gone, I pay the bill and finish my glass of wine. I can't help but imagine her lining her perfect lips in that pouty pink color. A color that makes it look like they've been kissed for hours. It's so cute how she plays with her bracelet when I ask her questions.

I move to stand as I see her across the room coming back to the table.

I don't want to leave it at just dinner and a shared dessert, but I don't want to be too forward and freak her out. I'm willing to take whatever she'll give me tonight. After one dinner I know that this woman is special.

Audrey returns to me with an expression I can't quite read.

"Ready to go?"

"Yes, I'm ready."

I stand and, without thinking, take her hand to guide her through the restaurant toward the front door. When the zap of lightning hits my forearm, I realize I'm a goner.

I drop her hand quickly. "Sorry."

"It's okay." She slips her hand back in mine and gives me a dazzling, yet soft smile. I smile back at her. As we walk, I let myself enjoy the feeling of her smaller frame so close to mine. If I tucked her up against me, her head would rest perfectly against my chest. Her hair swings as she walks, gently grazing my arm and dusting me with the scent of her perfume. It's light and beach-y, like the perfect summer day. I hope by the end of the night some of it lingers on my shirt so I can fill my car with it on the way home.

Yep. I'm a goner.

Audrey is everything I thought she would be and more. She's funny, witty, smart, and beautiful.

Chapter Nine

AUDREY

Outside of the distraction of the restaurant, my head is spinning. It already had been so overwhelming, being out with a guy alone for the first time since my breakup, but after running into Pia on my way to touch up my lipstick in the restroom, it's a full-on tornado.

"Did you enjoy your meal?" She's so pretty with her perfectly small nose and her high cheekbones.

"It was the best crème brûlée I've ever had."

She looks over her shoulder toward the entrance to the rest of the restaurant like she's about to tell me something secret. "You know, Noah never brings women here. I've been head chef here for five years and the only woman I've ever seen him here with is his mom." That news bowls me over.

He brings close friends; he brings his mom. But he never brings women. "I'd better get back."

"So nice to meet you." She gives me that look that says *he likes you* before going back to running her restaurant. Half of me is flattered, lit up inside like a bonfire on a cool evening. The other half is scared shitless. I scuttled away, my head filled with unanswered questions that make me remember my list and why anything more with Noah Fox is nothing but a bad idea wrapped in tight-fitting jeans.

I had fully convinced myself that this was merely an apology dinner. That Noah was just a nice guy doing the right thing. We barely know each other. Before tonight we'd only said polite niceties to one another in the last six months. That leaves me between a rock and a hard place. A place I probably shouldn't even know about except for the fact that I got some insider information from my new bestie, Pia. He's playing romantic chess, and I'm playing checkers with my sad little list of reasons I'm not interested in dating.

He's certainly not like the influencers I've worked with. He wasn't wearing any flashy clothes or name-brand jewelry. Not even a nice watch. From my experience with influencers, it has to do with the fact that staying relevant and garnering attention is what makes them famous. I think as an NFL player, eyes are on you no matter what, but you're not worried about that. You're worried about the game, the next play, your teammates. You're an athlete first, and whatever else comes with that is second.

Now, we're standing outside The Lush, my phone in hand ready to call an Uber home. I'm about to thank Noah for a nice dinner and tell him that I'm excited to have a friend in class when he speaks up, hand behind his head. "Would you want to go to a bar? I would ask you to go for a walk, but it's hot as hell out here tonight." July in Houston is a slowly broiling oven. The breeze blows my hair off my shoulders but there's no cooling effect. It's just hot air moving the heat around.

"That sounds good." What do I have to get home to anyway? The girls will be fine for a while longer, and my inbox can wait until tomorrow. I would say Monday, but who am I kidding? I will definitely be checking it before then.

"We could take my car there, if you're comfortable with that? You can Uber home from there." He hands his ticket to the man behind the valet podium, who hands it to a younger man who takes off toward the parking lot.

"Okay, cool. Where are you thinking?"

"Have you ever been to Bobcat Teddy's?"

"No, I haven't. That's kind of a funny name though."

"It's kind of a funny bar." I see a black Audi A8 coming up the circle driveway and Noah walks toward it. "This is me."

He opens the car door for me as the valet gets out of the driver's seat. He thanks the man, palms him a tip, and slides into the car. The leather interior is smooth, and the car isn't as hot as you would expect it after baking in the sun. It's nine-thirty and the sun has just barely set, the last of the light dancing behind the clouds casting a golden glow over Noah, highlighting the perfect planes of his face. I feel my heart beating faster so I glance at the dash, focusing on what song is playing so I can distract myself.

He sees me looking and hands me his unlocked phone. "Here, play whatever you want."

What kind of man just hands you his unlocked phone? Some men are so secretive about phones, and on the first night we're getting to know each other he just hands me his? I open his music app and scroll through his playlists.

It's eclectic, more modern. Some rap, some pop, some Texas country. I select the Texas country playlist and Parker McCollum croons through the speakers. He might be big time now, but he grew up in Conroe, which is about fifty miles from here.

"I love Parker McCollum. I saw him when he was so small

he was opening up for the Josh Abbott Band at White Oak Music Hall."

He takes his eyes off the road to look at me for just a split second. "No way. I was at that concert too. Colin is a big Texas country fan, and he insisted we all go."

"That's so crazy. I swear to God, Houston is the smallest big city."

"When he did the acoustic rendition of 'Wasn't that Drunk', Colin went crazy."

"I can't believe Josh Abbott's never played the rodeo. It's like he's never gotten any bigger than he is right now."

Noah shrugs. "Maybe he doesn't want to be bigger. Maybe he's happy playing medium-sized venues and selling them out."

"Yeah, maybe. His wife was with him that night, too, which must be nice."

"Now you've been through my playlists, tell me what yours are like."

I laugh, slightly embarrassed. "I tragically never outgrew the music I grew up with. My Old Jams playlist is my most played music. I love stuff like Blink-182 and Ke$ha. Old Taylor Swift too. I drop off of her stuff right around the *Lover* album. Music back then just had more energy to it. Maybe I'm just attached to nostalgia, but there's something about it. That feeling of hearing a familiar song and remembering what it was like to be young... well, younger."

He nods as if that makes total sense to him. "I still remember the songs we warmed up to when I played middle school basketball. Sometimes I still play them just to remember what it was like before sports were serious." And I guess it does make sense. We both like music that transports us back to simpler times.

The Parker song ends and "Wasn't that Drunk" starts up. "Oh my God," I breathe. "What a coincidence. We were just talking about this song. It's kismet."

The drive to the bar is shorter than I would have liked it to be. Between the company, the music, and the air conditioning, it's hard to want it to end.

He pulls into a parking lot across the street. The sign says ten dollars. He gets out and hustles to my side of the car while I gather my purse and phone to open my car door.

"Thank you," I say as I step out.

"You're welcome. I'm going to go pay."

I stand beside him as he slides a card into the reader. It noisily prints a ticket and he takes it, sliding it into his pocket.

He gestures in the direction we should head and I follow him. Weaving through the cars, I say, "The fact that you can't walk anywhere in Houston, but there's also such limited parking, is mind boggling. It's like it's not a walking city, but it's not a driving city either."

He chuffs, amused. "Wyatt's in his first season here and he drives a big ol' truck. He's now taken to having me pick him up to go places 'cause fitting his truck in these little parking spots is such a pain."

I motion to the various vehicles around us both parked and driving by as we cross the street, of which about fifty-five percent are trucks. "And yet everyone has one."

We're so close to Bobcat Teddy's now that I can hear the music thumping.

There's a huge porch covered by a tin roof that's packed full of people despite the summer heat. You have to walk through the porch crowd to go inside to the bar, and Noah reaches for my hand again to guide me through the crowd.

The average age of the patrons is definitely older than us and the music playing reflects that.

We step up to the bar together. "What do you want to drink?"

"I'll have a beer. Whichever one you get."

Noah turns to the bartender, and I can't hear what he says as I dig through my purse for my card.

He puts his hand over mine. "No, this is still apology night. Drinks included."

I put my card back in the little bag and accept the beer he hands me. He leads me back through the crowd to a tiny table directly under a fan.

For one split second the silence is a little awkward. We've known each other for one night. We've already covered music and our friends. Now what? I sip my beer and take in the massive amount of wood surrounding us. The tables, barstools, walls and even the bar itself are wood like a house straight out of the eighties. Another classic rock song comes on and the older people in the crowd around us start singing along. "I know I said I liked old music, but not quite this old," I say.

"It was this or one of the eight bars where the music is so loud we wouldn't be able to hear each other talk." I've been to many of those bars for birthdays and girls' nights and spent the entire night screaming in my friends' ears. "They're also way more packed than this place is, and I hate waiting in line for a beer."

"Impatient much?"

"A bar is a bar and a beer is a beer. If the bartenders want to play the 'only wait on hot girls' game, I would rather take my business elsewhere."

"So you come here where you're guaranteed to be the hottest person in the whole bar?"

He leans his elbows on the table, bringing his face closer to mine. "So you do think I'm hot?"

I motion at him like *obviously*. "You're objectively attractive." I pause, considering my next words. "And very nice and charming."

"Thank you. You're beautiful. I always thought you were even when you were dead sweaty after class." This makes my cheeks flame like I just got out of said hot yoga class.

He points at my bottle. "Another beer?"

I don't even hesitate. "Yes."

I watch him walk back to the bar, taking in the way his tight jeans fit around his thick thighs and nice butt. He's a tasty morsel, that's for sure, but I'm glad we're spending tonight getting to know each other. I feel so at ease around him. I drink my first beer as slow as I possibly can, trying to drag out the time we have together.

When Noah returns, two more beers in hand, I pat his seat like I've been saving it for him.

I'm so lame.

Quickly, I try to recover by taking his mind off my awkward gesture. "What's your favorite TV show?"

"Easy. *The Office*."

I perk up. "Mine too. I always say you're either one of two people. Someone who watches it once and moves on, or you watch it over and over again for the rest of your life."

"I play it on a constant loop."

"Me too!"

"I skip the last three seasons with Robert California, though. I can't stand him." Another correct answer.

"I wish Will Ferrell had stayed."

Noah shakes his head. "He was already too big."

"Sure, but he was the best replacement for Michael."

"Glad we agree on that. I'm not sure I could even be friends with someone if they didn't like *The Office*. We wouldn't have the same sense of humor at all."

I take another sip from my beer. At this point it's going to take me all night to finish it. And I'm okay with that. "What about movies? Are you a Marvel guy?"

"Not really. I think all superhero movies feel the same."

I nod, I've seen a total of three superhero movies. "I'm the same way about movies as I am music. Nothing's as good as what they were doing in the nineties and two-thousands."

"They definitely don't make stupid funny movies like they used to," he says, and I nod in agreement. "I would rather rewatch an old movie I've already seen than watch any movie that's currently out in theaters."

"What's your favorite nineties' movie?"

"*Tommy Boy* with Chris Farley. We had it on VHS when I was a kid, and we watched it all the time. I basically have it memorized line by line."

"I have *Talladega Nights* memorized." Thank God he's not going to suggest going to see the newest classic animated movie remake.

"That's the perfect stupid movie. They just don't make them like that anymore. I love when I watch a movie and there's only flip phones."

"Did you have a flip phone?" he asks.

"Until I went to college. My parents thought if we were going to have a smartphone, we needed to pay for it ourselves." Needless to say, I was never the coolest kid in school.

"That's crazy."

I take another sip of my beer. "Nicole had a pink Razr and I was so jealous of her. I had a stupid ugly black hunk of plastic."

"I had the Blackberry with the full keyboard. I was always messing up my texts because my fingers were too big for the tiny buttons." My eyes drop to those hands, taking in just how right he is about their size.

I laugh out loud at the thought of his giant hands punching at little buttons like a caveman. Then I sigh. "Every now and then I think about going back to a flip phone, but I really need my Apple Maps. I am horrible at directions."

"No one wants to go back to printing out directions from MapQuest. My mom and I used to fight when she would miss a turn going to a football game. She'd be like, 'it said a quarter mile, that doesn't feel like a quarter mile' and we would have totally missed the turn already."

"You're right. That's the only technology we need." I giggle. I pick my beer up again only to realize it's empty.

"Another one?"

"I don't know. What time is it?" I reach for my little purse and look at my phone. "Holy shit, it's one-thirty! This place is going to close soon."

Noah rises from his seat. "I'll go close out." I can't help but watch him walk away again. I can't believe we just killed more than four hours at this bar. I don't think I've ever been able to stand being in a bar that long. I always get overstimulated by the music and am ready to go. That's when it hits me that I couldn't tell you a single song played after the one I heard everyone singing. I haven't heard anything but Noah's voice. My focus on him and our conversation let the night slip away like sand through an hourglass. I didn't even notice.

When I look up again, Noah is back, holding his hand out

to me again. "Come on, I'll wait with you while you call an Uber."

I nod and take his hand.

We stand out on the street, cars whizzing by and people jaywalking without a care in the world. I glance down at my phone, keeping an eye on Matt in a white Mazda as he moves slowly down this street on the map. Noah squeezes my hand to get my attention. I look up at him and he's smiling. "I had a great time tonight."

I smile back. "Me too." And honestly, I'm not sure how to leave this. It's been years since I talked to someone whom I had any physical interest in. When I was with Hunter, I was extremely loyal and never looked anyone else's way. After our breakup, I swore off men and that led us to this moment. With this man who has been so kind and easy to talk to that I lost all track of time. I didn't even think about work except when I explained to him what I do. It's nice. More than nice. It's kind of addicting. I want to know what he thinks about everything. I want to know if he'll give up his coveted spot on the back wall and put his mat next to mine at yoga. But I don't say any of that.

When Matt in the white Mazda pulls up to the curb, Noah leans down to the open window. "For Audrey?" Matt nods in response and Noah opens the door for me to get in the back seat. I step off the curb and down to the car, making Noah tower even farther over me.

"Thank you for everything."

He leans in and places one chaste peck on my left cheek. "It was my pleasure. Let me know you made it home safe."

I slide into the car and set my purse on the bench seat. Noah shuts the door and steps back so the car can leave.

When I get home the house is dark and I realize I forgot to

turn the entryway light on before I left. I let myself in, kick off my shoes, toss my purse on the couch, and head straight to the kitchen for a glass of water.

While I sip it, I lean against the counter to text Noah. But when I open his contact, I have an overwhelming urge to call him. I can easily text to let him know I made it, but I'm still thinking about our conversation, sitting close at a tiny bar table, and how I never got to ask when he thinks he'll be back to yoga after training camp. When exactly does training camp start? I could hit that call button and have answers to all my lingering questions...

I hit dial.

I don't have to wait long. It only rings twice before Noah's smooth voice answers. "Hello?"

"Hey," I say, trying to hide how fast my heart is beating. Can he hear my blood rushing through the ear that's pressed up against the phone? "I made it home."

"Oh, good." I can hear him setting his keys down. I imagine he kicks his shoes off next.

"I had a great time."

"Is that why you called?"

I bite my lip. "I'm that obvious, huh?"

His low chuckle washes over me. "It's a good thing."

I hold the phone to my ear with my shoulder while I put more water in my cup. "I just got home and thought to myself: I didn't get all my questions answered." Honesty seems like the best policy at this point.

Ironic, I know.

"Hit me with 'em."

I head to my room and put Noah on speaker so I can get in my pjs while we talk. "When does training camp start?"

"The end of next week." I can hear the rustle of clothing on his end. If I imagine him rolling his shirt over his broad shoulders, then sue me. I wonder if he sleeps without a shirt. Somehow I now understand dudes who ask women what they're wearing when they talk on the phone. I'm barely tamping down the urge myself.

"So that's when you'll stop coming to yoga classes? Why?" I ask.

"It's a violation of my contract to do any physical activity not sanctioned by the team during the official season, which starts with training camp."

Oh. It's going to be a long six months of going to class and being disappointed that Noah's not there in his usual spot against the wall. Part of me is screaming to tell him that. It would be so easy to just say it, but the other half of me is warning me away. This is a professional athlete. He's busy, he's contractually obligated, he's... so hot. I quickly decided it's better to keep these feelings as inside thoughts for now. "Are you excited?"

I can hear the hesitation in his breath, considering how he wants to answer. I climb into bed, sans teeth care—even though I never miss out on flossing—while I wait for him to speak. I'll go back to the bathroom after we hang up and wash my face, brush my teeth, floss, etc. "I'm excited to see my teammates again. A lot of us live here, but go on vacation or travel to see family during the off season, so I haven't seen some of them in a while." He pauses again, seemingly to decide if he wants to tell me the rest of his thoughts. "But... to be honest, there's a lot riding on this season. My rookie contract is almost up, and I need to prove my worth to the team this season."

"What would happen if you didn't?" I lie in bed, covers pulled up to my chin, just the bedside lamp casting a warm glow over the rest of my room. I set the phone on the pillow next to my head so I can relax and listen to his voice.

"Anything could happen. I could get traded, or I could become a free agent and have to go try out for different teams. If no one wanted me, I might not be on a team next year." I can hear the uncertainty in his voice. That's a lot riding on one season of football.

"I'm sure you're going to be great. You could win the Super Bowl this year, you never know. It's only just beginning." I try to hold back my yawn, but it defeats me.

"You should go to sleep."

"No, I want to hear more about football." But I do close my eyes to let them rest. It's well into the night now and I am tired, but with the morning coming quickly I want to hold on to this while it's still just us. "Tell me about your regular day during training camp."

"Well," Noah starts, and I can feel the weight of sleep lingering over me, threatening to take me under. I can't help but think back to earlier tonight when I felt Noah's heated gaze on my lips as I took a bite of dessert, to later when he had me laughing over my beer at the weirdest bar I've ever been to.

There's no reason an apology dinner should be the best date I've ever been on in my life, but here we are. That's kind of sad, that no other date was as good as a dinner and drink. Considering I was previously engaged, I guess the bar is pretty much on the floor.

I have a feeling Noah will be making an effort to raise it.

———

The next morning starts way earlier than I'm ready for it to. When I turn my head, my phone hits me in the face. I pick it up and realize I'm still on the call with Noah. The duration of the call is over six hours and twenty-three minutes. I don't know what time I fell asleep on him last night, but from the tiredness pounding in my skull, I'm going to guess it was late.

Do I hang up on him? Should I say goodbye first? What if he's sleeping? What if he's *not* sleeping and he's just quietly sitting on the other side of this call waiting to see if I'm going to say something?

I hit the end call button and open my messages to send him a text, but I'm distracted by how many texts there are from Nicole.

> NICOLE
>
> How's the date going? Is he hotter outside of yoga?
>
> I'm assuming it's going really well since you aren't texting me back.
>
> Okay, it's been several hours, so you either made it home and are going to Pound Town, or you've already been murdered and dumped in the woods somewhere.
>
> …Seriously, text me back.

I shoot her a quick text:

> Am alive and home. All good.

My phone rings immediately in my hand and I answer it. "Hello?"

"Spill," demands Nicole.

"There's nothing to spill."

"Then why didn't you text me back last night?"

"We went to a bar after dinner for a few beers. I wasn't checking my phone, and it was late when I got home."

"But you had a good time?" she asks.

"Surprisingly, I did. I called to tell him I made it home safe and we ended up falling asleep on the phone."

"That's so cute," she sings. "So you're officially back out there. Audrey Dupree is back on the market, ladies and gentlemen!"

"I don't know if I would say that."

"You went out, with a man, to dinner and a bar—that's getting back out there."

I rip the covers off and roll out of bed. "I ripped the bandage off, sure, but that doesn't mean the cut underneath is totally healed."

"And that's okay. There's no rush here. Does Noah seem like the kind of guy to bounce in a week if you don't start putting out?"

"No. He's not." I pause, thinking back to everything he said. "He's incredibly kind. We talked all night, about nothing and everything. I couldn't tell you one specific thing we covered."

"See?" she says. "Don't count him out right away just because your expectations are so low. Give Noah a chance to raise them. He might surprise you." I dig through the top drawer of my dresser for a bra.

"Damnit, Nicole, why do you always have to go all Dr. Phil on me?"

"One of us has to!"

"It's only like eight-thirty in the morning."

"No time like the present," she tuts.

"And how's *your* dating life going?"

The words are barely out of my mouth before she's saying, "Just got home to the doggos, gotta run!"

I laugh and call out the word "Chicken" as we both hang up and I stare at the ceiling, bra hanging from one hand, phone in the other. Do I really have to decide today if I'm ready to let Noah Fox break my heart? Tomorrow? Even if he does call me, couldn't I have a couple more dinners to figure everything out? Even though last night felt so natural, we're still getting to know each other.

I can hear Nicole cackling in the back of my mind that she was right. It was time for me to get back out there.

Chapter Ten

NOAH

The morning is bright and humid as I move to my position on the line of scrimmage. The hustle and bustle of training camp is in full swing. Everyone is on the second practice field, some watching, some participating. Coaches yell and players stretch or vibe on the sidelines. We're learning new plays and running them against our own defense after a morning in the weight room and before an afternoon in the media room.

The second I woke up this morning I knew I couldn't hold off any longer. I needed to see her again. I waited what I feel is an appropriate amount of time—if one could call waiting a whole weekend to reach out playing it cool.

Audrey's been simmering under my skin since I woke up on Saturday. I close my eyes at night and see her smile instead of the darkness. To either torture myself, or to keep myself busy, I'm not exactly sure which, I texted her right before putting my phone in my locker and heading out to the field. So I'm out here wondering if she replied to me and when I can see her again.

Football is a symphony, and the quarterback would have

you think they're the conductor of the whole shebang. They're pretty important, but a band is nothing without every chair playing the right notes. Football is a sport where every man has to do their job perfectly for things to work. That takes lots of practice, good timing, and walking through the same plays at half speed over and over.

It does kind of all come back to the quarterback, though, as he's the first note you hear at the concert. The offensive line's job is to protect him. The receivers' jobs are to get open for him. Even on defense, the focus is on reading the quarterback and his offense. Football has occupied so much of my headspace for the last fifteen years that I thought my passion for the game would keep my wandering thoughts of Audrey at bay, keep me distracted from anticipating her text back. I wonder if my text was too lame.

> Want to go to the museum tomorrow? There's a King Tut exhibit running that looks super cool.

I want to get to know her and build a relationship. I want her to trust that I'm going to do what I say I'll do. Some guys on the team would probably drop dead hearing me talk like that, but my mother raised me right. Hard not to when you grow up in the South saying, "yes, ma'am" and "no, sir." Houston may be a big city, but we have small-town friendliness ingrained in our very souls—which includes manners.

A museum meetup says *I hope we can lean our heads together over an informational placard so I can get to know your mind.* I hope the message doesn't get lost over text. I meticulously planned for the time. It's late enough in the morning that she will have had time to get to her more immediate business needs before getting ready to meet me. It's not too far from her place, so it won't take too much time out of her day to get there and back. I know her time is more precious than mine. I get paid regardless of my play time. I want to be respectful of her business. Of her life. Of the hurt she's experienced before. I want to fold myself up to fit in it. Anywhere and any way that she'll let me.

I will admit that it's not a great time for me to be so distracted by a woman. After coming off an injury, I really need to prove my worth. My four-year, five-million-dollar guaranteed rookie deal is hanging over my head. It's year four already and I was injured in year three. I really want to stay in Houston, so I have to show them that I'm worth another contract.

Houston is home. Playing here is my dream. A broken ankle is a bump in the road, but not a death sentence. So I still have one more season to prove that I'm too good of a producer to be traded.

A girlfriend is a sure-fire way to get your head out of the game. Even in high school, I never had time for girls. I had a date to prom, sure, but she wasn't my girlfriend. Just a friend. Dad put so much pressure on me to put as much time as possible into football. In college, all the solo weight room sessions and lonely drills on an empty field gave me the best chance at getting into the NFL. When everyone else was sleeping in, hungover from a win, I was running suicides on the field because Dad would call and ask if I shouldn't be "making up for dropping that pass."

Now that I'm living the dream, it's an ongoing fight to stay relevant. That's the curse of playing at this level. It's a next-man-up mentality. There's always someone behind you, working hard to take your spot. All those years of pressure have worn on me mentally. Pushing yourself that hard without ever looking around and realizing you've made it to where you once only dreamed you could be is exhausting. Luckily, my therapist helped me recognize I made it and helped me take it all in. She can't help me with how lonely it is to not have a partner to share it all with, though. Plenty of NFL players enjoy the money and the bachelor life well into their thirties before settling down, but if there's a girl out there who perfectly fits into my life, I don't want to simply walk away from that chance.

I truly love the sport, but I'm not blind to the realities of it. It's fast paced. Weeks on the road. During the season you work eighteen weeks with only one break. No holidays. Night after night of shitty sleep in four-star hotels, lying awake wishing you were in your own bed. Your fate is always hanging in the balance. The one thing I can't offer Audrey is stability, and isn't that what everyone wants?

Hours pass under the hot Texas sun as I soak up time with my team. Getting ready for the start of the season is no joke. You're not in the shape you were in January. Your body isn't used to taking hits anymore. Rebuilding that muscle memory is like forging a blade. Melting down the metal and hammering it back into place.

I make myself wait until after my shower to check my phone, just to drag out the sweet heat of anticipation a little longer. Well, for that reason, and because I can smell myself.

When I finally grab my phone out of my bag, my heart leaps when I see her name on my home screen. She agreed to see me again.

AUDREY

I low-key love Egyptian mythology. What day?

I pump my fist to my side in victory. Unfortunately, that catches the eye of some of my nosier teammates. I quickly move my shoulder to block the screen from their sight. Colin notices that too. "What do we have here?" A slick smile splashes across his face.

I straighten out my smile. "Nothing."

"Doesn't look like nothing to me. You've had a goofy grin and a distant look on your face since the second you walked on the field." He knows me too well.

"Okay, fine. The dinner with Audrey last week went amazing. I wanted to see her again, so I asked her out and she said yes."

"You think that's a good idea? I mean, dinner was for sure, but seeing her again? Making this a thing? I'm not sure now is the right time," Wyatt pipes up.

"And what makes you say that, asshole? Besides the fact that you're in love with Nash, but it's 'not the right time' for you either." Wyatt has been harboring his undying love for his college best friend for years. Yet, even after all this time, she still hasn't noticed him.

"Did you forget how contracts work?" He's on the defensive now—ironic since he plays defense.

"Of course I didn't. My first priority is my career and this team." I shrug my shoulders. "I can have both."

At least, I have to try.

"I'm not trying to be a dick, and I know you're not either. I just want to make sure that you secure your place here next season. I would hate to be a Hurricane without you."

I nod. I appreciate him telling me my friendship does, in fact, mean something to him.

I've always had an easy time telling my friends I care about them. Whatever issue other dudes have when it comes to that,

I don't have. Maybe it's the way Mom raised me, evening out the overly manliness my dad tried to instill. She always made sure after giving or receiving the hardest hits on the field, I had a soft place to land with her. It kept the sharpness out of some of my edges. Or maybe it's my undying loyalty. Mom had her hands full with me as a kid. I had a lot of passion, a lot of testosterone, and not many places to go with it. Any dumb kid who ran his mouth about my dad had my fists flying. Got me into trouble, but eventually I learned to control it. Channel it into something useful.

I pack my bag and prepare to head home, my mind wandering to when I'll see Audrey tomorrow. Maybe I'm pushing it by making the next date so quick, but I don't care. I also don't care that it's a Tuesday. Football keeps a weird schedule, and it was easier to set a time to see her. Even if I catch a fine for being late, I'd still see her because after years of focusing on nothing but the game, I'm ready to take a chance at something more.

Chapter Eleven

AUDREY

On Monday morning, there's a knock at my door, pulling my focus from my spreadsheet. When I get up to answer it, I find Mom there. Sally Dupree is my equal height with curls from the eighties and too much perfume. She has a penchant for showing up at my house unannounced even though I haven't lived at home since I graduated college. The only resemblance we bear is in the shape of our faces. Otherwise, I take after my father.

"What's up, Mom?" I lean against the door, trying to squash any idea of her coming in. I have a meeting in forty-five minutes that I need to get ready for and can already see her peering around my house, assessing.

"I was just on my way to the shop, so I thought I would drop by." Mom is at the shop on Rue Calais Street on Mondays, so this is kind of on her way there.

"That's nice."

"What are you up to?" She attempts to move through the door, and we have a two-second standoff when she realizes I won't budge so easily. "Aren't you going to offer your mother a cup of coffee?"

Mom is relentless in all her pursuits. Whatever she's here to do or say, she's going to do it, so I sigh and open the door wider.

She sweeps through the threshold and into the living room. "I see you weren't expecting company." She purses her lips. "Otherwise, I would think you'd have cleaned up a little." She pointedly looks at the basket of unfolded laundry in front of my sofa. I feel the impulse to explain that this house is lived in, but bite my tongue. Hard to keep something spotless when you work from home. I suppose she wouldn't understand that because when I was a kid, I did a lot of the cleaning. "I was working."

"I see. How's business?" The way she says "business" belies her wish that I had stayed with the shop.

"It's keeping me super busy." I hit start on the coffee machine, and it whirs to life.

I follow Mom's eyes to the trash. "You've been eating out a lot, I see. You shouldn't be working so hard that you don't have time to cook."

"It's a tradeoff. Work more hours, make more money, and have less time to cook. It won't be forever. Eventually I'll get an assistant."

"Sure, sweetie."

I hand her a mug full of coffee. Passing her the milk, I restate my first question. "So, what's up?"

She blows on her coffee, taking a tentative sip. "Well, Sarah and Tyler are fighting again. He's taking the custody case back to court."

Tyler and Sarah were high school sweethearts who got pregnant their sophomore year of college. After a few years in the real world, things weren't as good as they had been in college. They split when my nephew was two. Since the divorce, it's been big dicking and custody battles out the wazoo. Tyler likes to fight for his time with Mikey, only to leave him with his mom while he and his new girlfriend (his former secretary) go out and "get a break."

"That sucks. I hope they figure it out quickly."

"Me too." She stirs her coffee. "You know, it would all get settled so much faster if Sarah could afford a better lawyer." I internally roll my eyes. It's all clicking into place. Mom is here because she would never air out Sarah's dirty laundry where anyone could hear.

This isn't the first time she's hinted at Sarah needing financial help. "She could always DoorDash while you watch the kid."

Mom waves her hand, chasing that suggestion away. "Nonsense. That's much too dangerous. She should be able to be at home with her kid. You must have some discretionary money since you've been working yourself to the bone." Doesn't she herself have three successful auto parts shops? Have they asked Lane for money? No, because they know exactly how much he makes.

"Even if I did..." I start, very annoyed. "That's not the same as paying for a lawyer, and you know it. I want to help Sarah, I do. Maybe I could babysit so she could take on more tutoring hours?"

"If you had a maternal bone in your body, you'd have more sympathy for a single mother. Who also happens to be your sister, Audrey."

"I wish she could get everything magically straightened out, but I don't have the money to help."

She sets her coffee cup on the counter. "I have to run, but we'll discuss this more at Mikey's birthday dinner."

"I'm not sure there's more to discuss. Money doesn't grow on trees, as they say."

"We'll see." She slides her huge bag over her shoulder and starts toward the door.

When she's gone, I lean my hands against the cool granite countertop. I don't want this to linger and ruin my time with Noah tomorrow. You would think it wouldn't be hard to tell my mom that I won't ever loan Sarah money because it makes family things too messy. I'm still not sure why she can't give Sarah the money that she needs. That's the parents' job, not the siblings. That's the thing, though, they never actually ask for money. There's never a "please" or a "could you?". It's like there's a knot in my chest with a string tied to my family, and I'm useless as it pulls me along. I've learned many times throughout my life that if you don't bend a little when people pressure you, you'll break. It's for everyone's benefit to just give a little. Right?

I slump into a chair, exhausted. I want a relationship with my mom like you see on TV, but sometimes I feel like we're watching different channels. Maybe it would be easier for me to figure this out if I had someone standing behind me, holding me up. I thought Hunter would be that man, but he's spineless.

I smile to myself because I know in my heart that Noah is nothing like that, and instead I choose to focus on our upcoming date.

———

There's a knock at the door just like earlier this morning, but this time it's heavier, slower. He's here already and I haven't had time to settle on whether I want this to be a date or not. I'm just going to have to set all the worrying aside and try and enjoy myself, get lost in the conversation like I did last Friday.

"Hey," I breathe. My eyes drink him in like someone who's been wandering the desert.

"Hey." I see him eye me from head to toe. I'm glad I picked something more casual today. My tight top is the perfect pair to my baggier jeans and Converse. "I'm glad we're hanging out again."

I nod. "Me too. It's nice to have someone other than Nicole to hang out with. She can get really busy sometimes with all the extra shifts she picks up."

"I'm happy to be of service." His smile is genuine and patient.

I step out to meet him on the porch, locking the door behind me.

"Ready?" he asks.

I gesture down my front walk. "Lead the way."

His Audi is parked next to my modest Camry on the cracked driveway, and he hurries around to open my door for me. I look at the ground as a blush colors my cheeks, not wanting him to see. How can I explain to him that the guys I've been out with before were so shitty they never bothered to open the car door for me?

The car smells like Noah and leather combined with something else. I glance down at the cup holder as I buckle my seatbelt and see two Common Bond coffee cups smelling sweet and pouring steam into the chilled air of the car. "Is one of those for me?" Noah nods, and I pick it up, wrapping my hands around it and savoring the warmth against the blasting

AC in the car. I take a sip, and I'm hit with oat milk and hazelnut. "How did you know this is how I like my coffee?"

Noah backs us down the driveway. "I've seen your order on your cup when you bring it before yoga."

I smile with the cup just touching my lips. "Thank you. This is perfect."

"Thought you'd need a pick-me-up. Figured you'd already worked all morning. Sorry, for planning something on a Tuesday. Practice schedule is crazy, and this is my classroom day, so I was able to get here earlier."

How was I supposed to have any fun today if I had a to-do list with unchecked boxes taunting me at home? I'm not going to tell him he's right, that I did work all morning. That's workaholic Audrey. This is fun, playful Audrey who is totally fine with not working a full day even though it's a weekday (eye twitch).

"You would figure correctly," I say. "So which museum are we going to again?" Houston has several, plus NASA, and a great zoo.

"Houston Museum of Natural Science."

"A classic."

"Did y'all go there for a class field trip in sixth grade?"

I sit up in my seat, remembering. "Yes! And they made us all watch someone dissect a cow eyeball!"

"I swore I was going to throw up the whole time!"

We're both belly laughing now as I gasp out, "What were we supposed to learn from that? What did we need to know?"

"It's been fifteen years, and I still have no idea."

I settle back against the soft leather. "I bet they don't do that anymore. Parents probably thought it was too gory."

"I have it on good authority that they do not, in fact, do that specific activity anymore. But they still teach square dancing in elementary school." I raise my brows at him. Does he have a kid he's failed to mention? He notices me doubting his sources and says, "Teammates have kids in school."

I nod. "I remember writing in my journal that I desperately wanted to be paired with my crush in square dancing, and how every week he got assigned to a different girl. Never me," I pout.

Noah pats my hand over the center console. "You poor thing."

We're about to pull into the odd-shaped parking lot of the museum, but talking about crushes sparks my interest. "Who was your first childhood crush?"

"You're going to laugh…" he starts, shy all of a sudden.

"I bet you I won't. Tell me and I'll tell you mine. You would never guess."

He hesitates, draws a breath, and then whispers, "Lara Croft."

"Oh my God!" I burst out laughing, then immediately cover my mouth.

"I told you it was lame!"

"No. I mean—yes. It is lame. But mine is Ash Ketchum." I move my hands from my mouth to cover my eyes.

"Anime? Really?"

"Like you're one to talk, mister triangle titties!"

He's crying laughing now, tears streaming slowly down his face. "So pointy."

This feels good. Better even than the times Hunter and I did stuff like this. He didn't see the charm of the science museum, and he was too cool to talk about silly things like crushing over video game characters.

Noah puts the car in park, quickly unbuckles, and takes off

around the car to open my door while I grab my purse from the floor.

"Shall we, milady?" His so-formal comment after the belly laughs we just shared almost makes me blush.

We walk into the museum, and I find none of the normal hustle and bustle. Where are the families with diaper bags and strollers lined up to buy tickets? Where are the employees who stand at the front to direct you this way or that? For a split second, I'm a little weirded out. "Is it closed? Did we miss something?" I glance back toward the exit.

He chuffs. "No, they're not closed. Well, not for us. But they are for the public."

"You did this?"

"I did." He smiles.

For the next couple hours, we wander around the museum, hand in hand. Talking about nothing and everything. Taking turns reading the placard out loud.

When we get to the Egyptian part, I get the heebie-jeebies around all the mummies.

I point to the one in front of me. "There's a real body in there."

Noah peers over my shoulder at the crusty shape wrapped in cloth. "Pretty cool."

"It's so gross." I read the name of the mummy aloud from the placard. "Did you know that the Egyptians believe the first act of creation was through masturbation?"

Noah whips his focus toward me, ripping it away from the mummy before us. "What?"

"One of my fun facts."

"How did it work?"

"It was believed that their first god masturbated, and through that act twin gods were born."

Noah looks at me like I'm crazy. "Why do you know that?"

"I took a mythology class as an arts elective in college. It covered Egyptians, Mesopotamian, ancient Greece and Rome, and the Norse."

Noah laughs and puts his arm around my shoulder as we walk to the next mummy. "You're something else, aren't you?"

———

There's so much to take in that by the time we get to the dinosaurs my mind is melting.

Noah takes note of my dragging ass. "Ready for a break from the never-ending search for knowledge?"

I nod, exhausted. "So much reading and walking and thinking."

He leads us down the stairs toward the main area. I always thought the design of this building was so interesting. When you walk through the front doors, the main hall is one long rectangle with thirty-foot ceilings. The doors in the very back lead to the butterflies, and the doors down the longer right side lead to the other exhibits. There's only one restaurant in this museum—McDonald's. It's been here for as long as I can remember. I don't think it's ever been anything else.

Noah pulls me toward it, and I follow.

"I hope you aren't disappointed in this meal after The Lush."

"No way. I love McDonald's, and I'm starving. I would eat anything at this point." Which is maybe how this Micky D's has been here so long.

We approach the counter where a lone employee is waiting to take our order. Her nametag says Natalie. Noah shuffles me in front of him so I can go first. "Hi, can I please get a McChicken and a double cheeseburger?"

The woman puts the order into the computer. "And to drink?"

"A Coke."

Noah steps up and I can feel his whole body behind me. "I'll have a twenty-piece nugget meal and nine sweet and sour sauces."

"And for your drink?"

"Sprite."

"Okay, perfect. You can put your card in the reader when it blinks green."

Noah pays and I collect our cups. Normally I would try and insist we go Dutch, but I was too distracted by hunger. It was all I could do not to drool.

We sit at a table, and it feels odd to be here alone compared to how packed this place usually is.

Natalie comes out with our tray of food. She has deep brown eyes and even darker hair pulled back under her McDonald's hat. "Thank you," we both say.

I set to work getting my meal ready. Opening both the sandwiches and putting the chicken in the middle.

Noah catches on. "Seriously? A McGangBang? What are you? Twelve?"

I stiffen, ready to defend myself. "I used to get them all the time when it was cool, but grew out of them. Like two years ago I realized I was still ordering the same thing anyway, and I just went back to putting them together. They're not full-size sandwiches, so two basically equals one anyway." I glare pointedly at his huge pile of sauces. "Like you can talk."

He holds his hands up in surrender. "I can't even defend myself. I love this shit."

"There is a certain je ne sais quoi about McNuggets at the science museum."

"Tastes like childhood," he agrees, putting a whole nugget in his mouth and I giggle.

We down our food in record time and start to clear the table.

Noah looks at me. "Are you ready for my favorite part?"

"The only thing we haven't done yet are the butterflies."

"I couldn't tell you why, but yeah, they're my favorite." He reaches around to rest his hand on the back of his neck. "Maybe it's the atmosphere or the beauty?"

I roll my lips between my teeth. This man is literally perfect. "It's my favorite part too."

The first thing that hits you in the butterfly exhibit is the humidity. I can feel my hair immediately poof. Houston's humidity is no joke, but in here it's cranked to ten. I bask in the familiar feeling. The smell is different. The vegetation is more exotic than the normal grass that colors the summer.

It looks the same as it did when I was a kid. The stairs are bordered by walls made to look like stone, and the tropical trees reach high above our heads.

I grab an identification card from the holder, look over at Noah and smile, preparing myself for the magic.

Chapter Twelve

NOAH

My mom used to bring me here when I was younger, maybe when I was eight. It was our thing. We'd go on a Saturday morning when football season was over, and we'd be so excited if it coincided with them having a new exhibit. She always said my dad got so many Saturday mornings with me because of football, she wanted to have something for just the two of us to bond over too. I've seen many different exhibits over the years, including death by natural causes and extreme weather. Mom would move as fast or as slow as I wanted through all the physical exhibits on the right side of the building. Then we'd eat at this same McDonald's. She'd ask me what my favorite thing we saw was while I munched on my kid's meal. Back then, dinosaurs were my favorite, but now that I'm older I realize it's always been butterflies for me. The amount of money and work it takes to keep these butterflies and plants happy and healthy must be exorbitant. The balance of the food and the air and all the living things are so delicate. Yet the staff here just does it. All for beauty and joy.

Well, that and to sell memberships and tickets.

Audrey and I walk slowly on the winding path through the brightly colored plants. Stopping to read about each species.

When we turn down the next path Audrey points out hot pink flowers. She looks up at me. "I saw flowers like this when we went to Hawaii a couple years ago on vacation."

She snaps a photo of a butterfly resting on hot pink flower petals. She's inspecting the oval leaves that come off the stem like corn on the cob. "I bet it was beautiful," I say and move to stand by her and read the sign. "Who did you go with?"

"Me, my parents, my brother, my sister, and my nephew."

"Wow. That's a lot to travel with."

"It was crazy. My nephew was only three, but my sister insisted that she didn't want to miss out on vacation." She hesitates. I see a flash of something behind her eyes. Something that leads me to believe this vacation wasn't as fun as it should have been for her.

The sun coming through the huge glass-domed ceiling warms her face. "Crazy how?"

Audrey turns and heads toward the next blossoming plant. "There was a day when we were at the resort pool, and when I looked up my family was gone. It was just me and my nephew. I had been reading and hadn't noticed them walking off. They didn't say anything either. Just took off."

I can't hide my surprise. "Where did they go?"

"To an adult-only swim-up bar. They came back like two hours later drunk as skunks, ready to pack up for the day."

"They just left their kid?"

"They said that since I was there by myself, I could help them out by watching the kid so they could have a 'real vacation'. They knew I was trustworthy."

"But it was your vacation too."

"Yeah, I paid my own way."

"And they just thought they'd brought free childcare with them?"

"They weren't entirely wrong. It was just me, and I wouldn't let the kid run amok."

"What about your brother?"

"He's taking over the family business, so he's never expected to do anything else."

"And your sister?"

"She's his mom, so she apparently deserves a break."

"Your family is something else." I hold my hand out to her. I thought me and my dad's relationship wasn't that great, but this is next level.

"Don't worry." Her smile is small. "I've learned to temper my expectations over the years." Hers is a quiet heartbreak. The kind that happens slowly over time. Regardless of my differences with my father, he has always supported me. Would I still be able to say that if I hadn't wanted to play football? That's certainly something to think about.

We walk a little farther in silence. I can see the exit ahead and it makes me a little sad knowing that we're this close to the end of our day together. If I think back to where we were just a week ago, I'm startled by how much Audrey has come to mean to me. I'm not one to fall hard or fast, but I trust my gut when it's telling me something.

"Noah, stand still," Audrey exclaims, and I freeze, worried I'm about to smoosh a butterfly resting in the path.

"What is it?"

"There's a butterfly right on your shoulder." She points to my left side, and I look down to find a black and white butterfly lounging comfortably on my shirtsleeve. "It's so beautiful. Hold still!" The camera that just a second ago was taking photos of the flora and fauna is now trained at me. "Smile," she says, and I look at her over the top of my shoulder. How could anyone not have a smile on their face right now?

The butterfly garden is magical, but soon I'll be traveling more often, and I need to have solid footing between us before that begins. I've seen how hard the regular season can be on relationships, and having one in its infancy stage could be a recipe for disaster. "Speaking of expectations…"

"Yes?"

I gather my courage to ask, walking in a slow circle around Audrey, making sure there are no hitchhiking butterflies trying to catch a ride to the outside world, careful not to disturb the one hitching a ride on me. When I land back in front of her, I take her hand again. "Where do you think this is headed?"

She opens her mouth, no doubt to instinctually say whatever first comes to mind, but quickly closes it.

I wait for her to speak.

She starts her slow circle around me. Checking me over and biding her time. Just the sense of her eyes roving over me sends shivers down my spine. "I really like you…"

My heart beats one big thump at the words. "But?"

"But… this is very new." She sighs as if giving in to her own doubt. "I can feel this thing between us growing and it's terrifying. I have lived all the highest highs and the lowest lows that you can in a relationship, and I don't know if I have the strength to do that again."

"You do." I take her by the shoulders. "I won't hurt you."

"You can't guarantee that." She looks defeated. Like she spent too many years trying to get people to see her, and everyone insisted on wearing blindfolds.

"I'll do anything to make you feel safe with me."

"I thought about it earlier, and all I can offer you right now is friends." I take a step back from her, dropping my hands from her shoulders.

"So, no to being my girlfriend?"

"Not yet."

"But yes to hanging out?"

She nods. I pull her to my chest and wrap my arms around her. "We can talk as long as you need. I'm not in any rush, Audrey. I'm willing to take whatever you're willing to give."

In order to do that, though, I need to be in Houston, which means I cannot fall prey to the distraction that working to gain Audrey's confidence will provide.

———

"Don't be nervous," Audrey says as she guides my hand where she wants it. "They don't bite." Her guinea pigs dance below, excitedly awaiting the carrot in my hand. They stand on their hind legs and snatch it from me as soon as it's within their reach. I never really thought that much about guinea pigs before now, but in person they're so cute. Their little faces and their squeaks do bring a smile to your face. We lean over the cage, shoulder to shoulder, and watch Reba and Dolly tug the carrot back and forth between them, both trying to take more bites.

"Enough, girls. There's plenty to go around." She puts another carrot on the bottom of the cage.

"This cage is huge." It takes up all the space on a huge built-in between the kitchen and the living room. It has hiding spaces, hammocks, beds of hay, and it's lined with fleece.

"The cages they sell at the store actually aren't big enough. They're social creatures, which means you need to have more than one, which means more space." She gestures at the big cage.

"Do you take them out?"

She laughs. "Of course, they're staples of Nicole and my's *Survivor* nights. We all sit on the couch with our food together."

"Do you ever make games for them?"

She gives me a mischievous smile. "Do you want to make them a maze?"

"Absolutely I do."

"Be right back." I watch as she goes out the side door and into the garage. She comes back carrying a huge cardboard box, a roll of tape, and a pair of scissors. We lay out all the supplies on the living room floor.

"So, this big piece will be the bottom, and we'll use the other pieces to make walls, then tape them together."

I sit on the floor next to her and start cutting pieces of cardboard. Audrey picks up the pencil she brought and outlines where the walls should go. I look at it over her shoulder. "Two dead ends? You're harsh."

"They're smarter than you think. They'll crack it in no time."

The sounds of tape ripping and cardboard cutting fills the air, and an easy silence falls between us. As we tape and make walls, I feel a warmth grow in my chest. This doesn't feel like a date. It feels more like a glimpse of what a regular weekend evening could be with Audrey in the future.

I watch as Audrey puts the last piece of tape in place and sits back on her heels to admire our handiwork. "Do you want to pick one up and bring her over?"

I put my hand behind my head to rub my neck, a little nervous. "Sure." These are her furbabies and I've never picked one up before. What if it squeals or bites me or jumps out of my hand? We stand by the cage again.

"You'll get Dolly, she's better with new people. I'll get Reba first and show you." She brings her hands into the cage; it's at waist height for her so it's an easy reach over the plastic walls. "You want to put one hand under their butt and one under their front legs." She does so to Reba, who easily allows herself to be lifted. She holds the guinea pig toward me. "Ta-dah. Your turn."

I step up to the cage and put my hands in. Dolly doesn't even flinch. It's almost like she's on my side here, being extra calm to help me out. I put my hands underneath her and she's so small that there's plenty of extra room. I scoop her out and bring her to my chest like Audrey did with Reba.

We move back to the maze, and with one hand Audrey puts some parsley at the end where the winner will finish.

"Okay, to the start." We both kneel down with our respective pig in hand, holding them close to the floor but not letting them go yet. "On your marks," she says. "Get set... go!"

We both put our guinea pig down at the entrance to the maze and they take off. Their little feet make pitter patter noises as they walk across the cardboard floor. Their squeaks of intrigue are quiet but cute.

I'm a competitive son of a bitch; there's no two ways about it. "Go, Dolly, go!"

They twist this way and that. Reba hits a dead end, and I yell, "Ha!" but she quickly turns around, heading in the right direction. Dolly is slow and steady, a tortoise doing its best to beat the hare.

But it's not enough when they round the final turn and Reba gets a whiff of that parsley.

"That's it, Reba," Audrey cheers.

Just like that, Reba wins. "You gave me Dolly on purpose 'cause you thought Reba would win!" I teasingly accuse Audrey.

She scoffs. "I did not. It's true that Dolly is better with new faces. We could have switched if you asked."

I scoop Dolly up from the maze where she's still looking for the prize and tuck her into my chest. "It's okay, girl. You're still a winner in my eyes." When I look up from consoling Dolly, Audrey's eyes are glued to me and full of affection.

Reba might have won the maze, but in the war for Audrey's heart, I might just come out the victor.

———

The days I get my full routine in are the best kind.

I love an early start to work because I can eat a second breakfast at the facilities. My protein shake at home only lasts so long.

I dive into the spread. Fruits to eat, fruits to make smoothies. Yogurt with one-million toppings. Pancakes, waffles. You name it—it's here. Apple juice, orange juice, grape juice, sparkling water, and coffee.

Teammates mill around filling their own plates and cups until we all start corralling toward the big room. Two double doors open into a room capable of fitting one-hundred people. This is where we meet Coach so he can talk to everyone at once. There are tons of coaches here and they all have assistants. The room is jam-packed with an extra fifteen or twenty guys since they haven't made cuts yet. I scan the room and take in the faces getting more familiar every day. It's going to suck when they get cut, but that's a future problem. You can't worry too much about the future in football. You can only work hard today.

If it were up to me, I'd want to keep all the new guys. That's why I'd be a terrible coach. My exterior is tough, but the inside is gooey.

Speaking of gooey—I spot Colin, who is equally as softhearted as me.

I sidle on up next to him, dropping my bag on the floor. He's already settled in with a plate piled high with fruit. I snort internally. Quarterbacks don't need the kind of calories the rest of us do. My plate is nothing compared to Wyatt's. The O-line takes pride in their heft. It helps to beat the guy across from you if you're bigger than him.

Colin's got his notebook out. I get mine and a pen.

We're just in time for Coach to start. Thank God; the fine for being late is something like eleven-thousand dollars a minute.

"Gentlemen. Welcome to week three of training camp. I hope you're all settling in and taking care of your bodies." He pauses to take in the room. "Today we are going to go over the game plan for the week, but first a couple of housekeeping things." The screen above him changes to the next slide. "If you're stiff or sore, make sure you're seeing the training staff. Nothing is too small to have looked at or worked on. They will decide if you need more stretching, more time on the warm-up bike, or ice baths. That's their job. Let them do it. They can't help you if they don't know what's going on." The slide changes again. "Monday is meetings. Starting here with everyone, then breaking into small groups for your position. Make sure you are taking legible notes. You might not be in pads, but this is not breaktime. If you are having trouble remembering plays, ask a teammate to help you study. This is your responsibility in your off time. I'll say this is especially true if you are fighting for a spot here. Running the wrong route in front of everyone will leave a sour taste in the staff's mouth. Media is still on Thursdays. Make sure after field practice you grab a shower and head that way. Grace will let you know if this is required of you, or if you are an alternate." He glances at his assistant. "Did I miss anything?" Jalenski shakes his head no.

"This team has fallen short every season since I've been here. And I'm sick of it. I'm fucking sick of it, guys. That ends this year. We have the talent. We just need to get the mindset. One rep, one play, one day, one game at a time. That's what it takes. We're going to have a take-it-to-them attitude. I can stand up here and talk shit all day. It's up to y'all to actually do the work and execute."

As Coach finishes up, the sounds of guys packing up around me increases. I think about what he said. Taking things one step at a time can apply to a lot in life. It's no use worrying about the future. Years of therapy continue to remind me of that. I think the same can be applied to Audrey and me. She can't help but look too far into the future. She's lost her trust. I have to earn it. I can live in the moment, be thankful for a movie here and a dinner there. Enjoying the time we spend together. That mindset comes with a lot of work. I do a lot to keep it up—journaling, meditating, and yoga. If it's important in my life, then I work on always improving. And the same can be said for my feelings about Audrey.

The rest of the day goes by in a familiar, steady rhythm, and by the time we are breaking it down in the tight end room to head out for the day, I'm ready to get home.

The house is quiet when I walk in. The housekeepers were

here today, giving the house the clean, empty feeling a hotel room has.

The more time I spend with Audrey, the more alone it feels here. Just me in this big house.

Maybe I should get a dog?

No. That's not fair to the dog. I travel so much. I would need someone to live here and help me take care of it. My mind immediately goes to Audrey as an answer to that question, but I remind myself that we are just *friends* right now.

My routine isn't complete yet. The small room on the first floor was meant to be an office, but what do I need that for? I turned it into something much more useful.

The yoga mat is laid out perfectly in the middle of the room. The sun shines through a north-facing window. Plants hang from the ceiling supplying fresh oxygen. It's simply perfect in here.

I pull the yoga mat out of the middle of the room and replace it with the thick gray meditation pillow. Nothing settles the mind and helps you take in what you learned like mediation. It's part of my everyday routine. Twice on game days. Some guys like to eat something specific, wear a special pair of socks, or listen to a set playlist, but I like to meditate.

The best thing is it's the same everywhere you go because it's always you. You're just accessing yourself and your breath intentionally. I can't think of any time in life where this hasn't been useful. It's important to relax your brain... just like cooling your body down after a workout.

I settle into the cushion and get my legs comfortable. I have more freedom with how I want to sit here than I do when I meditate on the field before a game. The cushion is comfy under my butt as I pull up the mediation app I like, scrolling through my options. It shows my last session which is my favorite.

Momentarily, I'm pulled toward thoughts of Audrey. What did she do today? Did she think about me? What is she doing right now? The sound of the meditation brings me back and I have to shake those thoughts away. I imagine that they are a piece of paper on the wind, blowing right by. I acknowledge my need to talk to her and tell my brain that we will text her when we're done.

With a clear mind I hit play on the meditation I selected to wind down with and listen as the calming music comes over the speakers.

Chapter Thirteen

AUDREY

"It was great seeing you, too!"

"Say hi to your parents for me, now."

"I sure will!"

I turn back to my cart and refocus on unloading groceries onto the conveyor belt. I can't believe I ran into Mr. Ron at H-E-B. He looks good for being well into his seventies. I haven't seen him since Sarah's graduation party. He used to be in Space City Auto all the time, getting parts for his hobby renovations, but as it got harder for him to get around and his son got too busy, he hasn't stopped in as much.

While I push my bagged groceries out of the store and into the parking lot, I pull up the family group text. Mom would love to hear this.

ME: You'll never guess who I saw in H-E-B today! Mr. Ron! He says hello to everyone and hopes to stop by the store soon!

I don't wait for a reply as I load everything in the car to head home. Grocery shopping is the worst. It's so dysfunctional. Touch everything from the shelf to the cart.

Then the cart to the checkout. Then the cart to the car. Car to the house. Countertop to the fridge. It's never ending and it's completely inefficient.

Once everything is put away and the new snacks are sorted into their plastic pantry organizer, I check my phone.

No response from anyone.

That's cool. People are busy. The shop doesn't close for another hour anyway. Everyone will see it later when they're home for the evening.

I pop a frozen pizza into the oven because it should be illegal to have to cook food and grocery shop on the same day.

I find my mind drifting as I wait for the timer to go off.

I'm not sure what I'm ready for, and I'm still one hundred percent sure he's going to head for the hills when we get far enough into this that I tell him I don't want kids.

Just how far is that, exactly? Is it like part of the pre-sex birth control conversation?

Like, "Oh yeah, I've got an IUD because I don't ever want to reproduce." Then we have to stop sexy time for him to break up with me because he knows he wants to have a son to teach how to play football? No, no.

I figure I have at least three months, and even then, he might get sick of me for a variety of other reasons before that.

If I told Nicole this, she would tell me that I'm convincing myself of things that won't happen again, but I don't care. She's not here. And that's exactly why I'm not calling her right now even though I know she's on her way to her NICU night shift.

I continue to mull all this over while feeding the guinea pigs their dinner. Tonight's entree is all the ends of the green beans I trimmed for dinner yesterday. Then I watch this guy on

YouTube waste scammers' time while I eat my BBQ chicken pizza. This time he was testing to see just how long they were willing to stay on hold. One guy did it for six hours before the YouTuber hung up on him.

I clear my plate and wash the sheet pan. When I check my phone again there are a couple messages in the family chat. I check them, expecting acknowledgements about me seeing Mr. Ron, but it's Sarah sending a picture of Mikey in his tee-ball uniform.

> SARAH
> Batter up!
> MOM
> How precious!
> LANE
> He's got his uncle's athleticism.

That is a cute photo of Mikey. I'm sure Mom read my text and said something to Dad, which made her forget to text me back.

I don't know what to say, but I don't want to be rude, so I just heart react to the photo and put my phone down on the counter.

Then I pour myself a glass of red wine.

Should I text Noah? I glance at my phone on the kitchen counter and consider snatching it back up and messaging him. I could tell him that sometimes it feels like my parents don't care what I think or have to say if it doesn't revolve around grandchildren. I could ask him what he ate for dinner and what his plans are for tomorrow and let him take my mind off my family. The first option will definitely end in questions I don't want to answer. So I decide not to text him as I take my wine and my phone with me to the dining room table.

It's still early enough to get some work done before bed.

And why not, it's not like I have anything else to do.

Chapter Fourteen

AUDREY

AUGUST

The time I've spent with Noah the last couple of weeks has been nothing short of amazing. We've mostly just been keeping to ourselves. Seeing movies and sitting way in the back. Hanging out at my house, making desserts and watching TV. Taking really long walks on days that Noah's feeling tight after a tough workout—which now that training camp is over and they're playing preseasons games is pretty often. But mostly, we've been getting to know each other. Taking things slow.

Is it a red flag on my part that I have yet to tell him why my relationship ended? Probably. I'm still not in a hurry. It feels like as long as we don't have that conversation, then we're not serious and this stays fun and just friends hanging out. And if we aren't ever serious, then there's no reason to have that discussion.

Despite that, I can't help but crave being around him.

There's such a caretaker presence about him. He brings a calm with him wherever he goes. It's like if shit is going to go sideways in my life and he's around, he's going to weather the storm for me. He won't let me get into a hard place and will be the rock in my life.

It's Michael's fifth birthday this Sunday. His big party with all his little friends is next weekend, and this is just the family celebration. As I pull up to my parents' house, I'm pretty confident in how things will go. I'll quickly open a bottle of wine to get me through the entire day.

I love my family, but... when we all got together for my mom's birthday a couple months ago, I walked in to find her hairdresser's son waiting to greet me at the front door. They thought I should get to know Sean. Apparently, he has a master's in mathematics and wants to work at NASA. What's not to like? Except the fact that this was only three months post-engagement blow up, and I was in no way ready to be set up with someone. I wish my mom would have known that it was too soon for me. But it never even occurred to her, I guess.

My parents are pushy, but they only have their life experiences to go off of, so that's what they think everyone should have. It doesn't come from a place of negativity, just a bootstraps mentality. It worked for them when they were younger (and the economy was better and everything was all around cheaper). But literally, times are so different now, yet they don't acknowledge that.

Mikey plops down on the sofa next to me and heaves a sigh only a kid who has no real responsibilities is capable of.

"What's up, bud?"

"Why don't I have any cousins?" Mikey is very upfront, no decorum.

"Because Uncle Lane doesn't have any kids yet."

"But you could."

"I could, but I don't."

"Why not?"

I stall, thinking how to best answer. A four—sorry, five-year-old—isn't going to understand sexism, misogyny, and reproductive freedoms. I go with the age-appropriate truth instead. "Everyone wants different things in life. Some people want to have kids, other people want to focus on their careers. I have different things that bring me happiness. Like hanging out with you." I tickle his side teasingly. "Besides, you'd have to share your cake."

He thinks for a second, the wheels behind his big brown eyes turning. "You're right. More cake for me."

"Exactly." I nudge him to the edge of the couch. "Now go wash up for dinner."

Dinner is only mildly chaotic. The chicken and the sides aren't done at the same time, and Mom's in a tizzy that waiting for the potatoes will dry the chicken out. My nephew is pretty unenthusiastic about being ripped from his iPad to sit at the dining room table.

The chatter at dinner is lighthearted, though. Everyone's in a good mood for Mikey's birthday. I don't care because I can drink my cabernet and eat my meal in peace. I would rather hear one-hundred times what Michael hopes to get for his birthday than let my parents turn their attention to me.

No one gets up from the table until Dad is done eating. That's the way it's always been. Once he pushes his chair back, the rest of us stand and start grabbing dishes. We all file into the galley kitchen. Mom shoos Dad and Lane away from the dishes, insisting that we will handle them after dessert. Sarah is quick to send Mom with them since she cooked, leaving Sarah and me to get the cake out and put candles in it.

I grab the gloves and the sponge to get to washing. We'll serve the cake right after. Sarah loads the dishwasher and prepares to dry. We first decided to do it this way in middle school. Sarah hated scrubbing, and I didn't mind washing with gloves. As I wait for the water to get hot, I can't help but think that maybe Sarah and I would be closer if I weren't so much older than her. Maybe it's her strong calling to motherhood, teaching, and everything kids. Her introduction to it at such a young age. Maybe it's my nonexistent motherly instinct.

I read once that motherhood is a spectrum. One side is the kind of person who knows from a young age that they want to be a mother. The other end is someone who doesn't have any interest in mothering or parenting. The lowest level won't even take care of pets. They don't want to be responsible for any living thing. I probably fall around the okay-with-taking-care-of-dogs level—or at least guinea pigs—but am uninterested in children.

"So…" Sarah knocks me out of my thoughts with her pointed tone. I grab a pot and start scrubbing.

"Yes?" I ask.

"Who's the boy?"

"What boy?" I make sure my tone is even.

"A certain six-foot, dark-haired man I saw you with at the movies."

"How did you see us at the movies?" I look up from my hands. "Why didn't you come say hello?"

"You two looked awfully occupied. You were hanging all over his arm with a stupid look on your face. Obviously, you guys are together."

"I wouldn't say that."

"What does that mean?"

"It means that I'm not interested in getting hurt again."

She nods slowly. "Right."

I already know where she's going with this. She didn't understand why I had to leave Hunter over something she didn't think I could be sure of. "If you weren't so stubborn, you wouldn't have to be so worried."

I rinse the pot I'm working on. "We've had this conversation before, Sarah. I feel the same way today as I did then."

"And you're worried that opening that can of worms will scare him away." It's not a question. Like she knows all the secrets I'm keeping from Noah, and from myself.

I decided to play dumb. "You don't know that he doesn't already know."

"I do," she says, and I stop washing.

I continue to look at the soap covering my hands. I want to bluff, but she's right.

She sighs like all her investigating of my dating life has tired her. "I know everything."

"What's everything?"

"I know he plays for the Hurricanes. I know you've been hanging out for weeks."

"How?"

"I saw you and Noah at the movies when I took Mikey to see that new cartoon movie with the cats. I did some sleuthing after. I knew I recognized him from somewhere. Once I got to googling, it wasn't hard. Tyler used to watch the Hurricanes all the time."

I thought I saw a blonde kid with light up Blue's Clues shoes when we were there, but was too engrossed in Noah to really pay attention.

"You're not going to say anything, are you?" I drop my eyes back to the sink. "I'm going to tell him eventually. We haven't gotten to that point yet." I grab the next pan and try to calm my racing heart.

"Of course I won't. Besides, it's not like I'll run into him or the two of you again," she says and my head perks up. "I'll keep it a secret, though, if you help me out a little."

I side eye her suspiciously. "With what?" I already babysit whenever she needs it.

"Tyler is fighting me for full custody. He got his high school friend who's a big shot lawyer involved."

"Mom told me, and I said no." I put the pan I was working on down and leaned my hands against the edge of the sink.

"I need help." My heart hurts at the desperation in my little sister's voice.

"I can't help with that, Sarah. I only have so much. Need I remind you that I work for myself? Why can't Mom and Dad help out?"

"They put all their money back in the business."

I snort. "Okay." That's such a copout.

"You work for yourself, and you've been working a lot, so either you already have some money to spare, or you can take on a couple extra clients to help me out."

"Where am I supposed to find these extra clients?" I wave my soapy hands around as if conjuring up said clients.

"Oh. You'll only need *one* more client, I'm sure. Specifically, one who plays professional football."

The shock of what she's suggesting hits me and I shake my head. "No. I'm not going to do that."

She puts her hand on my shoulder. "Of course you will. You're my big sister." She finishes drying the pan in her hand, sets it down, and leans against the counter. In the space of my silence, she drops the dishtowel on the countertop. "You're a smart girl, I'm sure you'll figure it out." She walks to the fridge and starts getting Mikey's cake ready.

I marinate in my own disbelief as I wash the rest of the dishes. When Mom said something to me a couple weeks ago, I thought she was acting of her own accord, but maybe she was put up to it by Sarah and just didn't do a very good job probing me. Obviously, Sarah has decided to take matters into her own hands and jumped at the opportunity that was presented to her after seeing us at the movie theater.

I move into the kitchen to gather around the table. Everyone is here watching while Sarah lights the five candles on Mikey's dinosaur cake. Mom snaps photos of him smiling while we sing. "Happy Birthday" rings in my ears as I stare blankly at my nephew's face lit up by the glow of the candles. The celebration around me is a stark difference to the thoughts running through my mind. I'm actually really livid that my family is putting the burden of Sarah's legal problems on my shoulders.

I have no idea what I'm going to say to Noah. I didn't want to get serious, and he wouldn't be interested after getting to fully, truly know me anyway. Even if I didn't want to keep everything on the D.L., helping my family is my only option here, otherwise I look like the villain. Noah is a good man. I'm sure he will understand. How much I feel for him already scares me. Maybe this is a gift from the universe—a push in the right direction. A way to hurt just a little now instead of enduring devastating heartbreak later.

Sarah might be self-serving, but I needed to have some sense knocked into me.

This can't go any further. Not without laying myself bleeding before him. Messy and distrustful as I really am. Even if there wasn't pressure from Sarah, I wouldn't have been ready for that. Despite my very real feelings for him, I know in my heart that this is still too new and I'm too scared.

I plaster a smile on my face and head to the living room with my little slice of cake, which crumbles like dust in my mouth. The chatter around me is more like the hum of an annoying mosquito than comforting ambiance.

After gathering up all the empty cake plates, I pretend to check the time on my phone. "Oh, would you look at the time?" I stand and grab my purse, moving swiftly toward the front door.

"Happy birthday, Mikey. Bye, Mom. Bye, Dad," I say quickly. Before I step out of the door, I realize Sarah didn't even bother to walk me out.

Mom and Dad look confused, but they both hug me goodbye. Just as I turn toward my car, Mikey comes running out of the house. He slams into my legs and wraps his arms around them. "Goodbye, Auntie Audrey." He pulls back and looks up at me. "I'll see you soon?"

I put my hand on his head and ruffle his hair. "You bet." Then he's off, running back into the house, taking any defiance I had left with him.

Even when we fight, she's still my sister and I want to help her.

———

The days that follow are unlike any I've ever experienced. Work feels like an eternity. Yoga classes feel like a blink. Time between Noah's text messages and mine seem to contract and expand without reason. It takes me hours to respond to him because what is there to say? I'm seriously considering breaking this off, just when it's starting to get good.

If I tell Sarah to get lost, she'll tell Noah everything, and I'll lose him for good. Which is a really shitty thing of Sarah to threaten me with. If I give in to Sarah now, there's no telling what else she'll want. It could set me up for more of this in the future. Where would it end? How long could I keep the façade up? How long can I keep hiding from Noah anyway? The lies would eventually bring us crashing down and it would be my fault.

It's going to be my fault either way. I can hurt us both right now and save us some pain in the future, or I can continue on this path and eventually break his heart when he learns I wasn't honest with my intentions.

Doesn't seem like I have much of a choice.

———

I spent this morning clutching my coffee cup, worrying about how to ask Noah to see me again knowing what I'm about to do. I find myself swinging wildly back and forth between being relieved to have a reason to bolt, and bracing for how much this will hurt. The fact that my feelings for him are this strong after only a few dates scares me. This is a man I could get attached to. Which means I need to get out at all costs before we get to the point in the relationship where he starts telling me what he thinks I want to hear instead of the truth.

I remember what Nicole said, *Noah is not Hunter*. I want to believe that, I truly do, but after just six months of being newly single, I'm not sure I'm ready to test that theory. Being told he's okay with something when he's really not—for years— kills your trust in any human of the male variety. Is Noah a man who would be willing to do the hard work and build that trust back up? Maybe. But if I do what Sarah asked, I won't be giving him that chance. I'll be making the decision for him.

I'm saved from my own thoughts when Noah's text asking me to coffee tomorrow lights up my phone. It's a tight turnaround. To be ready to onboard a client and break your own heart in the process of twenty-four hours is a tall task.

I have no idea if he would even want to hire me. What if the team already provides a social media manager for him? It's more likely that there's someone who does the team's social media, but their personal pages are up to them. Either way, if he already has someone, then this is pointless, and it might ruin his image of me. He could think I'm just trying to cash in on his notoriety, which I'm sure would leave a bad taste in his mouth. We might be friends, but we've never talked about business.

The math is simple. Most athletes make a guaranteed amount from their contracts, but often take sponsorships on the side to make more money. There's only one famous tight end I can think of off the top of my head who makes a low salary as far as the NFL goes, but he more than makes up for it in commercials and sponsorships.

What if he moves on and I have to see him dating other people? My heart drops into my stomach. I'll have to see him happy every day and constantly be reminded of what we could have been had I (and my sister) not gotten in the way.

Besides, there's no way he'll stick around when he figures out I'm not looking to settle down and immediately pop out some kids. So as far as I can see, having him at arm's length is better than not having him at all. This way I can shove my blossoming romantic feelings down, down, down.

————

I wake up the next morning shaking off one of those dreams that feels so real, but the second you wake up it gets wiped from your memory. After brushing my teeth and hair, I step to the closet where I hung the business casual outfit I agonized over last night with a hefty glass of wine clutched in my hands. The straight leg jean, ivory silk blouse, and black blazer combo with my nude heels gives me the boost of confidence I need to push myself out the door.

Common Bond is bustling when I arrive. Not sure if I'm glad of the subtle buzz in the shop or mortified by how many people could bear witness to this. I glance around the room, the scent of fresh ground beans filling my nose. My heart absolutely sinks when I spot Noah already at a table. I take a deep breath, trying to push the nausea away. He went out of his way, like he always does, and I'm here to pump the brakes.

My heart pounds as I realize I spent so much time agonizing over ending things, I never considered what I would do if he said no to me working for him. Worst-case scenario, I leave here completely empty-handed. No Noah, no money for Sarah. Just me.

Noah's green eyes shine as they meet mine and I take a seat across from him. I drop my laptop bag on the ground, the weight of it dragging me down even more than I've been the last few days. He slides my coffee and a blueberry muffin across the table to me and eyes the bag. "Coming from a meeting?"

I smile, but I'm sure it looks more like a grimace. "No, I thought maybe..." I take a deep breath. "We could talk about work?"

"Sure, if that's what you want."

"I think you're great," I wince at my own cliché, "but I feel like we might be better as business partners than life partners right now."

Noah stares at me blankly for a second, like the words I'm saying haven't sunk in, then he leans toward me. "Are you okay? You seem kind of off."

I should have known Noah would be smart enough to read through this bullshit. That's what this is, and right now I'm the queen of it.

I can't even bring my eyes up to meet his. "I'm fine." It comes out almost a whisper.

"You're obviously not, Audrey." He leans back quickly in frustration and sits silently, arms crossed over his broad chest while I set my laptop on the table and unlock it. I know he doesn't understand what's happening.

"Did I do something wrong?" He gestures to the laptop.

"No." My voice wobbles.

"Audrey," he pleads, "Please tell me what's going on."

I breathe hard. "I can't." He reaches for my hand, and I pull it away. "Please, Noah. You have to let me do this." I hope he can read in my eyes the confusion and the conflicting emotions.

I'm afraid of losing him.

I'm afraid of keeping him.

I see his eyes harden. "We can do whatever this is, but how can I trust you when I know you're lying to me right now?"

"I don't know." How does anyone trust at all these days?

If this had scared him off it would have solved all my problems.

If there's no Noah in my life, there's nothing at risk here.

No Noah, no heartbreak.

If there's no Noah... there's no comfortable warmth. No clouds in the sky to take the sunset from orange to stunning pink. I try to hide the tears pooling in my eyes. He nods in response. Why am I even crying? This is what I wanted, right? I could have finally stood up for myself and told Sarah to fuck off and dealt with the ramifications of that with my family. I could have just told Noah about my aversion to having kids and let the cards fall where they may, but at my core I am weak.

So I start my regular speech.

"I have a variety of semi- to pretty-famous clients. They range from influencers to pro athletes. My goal would be to find brands that would align with your image and reach out to them and see if they were interested in a sponsorship or one-off ad on one of your social media platforms. When companies reach out to you, I'll be there to make sure you're getting a good deal. Your agent and I will make sure that everything is on the up and up." Noah's eyes stare blankly back at me while I talk. The excitement I saw there when I walked in is gone. He gives one curt nod and then turns his gaze toward his coffee, still half full on the table.

"I'll have to give my manager Arie a call and get his input." I nod, not trusting myself to speak. Noah fills the gap. "I'll do whatever you want me to, Audrey."

"Let me know what you two decide." I choke back my emotions. Holding in the tears threatening to fall and trying not to take off like a dog with their tail between their legs.

Noah's eyes stay downcast as he speaks. "Why are you doing this?"

"I'm protecting myself."

"From what?" He stares into my eyes now, searching.

"Everything," I whisper.

I gather my things, and stand. I turn back toward him one last time. His face is sullen and dejected. I hate that I put that look on his face. I hate being this way, but I feel like there's no way to break these chains.

I'm pissed at Sarah for putting me in this position.

The universe.

Even Noah for being so fucking unflappable.

But most of all, I'm pissed at myself for being weak.

Chapter Fifteen

NOAH

"Hello?" Arie picks up on the very last ring. He's always trying to finish whatever email or text he's working on before answering.

"Hey, it's Noah."

"I have caller ID," he says flatly. "What's up?"

"I want to take on a manager for my social media sponsorships."

I'm sure he can hear the dollar signs cha-chinging. "And why would that be?"

"It's a business opportunity," I say, though I don't think I'm all that convincing.

"Try again." Dammit.

"It's about a woman."

I can hear the creak in his office chair as he leans back into it. "There it is."

"We'd hit it off and we'd been talking nonstop, and then all of a sudden yesterday she showed up for coffee with her briefcase talking about sponsorships." I trail off... I don't really know anything else.

"This is a weird way to gold dig."

Anger pinks my cheeks. "She's not a gold digger." I try to calm myself so I don't bite my agent's head off. "She's already pretty successful at this. I've checked her website, looked at her client list."

"So if she doesn't need your money, then what's this about? She could have just let you down easy if she wasn't interested in dating."

I run my fingers through my hair. "I don't know, Arie. But I'm going to find out, and to do that I need you to approve this and sign the papers."

"I don't know if this is a good idea…"

"I will give you double your usual percentage. I'll take some from whatever I get, and I'll double yours. Just don't fight me."

Arie heaves a dramatic sign as he's wont to do. The man lives off of hysterics, but is ultimately controlled by cash. "Fine. But when this all blows up in your face and she leaves you high and dry, don't come crying to me."

"Oh, I won't. I can promise you that." Because this is the real deal, and this is how I'm going to prove myself to Audrey—and get to the bottom of whatever is going on with her.

———

I'm worried about Audrey. Not about her and my future, but in the sense of whatever happened to make her pull a one-eighty on me. I could see in her eyes that she needed me to go along with whatever this was. I almost asked her to blink twice if she was being held hostage because it was so unlike her to behave this way. The woman I was getting to know was not who was sitting across from me at Common Bond the other day.

If she thinks this shtick is going to keep me away from her, she'd lose that bet every day of the week and twice on Sundays. I'm determined not to let her forget how good we are together. How good we could be.

I genuinely don't have any skeletons in my closet. I'm not a one-night-stand kind of guy. I don't have any crazy exes. No one could have contacted her telling her I've got other women on the side or anything. I'm in no rush. If this was really in the shitter, she would have straight up dumped me.

But for some reason she needs me to be her client. And for that reason alone, I will go along with this and get to the bottom of whatever is wrong with her.

But the end of summer is fast approaching. The heat is still lingering and there's no sign of fall. It will make its tardy appearance sometime in late September. The only note of time moving along is the end of the preseason games quickly approaching. There's only one preseason game left. I've been focusing on getting fully in gear and keeping my mind off the fact that Audrey isn't completely mine. Sweating my ass off as we run new plays over and over is doing the trick, though... for the most part. Bonding with my teammates and the rookies just drafted to the team is covering the rest of my downtime.

Tonight, we're eating a team dinner in the private party room of a nice-ish restaurant in the city. We were all cut loose an hour early to have time to shower, change, and get here for dinner. Appetizers are being passed around. Crab cakes, meatballs, bread and butter galore. The chatter is amiable and friendly. Big, booming laughs drift down the table from the defensive linemen. The tables all have white linens on them and our burly, bruised, and tattooed bunch stands out against their starkness. I've been on the Hurricanes for more than three years now, and even if I don't feel comfortable with my position and the fight I've put up for it, I do feel comfortable with the men surrounding me. For the most part, they're good guys. Some of them are still learning to not indulge too much in all the special privileges that being an NFL player comes with, but sometimes you have to get burned to know.

Colin hands me a plate of meatballs in a tomato-y barbecue sauce and I scoop a whole one onto my plate. He takes the chance to ask, "How's the girl?"

"She's not my girlfriend," I snap.

"That's not what I asked, asshole. Geez, someone is testy today."

I'm not going to admit it's in spite of my best efforts. I've been the best damn client anyone could ask for.

She sends me the contract? Immediately signed. I send it to Arie, and just as he promised, no questions asked. "I'm not. I just don't want to talk about it."

This pricks the ears of the other guys on our side of the table. The kicker, long snapper, and the entire offensive line look my way.

"Don't want to talk about what?" Mack asks.

"Not what," Colin answers with a pointed finger. "Who."

"Nobody," I mutter. I have a recurring therapy appointment, I don't need to rehash things at our team dinner too. It doesn't matter that I don't answer because Colin quickly fills everyone else in on my romance turned strictly business. Nothing stays between two teammates here for long. Everyone heard me say I was taking Audrey to The Lush last month, and it seems like they've been talking about it among themselves since then.

There's a mixed bag of reactions.

Jaden snorts. "If she doesn't realize what a catch you are, then she's not worth it. You deserve to be fully wanted."

I rest my chin on my hand and my elbow on the table, listening. Finally, I lean back in my chair. "I have to respect what she wants."

Mack is the first to speak, shaking his head. "No, that's not what this is. Women want to know you want them. To know you're willing to put in the effort to win them over. She's obviously interested, and you got along great at dinner. So I don't think you should give up on this."

I scoff. "I think she wants to be with me. I can't just disregard whatever is going on with her and scare her away."

"No, no, no, no." He shakes his head vehemently. "That's not at all what I'm suggesting. I have... a plan..."

If this was a sitcom and there was a camera, I'd look right into it with my mouth wide open. "Yikes."

Chapter Sixteen

AUDREY

If I waited a few days to call Sarah and tell her that I'd done what she suggested, it's because I was waiting for Noah to talk with his agent. At least, that's what I'm telling myself. Maybe Sarah could have won the lottery in those couple days and wouldn't have needed money from me at all. But she didn't, so I unlocked my phone and hit dial on her number.

"Hello?" she answers.

"Hey," I start. This isn't a phone call to catch up or inquire about Mikey. This is strictly business, and if she expected anything else, that's her fault. "I just got off the phone with Noah's agent and he's officially on my client list."

"Oh, good," she croons like this is a legitimate thing and I'm just taking him on to elevate my status as a social media manager, and not as a backhanded way of her getting the cash she needs.

I stick to business. "I work on commission, so there won't be any money to give you until after he books a sponsorship. Even then it's split three ways. He gets a cut, his agent gets a cut, and I get a cut. So whatever big number you have in your head, you can go ahead and slash that way down."

"Sounds like you need to get to work then." Her tone is lighthearted, but there's a threat laced beneath it. *Get this done or I'll ruin you.*

"We already have a meeting planned for next week, and I have a few brands I think would be good for him."

"Sounds perfect, I'm sure he'll get whatever brand he wants."

"We'll see." I grunt. "I'm not a magician and I can't make him do whatever I want. He has to agree."

"That's not my problem, is it?"

"It is a little bit," I say.

"Thanks so much for calling and letting me know." Her voice drips with false niceties.

"Congrats again on the new client. This could take you to new heights!"

My gut twists at the way she's talking, pretending like everything is fine between us. I wonder if she's at the shop with mom. She could be putting on a show like this for her sake. I want to speak up and tell her to get lost. To ask Mom and Dad for money again or do what most of America does and take out a loan, but I bite my tongue and say "Thank you. Talk to you later" instead.

"Bye," she calls like the phone was already halfway from her face, ready to click the end button.

Then she's gone and I'm sitting alone in my house again. My sister and I now have a fake relationship, which is worse than it used to be. Before, we just weren't in the same place in life. Now, we might be enemies.

But I can't focus on her a minute longer as I have an

imporant meeting with Noah tonight that I have to prepare for.

––––––

Noah is my easiest client by far. He never questions my ideas or opinions. He's always on time and always polite. He has a twinkle in his eye that lets me know he might be up to something, but I mostly just shake that off. I could be convincing myself of it because it's better than seeing him give up on me. I don't have time to be worried about what that man could be doing. *Please don't let it be another woman.* I know I have no claim to him, and dating is well within his right, but there's a part of my stupid heart that would burn if I had to hear even one mention of his latest conquest.

I shake off those distressing thoughts and focus on the slide deck in front of me. Tonight, I'm headed over to Noah's house after he's done with football to pitch him a couple of partnerships I think would fit his image. The timing is perfect. A new season right around the corner means the hype for football is high. Right now, it includes a kombucha company, Nike (which, I'll admit is shooting for the stars), and a hydration supplement similar to Gatorade, but with less sugar. I'm interested to hear his thoughts on these potential brands. I've done the market research and taken into account what I know about him, but obviously he has the final say.

Regardless, I've done the work for this client and am confident one of these sponsorships—or maybe more—will pan out.

––––––

Later that night, a huge gate whines as it lets me through. I step out of my car and onto the gravel driveway of a beautiful house in a nice area of downtown. The sidewalks are perfectly trimmed; the oak trees are huge and lush. I turn to face Noah's house. It's exactly how I expected it. White stucco, light gray plaster, with modern black accents and dark brick. I walk up the front steps and the door swings open. Noah walks toward me, hands out to take my laptop bag from my shoulder and the stack of folders out of my arms. He leans in and kisses my cheek like he literally can't hold himself back from it. It might be a little more than acceptable for someone's "business partner," but we've thrown most normal things out the window already. Plus, I'm not about to fight him. I missed the feeling of his nearness. This deal is working for us both, but I know he feels the undercurrent of something else running between us. The same current that had us falling asleep on the phone. This feeling is almost a tactile thing—it crackles in the air.

Noah steps back. "Come in. I just put the rice in the jambalaya." Of course he's making us dinner. I would expect nothing less from a man as in touch with everything as Noah is. His family, his team, himself, and his connection to food. I'm sure he appreciates the time it takes to make a dish where you have to build levels of flavor. First searing the chicken and sausage, then softening the holy trinity (onion, celery, and green bell pepper), before adding in tomatoes, spices, and broth.

I step in behind him, giving his taut body a quick once over while I have a second. He's in casual athletic clothes. Like what anyone would put on when they get home after a day of work. Only difference is the blue and white Hurricanes logo. "It smells amazing, I can't wait."

Whatever the opposite of a bachelor pad is, Noah's house is that. There are photos hung on the wall, throw pillows on the couch, and a basket of neatly rolled blankets near the big screen TV. He sets my bag on top of the coffee table. "You can plug your laptop in here and put your slides on the TV when we're done eating." He turns and heads into the kitchen and I follow, trying at the same time to take in the rest of his house. Being alone with him is something I've been nervous about. I'm not a Netflix and chill kind of girl, and I didn't want to give any mixed signals. Now, I'm here for the first time under different circumstances than I had originally thought.

His kitchen is a reflection of him. Dark but warm. Clean-cut but soft around the edges. There's black cabinets and gleaming white quartz countertops, but the fridge is covered in save-the-dates and family photos. Noah is a man who isn't afraid to show you his gooey insides. I imagine that the Noah I'm in the presence of now is quite the contrast to number 49 on the field. I come back to reality while he's mid-sentence and I realize I missed what he was saying.

"–can eat at the table."

I nod. "That sounds great."

I start picking bowls up off the island. I turn to carry the salad and dressing to the table, and when I round the corner from the kitchen, I stop in my tracks. The far end of the long dining room table is covered in candles. At least fifty of them. Two chairs are set up at one end. The head of the table and the first chair to the right side. So many candles lay out before them, all the way down the long oak table. I'm sure I gawked for way too long when I feel the heat of Noah's body behind me.

"Too much?" His voice is low, a soft breeze against my ear.

"Uh, no. It's beautiful. Does everyone on your team get this treatment?" I joke, attempting to lighten the mood, lift the weight of the lust between us and remind him that this is just professional right now; that it can be nothing more.

"No. Just those I really care about."

Oh. My stomach drops to my feet. I wasn't prepared for his brutal honesty. His unfiltered interest. I whirl on him, and he smirks.

"This is a personal dinner, Audrey. The business meeting is after."

"You think you're so smart, don't you?"

"I do." He nods. "And I'm nothing if not persistent."

I scoff and march myself to the seat at the right of the table. Noah is immediately behind me, pulling it out for me. "Thank you," I mumble.

He sits next to me and spoons a scoop of jambalaya into my pasta bowl. We eat in silence at first.

I came prepared for a business meeting and I was instead surprised with a gorgeous man making me a hot meal. I peer at Noah over my spoon and watch as he blows lightly on the rice and meat mixture on his. Since I've got the green light for this being a "personal dinner," I'm going to take advantage.

"Would you rather fight one T-Rex-size chicken or one-hundred chicken-size T-Rexes?" He chokes on the food he just put in his mouth.

"What?!"

"Answer the question, Fox," I say, mock seriousness in my tone.

"One-hundred chicken-size T-Rexes, obviously. I could punt them."

"That's the correct answer."

"Would you rather be able to see ten years into your own

future, or six months into the future of the world?" he asks. I pick up my glass of wine while I consider the question.

"See ten years into my own future. If the inevitable heat death of the universe comes between now and then, it would affect my future too. If my normal life in ten years involves carrying a backpack of fresh air because money-hungry politicians sat back and did nothing while corporations destroyed the environment, then I would know the fate of the world and myself."

"Well thought out," he chuffs. We refocus on our food again, hints of smiles on our faces.

After finishing salads and the main course, he pushes back from the table and heads back into the kitchen.

What else could there be?

My eyebrows raise when he walks back carrying two beautiful, golden crème brûlées. He winks as he sets mine in front of me.

"I thought we were just friends?" These delicious little pastries are a lot of work.

"We are." He hands me a spoon. "Doesn't mean you shouldn't have what you like."

"You made these?"

"No, of course not. I ordered them from The Lush and picked them up earlier. I only toasted the sugar. Baking is a science, and that freaks me out."

So he's not a baker. Just thoughtful. Got it.

If his plan was to make me remember our first dinner together when I tasted the best crème brûlée I'd ever had... it's working. The look on his face as he lifts the spoon to his mouth tells me this was in fact his plan, and that he isn't immune either. In an effort to cut this off and rein in whatever is left of my professionalism, I scarf down the rest of my dessert in record time.

My chair makes an awkward scraping noise as I push back to stand. "I'll get the slide deck set up and meet you in the living room." I dart out of the dining room without waiting for his response. I'm literally trying to run away from my feelings. Yes, I realize how crazy that sounds and I don't care.

I'm cramming myself between the back of the TV and the wall, trying to blindly shove the HDMI cord in the right spot when a warm hand takes the cord from me and effortlessly connects it. I duck back out and pull on my professional Audrey persona. "Please take a seat. We'll get started." I pause while he sits, grabs a throw pillow, and puts it in his lap to rest his elbows on. He's the picture of comfortable except for his shit-eating grin. I'm swallowing too much in a poor attempt to keep my nerves under control. I've done the market research, I know the going rates, and I think I know Noah, too.

"Today, I'd like to talk about a few key brands I think would fit well with your image and your social media presence. If we agree on a couple, we can reach out." I hit the clicker and the slide changes to reveal the kombucha brand.

I jump when Noah snorts. I press on, "You're an athlete who enjoys yoga. You have the vibes of someone who takes care of themselves inside and out. The Bouch will be interested in working with you because right now it's very much a niche product. When people see you drinking it, they will consider it as a drink alternative for athletes besides Gatorade or Muscle Milk."

"No way."

"Excuse me? What's wrong?"

"This is not where I thought this would be going."

Hands on my hips, I say, "Well, I have two more brands to

pitch if I may continue?" Noah slaps his hands on his thighs and rises.

"Actually, no. It's my turn to talk. I've already been in touch with a brand, and they were extremely eager to work with me."

"And what brand is that? Herbalife?" I laugh at my own joke. Noah is not nearly that desperate.

Noah looks at me seriously, honesty in his green eyes. "Why are you here, Audrey?" I look at him. We stand toe to toe, blinking at one another. I know it's on me, so I break away first, fiddling with the hem of my shirt. "That's what I thought."

He turns and heads up the stairs. I stand there stunned. Am I just supposed to wait here? At his beck and call? He winds me up with that gentleman act over dinner and then just disappears on me right after calling me out? Rude.

I sit primly on the edge of the couch facing the stairs and whip out my phone. I'm not even checking emails. I just need something to do while I wait. Maybe five minutes pass when I see just a peek of feet coming down the stairs.

I see more.

Legs that are toned and tanned. No surprise there. I've seen all that before. Wow, it feels like a million years ago that we were at yoga together.

All thoughts are simultaneously wiped from my mind as Noah finishes his descent. My eyes bug out like a cartoon character. I'm pretty sure my jaw falls to the floor and my tongue rolls out of my mouth in shock.

Noah's wearing nothing but tight black briefs. They're not cotton, the fabric is something more athletic. They cling hella fucken tight to his thick thighs that flex and move as he finishes his stairwell catwalk. The band around the top has

SEDUXION written in white lettering. My eyes continue their heated stroll up his body. The V above the waistband of the briefs. Abs on top of abs on top of abs. How can a human have that many abdominal muscles? They're tanned just like the rest of him and—*did he oil them down for this?*

My eyes finally meet his and I'm stunned into silence. Very hard for me, by the way. I realize just how long I've been staring, and my cheeks ignite. I can feel the heat touching the tips of my ears, the flush over my cleavage. No way he didn't notice me giving him the eye fuck of a lifetime. Noah doesn't miss a beat, though. "You like what you see?"

I more than like. I'm tempted to search for the outline of his cock in the blackness of the fabric just to satisfy my curiosity, but I clear my throat instead. "What is this?"

He puts his hands on his hips, obviously proud of himself. "It's my first brand deal."

I put my elbows on my knees. "Let me get this straight. You skipped over all the normal athlete brand deals and went right to 1992 Marky-Mark for Calvin Klein?"

He points his index finger at me. "Exactly!"

I drop my head in my hands, shielding my eyes. "We can discuss this after you find some more clothes." He flexes his biceps at me, teasing. "Put that shit away." I wave him off. I can't think with him half naked like that, much less carry on a conversation.

He turns and heads back up the stairs. I mean, I'm only human, so I take a looonnnngggg last look as his tight ass ascends.

I need a second to catch my breath. Get my head on straight.

He set me up.

I'm one hundred percent sure no one else's Adonis client is

privately modeling products for them in their home after a nice dinner.

What is his angle here? Has he decided that since I'm so cut off from an emotional relationship that he may as well try and tempt me physically? Is it an act to try and make me break my business schtick?

Noah comes back down, pulling a white T-shirt over his head. "Okay, boss, let's discuss."

"You can do whatever deal you want, but keep in mind that the more family-friendly ones might not be as interested if you start with Seduxion right off the bat."

"I'm not worried about the family-friendly ones. My choices can reflect that."

"Whatever you say." I pause, giving him an out in case this is all a bluff. When he doesn't admit anything, I say, "We can get the ball rolling."

"Sounds good, but in the meantime, I think you should come to a preseason game. You'll have a better understanding of me, my image, and what kind of stuff I should be posting if you came. Maybe meet some of my teammates."

My smile is soft. Spending more time with Noah is what I want. As far as he knows, my agreeing to this is just business, so it can't hurt. "That would be nice." I cough quickly. "I mean helpful. That would be helpful. For me. To help you." I cringe. I can hear how bad I sound. Noah doesn't acknowledge my word salad and I'm grateful for it.

"We play the Phoenix Pirates at home this week. I'll send you the badges you'll need to get in." He guides me toward the front door. I'm ready to leave, but I'm not. I'm so at ease in Noah's presence. Like after the stress of everything, I can finally relax. I have to hold myself up against my clients and my parents and my sister. But when I'm with him, he's the one supporting me.

I also feel sped up, like everything between us is going one-hundred miles an hour on the highway and I'm not in control. But the thing is, putting business between us was supposed to help me get control back. I'm not sure that this is the outcome I was hoping for.

I turn around to get one last glance at his pine eyes.

This has been the overarching theme of my life. The loss of control. I'm a mistake, made with no maternal instinct. In order to make up for that, I need to be perfect in every other way. The perfect businesswoman. The perfect daughter. I will never be the perfect wife.

I can feel my mind fighting. The side that knows I'll never be good enough versus the side that doesn't care and just wants to take whatever it can have.

This man has the audacity to chuckle at me. He lifts his hand and touches a piece of my hair that's come loose from its ponytail. I look at his handsome face as he tucks it gently behind my ear. I inhale and it brings his cool, crisp smell to my senses. My hands itch to run through his hair and pull him to me.

I've got to get out of here.

I find my words. "I think that's my phone. Better grab it."

Noah cocks his head like a dog hearing a funny noise. "I don't hear anything."

"That's because it's on vibrate." I turn to step onto the front stoop. "Okay, bye!" I career down the steps leading toward the driveway. In my haste to get out of there, I totally forgot to show him the other brands I had selected. I turn to yell over my shoulder. "I'll email you the rest of the slides so you can review the other brands."

Mid-wave he calls back, "No need! I think we found the perfect fit."

Those boxers fit something perfect, all right. And it wasn't his branding image.

———

I'm an absolute mess. An hour ago, I'm not saying I ran to my car at Noah's house, but my stride was distinctly faster than a speed walk.

Now I'm lying on the couch, Dolly on my chest, Reba tucked in to my side, feet thrown over the top part, arm over my face as my other hand holds my phone to my ear. "I swear, he's trying to kill me!" I've been regaling the whole ordeal from tonight to Nicole for the last half hour. She knows a watered-down version of what's really going on, but she asks a lot of questions.

"Oh, he's trying to do something, all right. Bow chicka wow wow."

I roll my eyes. "Nicole, don't be the stereotypical side character in the romance novel whose only input is encouraging the female main character to sleep with the guy."

"So, Noah is your male main character? Your *hero*?" This girl is impossible.

"That isn't what I said."

"No, but it's what you're *not* saying."

"That's enough of that." I pet Dolly. She squeaks in satisfaction. "But to be honest, right now my entire focus is on not kissing my client when he struts his stuff." We both burst out laughing.

"At least you're getting good entertainment out of this, and probably tons of content for the clit closet."

I'm a grown woman with needs. "Stashing it away for a rainy day. I'll likely get more when I see him on the field."

There's something so funny about two grown women giggling on the phone about masturbating. We have truly fallen far from God.

"All those catechism classes couldn't save us." We cackle together at our own jokes until we're abruptly interrupted.

My phone pings in my hand and I hold it back from my face to check it. "Oh my God!" I gasp.

"What?"

"Noah sent me a pic." My voice is strangled, the sheer hotness of Noah's mirror selfie choking me. He's in his Seduxion merch, hip leaning against the bathroom counter. One hand holding the phone, the other behind his head, the bent angle showing off his biceps. He must have taken this right before he came down. I read the message aloud for Nicole. "'Thought you might need a free sample.'"

"He must be psychic and knows we are talking about him!"

"Ask and you shall receive," I snort.

We continue talking about how her last shift was, and a bunch of other stuff, but I keep sneaking glances at Noah's picture.

And realize that my clit closet is now overflowing with that one simple picture.

Chapter Seventeen

NOAH

I walk out onto the practice field with Colin, filling him in on how my business meeting with a side of modeling went. I'm really glad she's here, but I'm not sure it's the best day for her to come to a game. I need to start proving my worth immediately, and bringing my number one distraction to a preseason home game might turn out to be a huge mistake.

Next week the Dallas Outlaws will be here for joint training. They will practice with us Wednesday through Friday and then we will travel to play them at home on Sunday for a preseason game. These practices can get a little chippy because you spend so much time together and tensions are high. Testosterone is even higher.

"Knowing what a good dude you are, I'd bet she's also fighting feelings. Women love when you cook for them, and I've had that jambalaya. It's good as hell."

"I'm in limbo."

"You're not doing anything wrong." He shrugs. "You're just giving free samples. She's gotta decide that your flavor is worth putting all her money on. Then you can scoop her a big ol' serving of Foxy."

"That metaphor got way out of hand." I laugh.

He cringes, and rightfully so. "It did. I apologize for referring to you as something tasty to be consumed."

I clap him on the back as we walk up to the field and join the other men. "Apology accepted." We've got fifteen minutes until the game starts. Since it's preseason I did my meditation routine in the locker room, so now I've just got my finishing sideline stretches. "I'll catch up with you later, I've got to finish getting stretched out."

I claim a spot on the field. It may or may not be the perfect spot to catch Audrey in my line of sight. She's here, walking up the bleachers. There are tons of fans, but also spouses, families, and the press. I watch her ass sway up the steps and an idea comes to me. Why does the fun need to stop after our little meeting? She's seen yoga Noah, date night Noah, and model Noah. She hasn't truly seen football Noah.

Today, I'm going to give her a show.

Was I stretched by the trainers before even coming out here? Yes.

Would I ever miss a moment to put that sultry blush on her cheeks? No.

There are so many other people on the field, no one pays any attention to me as I approach the sideline, equipment in hand. Time to go to work.

Chapter Eighteen

AUDREY

I've just settled in my seat on the bleachers and put my water and iced caramel macchiato on the seat next to me when a perky blonde saunters up. "Is this seat available?" she asks, pointing next to me.

"Yes, it is. Go right ahead. Lemme get my shit out of the way."

She sits and heaves her gigantic purse off her shoulder, setting it on the ground in front of her. You would never know she's here to sit in the hot sun watching a low-key preseason game. She looks like she should be on the newest season of *The Bachelor*. She's got a perfectly straight smile framed by full, bright pink lips and artfully curled hair. She turns to me and extends her hand. "I'm Chrissy."

"Nice to meet you, I'm Audrey."

"So, which one is yours." She swings her gaze toward the field in front of us. The practice game field is way smaller than the stadium, so you can get a good look at all the guys' faces from here. "A rookie?"

"Technically? None of them. I'm Noah Fox's social media manager. I'm just here to get a taste of what being a professional athlete is like. You know, so I can make sure I understand his image."

"Damn, that's impressive. I'm with Colin, the quarterback. We got married last year."

"Congratulations!" I say. She tells me they got married at The Meadows in April last year and continues to talk about the ceremony and their honeymoon. I accidentally tune her out. I don't mean to. I just finally see Noah out on the field, and what I'm witnessing is making me dumb.

I watch him move at his own pace on the sidelines, stretching. It started off innocently enough. A couple hamstring stretches, some arm maneuvers. There's this one stretch that all serious athletes do where you bend one knee, straighten the other leg, and dip your fingers down in a circular motion. I've seen CrossFitters do it. I'm sure it's his routine, but watching a man made like that stretch is not something I get to witness every day. I swear to God, I could sit here for eons and never look my fill. Since Noah isn't my boyfriend, I let my eyes drift a little. It's a football field full of man candy. Like someone had gotten a football-shaped piñata for their birthday, but instead of Jolly Ranchers and bubble gum, it's filled with professional athletes. Even the coach is hot. He's much younger than the football coaches of Dad's age. Gone are the silver-haired old men. In their places are beautiful men with obviously high football IQs.

Almost as if he could feel my gaze leaving him, Noah ups the ante. My eyes follow his every step as he strolls over to the bench and grabs a foam roller. He greets some teammates, grabs a squirt of water, and walks back over to his warm-up spot. He places the roller on the ground and then lies on his stomach in front of it, hits a quick up dog, then rolls to his right side and drags the foam roller underneath his left thigh.

"Oh, God," I whisper. I thought it was just loud enough for me, but Chrissy definitely heard.

"What?" Her head perks up from her phone. She follows my gaze and her jaw drops. "Oh my God."

Noah is stomach down on the turf using the foam roller to massage and loosen his quads. Rolling those hips back and forth. His right foot is anchored to the ground, allowing him easy, rhythmic movement. He has a tortured look on his face, like the feeling is just too good.

I'm going to incinerate right here.

I can't rip my eyes away from him as he rolls off the roller, then over to his left side to repeat the movement. It's almost like I could feel it... the ghost of his body hovering over me, pushing me into the soft bed below.

"It's going to be a long fucking day," I groan.

"Yes, it is," Chrissy says. "Now spill. I want to know everything." For a split second I wonder if it's a bad idea to tell Chrissy everything. Her glossy lips and shiny jewelry don't scream "quiet confidant," but I decide if I'm going to be around the game, I might as well make some friends, and the fastest way to make a new friend is hot gossip.

For the rest of the afternoon, I'm tortured. Both by Chrissy's questions and by Noah's athleticism. I watch his calf muscles as he sprints to receive passes. I watch his arm veins bulge as he holds another man back on a block.

Then finally, I watch sweat drip down his face as he stands in the huddle and listens to whatever his coach has to say. I'm overwhelmed with a sweet sense of relief when they all clap together and head into the locker room.

But what I thought was the end to my torture actually turned up the heat. As the team was walking off the field, Noah made direct eye contact with me and fucking smirked— a grin that said he knew *exactly* what he was doing every second he was on that damn field.

Chapter Nineteen

NOAH

The air is a little tense as we file into the locker room. For some of the men around me, today will be their final day with the Houston Hurricanes. For the third time today, I thank my lucky stars that I'm still on contract and not fighting for my life out there right now. I expected to be distracted knowing Audrey was in the stands, but oddly, it was more like it improved my confidence. I ran my routes perfectly. In the plays where I blocked, I ran over the defensive end. All of that combined has me holding my head high as I grab my change of clothes.

I duck out of the locker room and head toward the area where they corral the visitors. There are tall bar tables covered with white cloth and people standing all around them. The general admission fans have been sent home, but those with multi-entrance passes given out only by the team are allowed back here after the game ends. Lots of girlfriends, wives, brothers, and mothers mill around the room. The ceilings are high, and the carpets are like that school hallway type, except nicer. Off to the side is a small table with sliced sandwiches, bags of chips, and cups of lemonade. I scan the room as other players file out of the team area and greet their visitors.

I spotted her from the field and was taken aback by her beauty, but seeing her up close, I have to suck in a breath. Her cheeks are pink from the late summer sun, and her hair is wild from sitting outside. Silver hoops glitter in her ears, and she ditched her usual silk shirt for the city's baseball team T-shirt under her blazer. However, her normal dark-wash jeans are still making their appearance. I'm lapping it up. I love seeing the way she fits into the room full of my teammates' friends and family. Like she could be that for me. We need to get her a Hurricanes shirt stat, though. Preferably a jersey with my number on it.

A thought strikes me suddenly—what are they telling her? She's been with everyone since this morning. They all sat in the stands and chatted while we practiced. What if they asked her questions that were too personal? If Chrissy asked her if she was into me, what would she tell her? I pick up my pace.

People greet me as I make my way toward Audrey. I clap my teammate's younger brother on the back, and I shake another one's new girlfriend's hand. The whole time I keep my eyes on her. Whoever she's talking to has their back to me. With thick, bleach-blond hair—it could be half the team's girl. I have no idea. She's talking animatedly about something, which I hope means she's had a good time today. I see the change of her smile when she notices me walking over to her. Seeing that reaction feels good. Like standing near the ocean and feeling the sea breeze on your skin.

I settle my hand on her back. "Hey, there you are. I've been looking for you."

"Hey," she says, smiling hard. "Chrissy was just filling me in on all the exciting stuff coming up during the season."

"Really?" I turn to Chrissy and lean in for a hug.

She smiles at me and tells me about the team welcome dinner they're hosting. She turns to Audrey. "I'll see you there, right?"

Audrey looks away, down at the floor. "I'm not sure I'm—"

"She'll be there," I interrupt. "She's my plus one." Audrey raises her eyebrows at me, her mouth a sweet little O.

I'd like to stick my—*whoa, hold it together, man.* I'm still at work and still being a gentleman.

Audrey recovers her shock quickly and gives Chrissy a friendly smile. "I can't wait. I'll see you there. Let me know if I can bring anything." They quickly hug, which catches me off guard since they've probably known each other about six hours maximum. I guess that's a lady thing.

Chrissy totters off in her skyscraper heels, and I turn to face Audrey fully.

"How was your day? Not too stressful, I hope?" Audrey asks.

I'm hyperaware of how close we are.

"No, it was good. I feel good. My ankle feels good." How many fucking times can I use the word good?

"I'm sure that's a relief."

"It is." I move my hand to the crook of her elbow. "So is having you here today." Feeling her so close to me, smelling her light and breezy perfume. Years of therapy have made me painfully aware of my feelings. Right now, they're very strong and they're all about Audrey. Admiration, care, friendship, and more. It sits in my stomach, and it's not the tittering of anxiety, but the pleasant fullness of finishing an ice cream after a meal.

It fills in all the cracks.

I'm pulled into her gravity with the weight of her gaze. We

stay like this for what feels like an hour, but in reality, is probably only two seconds.

She is startled when Gina interrupts us. "Hey, Noah. They need you in the media room." She smiles at the two of us. As the media coordinator for the Hurricanes, I owe her for stepping in. If she hadn't, I might have kissed Audrey in front of all these people, and I know that's not what she wants. Luckily, there are many ways to show her my intentions without PDA.

I let my hand continue its exploration of Audrey's arm as I bring my hand down to meet hers. "Come on, you can see me in action… again." I lead Audrey away from the room filled with friendly conversations and big, bellowing laughs.

I follow Gina's bouncing hair through the hall and to the right, toward the media room. It's like this all the time, but today might be a harder media grill than usual since it's the last day of preseason.

"You can stand at the back with Gina while I finish up." I stroll to the front of the room and take a seat at the plain white table saddled with a microphone. Cameras snap and flash from every angle. As soon as my ass hits the chair, hands go up in the crowd in front of me.

I nod at one of the reporters and she stands. "Ashley Thomas, ESPN2. As a returning player, is there anyone on the sidelines you see that has something special?"

"Yeah, I think Ian could be something special. He's from Cal State and he told me he deferred acceptance to med school to be here and chase his NFL dream. I think that's the kind of person we want on this team. Smart people with the tenacity to go after what they want in life even if other people tell them it's crazy."

"Thank you."

After she sits, I acknowledge the next one. "Robert Inglish, Gridiron Riff podcast. You're coming off a rough season last year, do you feel like you did enough in the off season to prepare yourself for playing at a higher level this season?"

I lean forward and put my forearms on the table. "I have an immense amount of focus. I've been putting in the work and then some." My eyes slide purposefully to Audrey's. "I'm also determined to get everything I want, on and off the field." I lean away from the mic and push my chair back. Gina pops in. "That will be all from Noah today. Thank you. If you'd like to wait, I'll have the next player in shortly."

Chapter Twenty

AUDREY

I blink.

Then blink again.

I can feel the heat in my cheeks rising from the look in Noah's eyes. I thought I was in control of this situation, that the lines were clearly black and white, but Noah is playing by his own rules. I stayed on the straight and narrow when he modeled his god-like body after cooking a delicious meal. I steeled my resolve against his warm-up routine that was essentially softcore porn. It wasn't easy, but that's just the physical stuff. I could write it off as lust, but there's more. On top of all those trials and tribulations, he's proven to me that there's a good man behind all that muscle.

Nothing he does is for show, it's all just him right at the surface. I push him away and he stays. I put other things above him, and he waits. A prideful man would have felt the sting of rejection and taken off to lick his alpha-male wounds while listening to an Andrew Tate podcast. Noah is not a prideful man. He's thoughtful, loyal, and persistent.

As he walks toward me, waving politely at the media

standing around the room, I realize that I'm fighting feelings as hard as I am fighting lust. I'm not sure how long I'll be able to hold out.

My right hand's full of obligations, my left hand's full of fear, and I realize that I have nothing left to hold onto Noah with.

He strolls right up to me, like that little show wasn't for my benefit. "Do you want a tour?"

I nod, barely able to focus on anything else but him. "Yeah, I'd like that."

He places his hand on my lower back and guides me out of the media room. Part of me is afraid that a photo of his hand on me will be splattered all over social media, but when I glance back, the entire room is focused on the front table where Colin now sits.

We leave the room and turn right. Noah walks so fast, his stride at least twice that of mine. I have to hustle a little to keep up, but as soon as he notices, he slows his pace. He wipes his hand over his mouth. "Sorry I'm used to being shuffled from meeting to meeting here."

He flips around and walks backward in front of me like a tour guide.

"If you look to your right and left you will see several conference rooms. These are meeting rooms for the different positions. All of the offensive line meets together with their coach to watch film and do team building. There's a room for every set of positions. Wide receivers on your left, quarterbacks on your right. This hallway is pretty boring." He keeps walking backward.

We enter a huge opening with big glass doors to the left, and to the right a painted brick wall with the Hurricanes logo on it. Over the hurricane image, Full Throttle, No Limits is written in white letters with a navy outline.

"This is the front entrance to the practice facilities. Basically, everyone comes through here every day. If you look up, you'll see the century chandelier. One-hundred years of teams are up there. The name of every man etched into the glass." I look up at where Noah is pointing. One-hundred, multicolored glass poles hang from the ceiling. They're red, clear, and blue. The light flows in from the huge doors, casting the color of the glass to and fro. "White means a winning season, navy means a losing season, and red is a Super Bowl." There's only one red rod, and it seems to be toward the beginning.

"Are you going to be up there?"

"I already am, I've been here three years." I look up at the three blue rods, the bottom of them labeled by the years. All losing seasons.

That must be so hard to see every day. You come in to work, looking for success, and literally hanging over your head are all the previous failures.

"Everything splits off from here. You saw the east side, let's go to the other side." He crosses the room in big, backward strides as I follow, taking everything in. This is what makes up Noah's days. I gaze at the shiny floors and the high ceilings and think about all the social media photo opportunities here.

On the west side of the practice facility, Noah takes me to a huge set of double doors painted navy. "This is the locker room. Probably the coolest part of the whole place." He opens the door and holds a hand up to me. Simultaneously, he puts his head through the door and yells "HELLO?" When no one answers, he gives a satisfied nod and pushes the door all the way open. "Had to make sure everyone was out for the day before bringing a hen into the roost."

I'm amazed by how nice the locker room is. Each player has their own cubby, probably four-feet wide. The top of them has their name emblazoned. Below that is a shelf that holds Hurricanes' helmets and brand-new cleats. Then a longer space that has hooks at the back. Everything is customized with the player's number. Some of the guys have family photos taped to the sides of their cubby, like when you decorated your locker in high school. I walk a slow circle around the room, looking at everyone's photos. Some have boxes with fan mail piled high. When I get to Noah's, the family portrait catches my eye. I see a younger Noah standing beside his parents. He has his arm thrown over his mom's shoulders.

As I scan, I feel Noah step closer to me. "That was my senior year of college on our last family vacation before I went pro."

"You look happy."

"I was." He pauses as if considering whether to say more. "I had finally done what my dad had always wanted me to do, but when I got to the league I was overwhelmed with the pressure and all the changes that come with leaving college."

"I'm sure that was hard."

"All that ever mattered to my dad was that I go pro, like him. That was always at the front of my mind. Reaching it was everything to me, and when I finally did, I was so stressed about the responsibility and expectations. It sounds so stupid because there's millions of guys who would kill to be in my position and I was anxious and insecure about it."

"Your dad was pro too? I can only imagine how hard that would be. The change between college and adulthood is huge.

It was hard for me too. Suddenly, you're out in the world. Before I started working for myself, I felt listless."

"I had a hard time handling it until I started seeing a therapist. She helped me get a sense of accomplishment for even making it this far, and gave me the coping skills I needed to be at this level."

"I'm glad you were able to see someone. A lot of dudes don't believe in that."

"My mom deserves the credit for that. She's a huge advocate of therapy for everyone."

"I love that."

He looks at me for a second and I can tell he's debating what he wants to say next. He wants to know something, but doesn't want to push it. "It seems to me like you've been trying to live up to your parents' expectations too."

I turn my gaze back toward the lockers, away from him. "My parents didn't understand why I ended my engagement. They thought my ex was a perfectly nice guy. To this day they mention him and ask if I know what he's up to."

"Ouch," he says, and I stare at the picture of Noah looking so happy with his parents. I remember at my engagement party, the same night I ended things, all the aunts were around squawking about breaking bows while I unwrapped gifts. The old wives' tale of however many bows you break is how many future children you would have. I made damn sure I didn't break a single one, carefully opening each beautiful package.

"What's your sister like?"

"She's the baby, and she has a baby. That also makes her a favorite."

"And what does that make you?"

"The eldest daughter." We're quiet.

I don't want to see the distance in his eyes anymore. I want to see the brightness they usually contain. And I don't want to talk about my family anymore. "Let's continue the tour."

We're on the north side of the facilities.

"This," he explains as we walk, "is where the training room is. Everyone gets stretched and taped up before hitting the field, which is directly out the back doors."

My mind sticks on what he just said. I realize that he was already good to go when he came out today. His performative softcore porn had a purpose.

That show was for me?

I'm speechless as he continues. After the training room is the weight room. He opens the door for me to peek in. "Two-thousand square feet of lifting equipment." I recognize a bench press, but most of the other machines are as over my head as aerial yoga.

I laugh. "I'm sure this is both impressive and expensive, but I have no idea what I'm looking at here."

One side of his mouth tilts up. "Let's go see the field."

When we walk out the double doors we're hit with the muggy heat of late August. Houston will get nice weather eventually, but it's probably still a month away. The hottest month of the year is almost over. Then we'll just get fewer hot days. You'd be surprised how nice eighty feels after months of high nineties.

A network of concrete walkways spread out in front is us leading who knows where. I follow Noah to the left one and he leads us toward the practice field.

"Didn't I see all of this today before the game?"

"Yeah, but from the field it's completely different."

It's huge. Not just a football field, but large sideline space too. The stands for the fans take up a massive amount of space. It's mostly empty now, the day having ended an hour ago. A few maintenance men making sure the white lines are solid and undisturbed. A couple of equipment managers are packing up the rest of the cones.

Noah turns to someone wrangling extra balls into a big mesh bag. "Brandon, toss me one." He holds up his hands. Brandon pauses and looks at Noah. He sighs. "I promise we will bring it back in when we're done. You don't have to wait." I startle as Noah catches the ball Brandon sends hurtling toward us.

Noah turns to look at me, his dark eyes full of mischief. "So, do you know how to throw a spiral?"

Chapter Twenty-One

NOAH

I'm about to take some thoroughly calculated risks and some possibly problematic liberties. I'm desperate for some of this space between us to disappear. I'm not the kind to turn down an opportunity when it's afforded to me. I spent all day watching Audrey laugh with my teammates, be friendly to their wives, and wear another team's shirt. I'm sick of this arm's length shit.

Her response knocks me out of my thoughts. "No, I can't say that I do."

I wave her closer. She takes one step.

What a fuckin' tease.

Impatiently, I take one massive stride toward her and close the distance between us. My body behind hers. All hard lines and rough hands. She's in front of me, all soft curves in her professional blazer.

I reach around her side and place the football in her hands. I watch as she tries her best to wrap her small hands fully around the leather. I chuff as I realize how incorrect her grip is and put my hands over hers. "Like this." I pick her right hand up and place just her fingertips on the laces. I put the left one on the other side to guide the ball. "Bring it up like this, use your left hand to guide it. Pull it back over your shoulder, then let it fly." I stand back just a bit, giving her the space to launch it and giving myself the ability to take a whole breath without my chest brushing up against her back.

She lets it loose and it's actually not horrible. "That was medium good."

She whips around on me, her face set in mock horror. "You mean I'm not the next starting quarterback of the Hurricanes?"

"I can lie and say that you are. If it means—" Maybe I'm not doing a very good job at being patient after all. Giving in to my attraction to her is too easy. But there's more than just attraction now, isn't there?

Since smacking her in the face with a door, she's done nothing but what she thinks is best for everyone else around her. Even at arm's length, I've learned things about her that I like. How determined she is to work for herself, how hard it is for her to let go and give herself what she wants. How beautiful she looks when she allows herself to indulge, whether that be in food or laughter. All I'm doing is encouraging that. She's the one who's set the edges.

That's her problem.

I'm shaken from my fraught thoughts when Audrey closes the space between us. Her face is soft as she looks up at me. The sun setting behind her gives us this picture-perfect halo of light.

"If it means what?" Her breath is a whisper. I pause a beat. Her words hanging between us.

You'll want me. But I can't say that, so I choke it down. Instead, I focus on her, what I think might be keeping her from giving herself to me fully.

"You can have whatever you want. There are no rules." I can hear the blood rushing in my ears. She might be good at doing what needs to be done at the cost of her own needs, but I'm not. I'm selfish when it comes to her. Needy.

Instinctively, I put my right hand to her face. Cupping her jaw, I draw her lips to mine. I don't give her a second to think. I know she can think her way right out of this kiss, right out of my arms. I feel her freeze, just for a split second, then she leans in.

I put all my emotions into my kiss. What I hope we can be, if she'll allow us. I'm standing in this field begging for her to let me be more than a paycheck. To inspect every part of me and find that I'm worth more than whatever is holding her back. To trust that she can tell me anything. That I'll be there to catch her when she falls.

If she'll just give me the chance.

When we break apart, she rolls her lips together like she's trying to savor the taste of our kiss, but I can read indecision in the lines of her face.

She reaches out and takes my hand by just my first two fingers. "Noah, I-I'm still trying to figure some things out. I can't go around chasing whatever my heart wants."

"Why can't you?"

"I have responsibilities."

"So do I"—I gesture at the field around us—"but I'm not going to let that keep me from living my life."

"You're living your dream."

"Now, yes. But at first, when I was a kid, this was my dad's dream. He wanted me to go pro like him. So this is my dream, but it's not playing football that fulfilled it, it's getting my dad off my back that did." It's my turn to look away from her. "I don't know what I would do if I hadn't ended up loving football too. Or if I hadn't been good enough to get drafted. Would my dad and I still be okay, or would he only look at me and see disappointment?"

She squeezes my hand, which makes me look back at her. "I'm sure no matter how much he loves football, he loves you more, and whatever you had decided to do instead he would become a fan of. Because it's you." Her voice trails off at the end like she's saying it to me, but part of it is reverberating around in her own mind. She's probably thinking about her own parents.

I squeeze her hand back. "Thank you." I check the time on my phone. "We should get back."

I jog fifteen feet to where Audrey's ball went and pick it up. I carry it with me as I guide her back in the direction of the main building.

That throw certainly wasn't a spiral, but my head is definitely spiraling out over her and what we are and where we're going.

Chapter Twenty-Two

AUDREY

Since our kiss on the practice field last week, I've kind of been avoiding Noah. I just need time to get my head sorted. That might be my problem, though. Thinking it's my head that needs sorting and not my heart.

My phone rings, breaking me of my reverie. *Sarah* flashes across the screen and I swipe to answer it.

I'm not excited to be talking to her considering our last phone call.

"Can you watch Mikey on Saturday? Tyler just called and bailed on his time with Mikey this weekend, and I already made plans to do extra tutoring Saturday night."

"Hello to you too," I say. "I have plans. A backyard BBQ thing."

"Good. Sounds like you can bring Mikey with you."

"It's not at Noah's house. It's rude to show up with extra people."

"It's not nice to lie to people either…" she admonishes.

"What if I tell him just to get you off my ass? Then what?"

"You won't." Her voice is confident.

I can feel my teeth grinding themselves down to nothing. "How do you know?"

"You can't help but put people before yourself. You do want to help me, and you want to keep Noah. This way, you're doing both. You're welcome."

She's not wrong. I'm still fully convinced that if Noah knew all of me, he wouldn't be interested. The way he kissed me the other day makes me think I could have everything. That if I asked for it, he would give it to me. I'm just not someone who asks for what they want.

"I have to double check and make sure it's okay."

"You do that." I hang up with Sarah and go right to my text messages with Noah.

ME: Hey, Sarah just called and I've got the nibling on Saturday night so I can't go.

There. Open ended, ball in his court.

I swipe away my texts, and turn back to my laptop. The bright red number over my email is giving me acid reflux, and I'm determined to get it down to zero before lunchtime. I'm about to type out my salutation when my phone rings again, Noah's name across it and a photo of him with a butterfly on his shoulder from the museum.

For the second time in five minutes, I swipe to answer my phone.

"Just bring him."

"What? Who?" My voice is tinged with confusion.

"Your nephew. Just bring him to the team dinner on Saturday night. It's at Jaden's house. Chill vibes, and family friendly. It's a pool and grill out kind of thing."

"I could never impose like that. I'm already your plus one, I couldn't bring another."

"Audrey, it's just one kid. I'm sure Jaden can spare an extra hot dog. There will be plenty of entertainment, and other kids will be there. Just have him pack a swimsuit."

"I'll need to clear it with his mom first," I hedge.

"Of course."

"And I would hate to be a burden." *Excuses.*

"You're not."

"But if you insist…"

"I do." He does.

"Okay, then."

"Okay."

"I'll see you Saturday."

"You will." The line goes silent.

I think we are both thinking about our practice field kiss. It was just a taste, like the perfectly small servings of gelato they have in Italy. He may have kissed me, but I stepped into his space first. I don't think either of us regrets it.

"We won't be kissing at the party. Regardless of whether or not I'm bringing Mikey. Just so you know."

"Mhm," Noah says, placating me. "It was a moment of weakness."

"For both of us."

"But you liked it."

My stomach drops as if trying to touch my toes. "Okay. Bye now."

I can hear the chagrin in his voice. "And you want to do it again."

I can feel the tips of my ears turning the slightest shade of pink. "Gotta go."

"And I really liked it too." Then he hangs up. I huff. The man is nothing if not persistent.

———

Saturday afternoon, I'm digging through my closet looking for the perfect team/family, pool party/cookout outfit. After putting on a light blue sundress and taking it off, I settle on my white jean shorts with sunflowers stitched on them and a strappy golden tank top. I throw a bikini in a bag along with some pool towels and sunscreen.

I open the front door and find Sarah and Mikey standing there. She's got jeans and a T-shirt on despite the heat. He's wearing swim trunks and a dino T-shirt.

"Hey, little man!" I lean toward Mikey. "Are you ready to go play at the pool?"

Mikey throws his little fist in the air. "Yes!"

"Okay, Mom and I are going to get your car seat in my car for the evening and then we'll get going."

Sarah puts a hand behind Mikey's head and steers him back down the walkway toward her car. "Why don't you sit in the car's AC while we get it switched." Mikey sits on the regular seat while Sarah undoes the car seat.

I open my car doors and lean in the opposite side of her to help her connect it. I could just keep one in my car, but I'd rather do the swap when I need to.

"What do you think you're doing?"

"Helping?" My brows scrunch together in confusion.

"No, I mean telling my kid that family isn't important, and he shouldn't have kids."

"I never said that." She doesn't give me any more space to explain.

"Honestly, Audrey. I don't know what your problem is. What kind of person tells a little kid they don't have to listen to their parents."

"What are you talking about?"

She points her finger at me accusingly. "You know exactly

what I'm talking about. That little stunt you pulled at Mikey's birthday?"

"You aren't letting me speak! I just told him that not everyone feels like they have to have a family of their own to be happy. That everyone gets their happiness from different things."

"So I ask for a little help with him and you're just waiting to undermine my parenting?"

"If that's what you want to take away from what I said, then I can't make you understand."

"I don't understand anything about you, Audrey. I don't understand why you left a perfectly good guy like Hunter, or why you won't take over the shop with Lane, or why you feel the need to be so... so... individual."

I sigh. I've known I didn't want to have children since I was a teenager. I babysat because it was the best money I could make at the time, but I didn't love it like my other girlfriends did. It really blossomed in college when I realized that there isn't a path you have to follow in life. Since then, I've been reading everything I can on women without children, which led me to feminism. I can talk about the patriarchy, capitalism, and the Witch Trials' effect on women's power until I'm blue in the face and she will never understand. She won't want to hear that any time I dream that I become accidentally pregnant, it always ends with me terminating the pregnancy. That I'm simply not cut out for her normal. That's okay with me. I knew that my other friends would get married, have children, and move on from me. Their days would be spent hanging out with other parents at gymnastics and dance classes. That's part of the reason I wanted to work for myself, be my own boss. My business is my baby.

We click the last of the straps into place and lean back to

finish talking over the roof of my car. "I know you don't, Sarah." I wipe my hand over my face. "Do you not want me to watch Mikey tonight? If you think I'm hellbent on uprooting your family, I certainly wouldn't want to infer my beliefs on such an impressionable mind?" My voice is drenched in sarcasm.

Sarah's "No, no. That's fine" is lickety-split. She wants to misunderstand me, but she doesn't want to lose my help. "Just don't answer any more of his big questions. He's only five and he should be hearing stuff from me."

"All right." I don't want to step in it again anyway. "Besides, I would rather fly under the radar and keep everyone happy with my free childcare."

She just stares at me, obviously annoyed, and straightens her shirt and heads back to her car to get Mikey out and buckle him in.

"I'll be back here to get him by ten."

"We'll be here."

She waves to him through the window. "Have fun with Auntie Audrey!"

He waves back as I buckle into the driver's seat.

I look at him in the rearview mirror. "Ready to rock?"

"Yes!"

As I drive, I can feel my anger bubbling up inside me. It's like now that I'm out of fight, flight, or fawn mode, my brain can finally make sense of what I'm accused of.

Sometimes it feels like my own family is intentionally misunderstanding me. How else could you explain Sarah taking what I said the way she did? I'm sure being a single mother is hard, and maybe she's a little insecure, but there's no reason to take it out on me. The emotional whiplash of being needed and trusted for childcare, to being berated for giving an honest answer, is painful. The sting of always being the minority fucking sucks. I can feel it beating in the back of my skull, hammering against my goodwill. I'm not sure what curse I was born with to have my whole family needing me, and at the same time never understanding me.

I take a deep breath to try and bank the flames of my anger as I pull up to Jaden's house at half past four. I can't allow the negativity in my family life to get in the way of enjoying time with Noah tonight. Even though it's a stark reminder of my spot in life right now. The part of me that desperately wants to be with Noah is being held back by helping Sarah out and the money that comes from Noah being my client. The part of me that's afraid Noah will reject me is being provoked by Sarah's reaction. Every time one of them makes a comment, no matter how inconsequential they think it is, it's a tiny cut in my skin. A reminder along with all the other tiny cuts over the years that I'm scared, different. The weight of everything is so heavy, it's keeping me rooted in place. Neither moving forward, nor back.

I hop out of the car and go to the back to get Mikey. He already has his goggles perched on his blonde head. Ready to go. I take a breath and steel my resolve to have a good time as we walk up the front path. This house is just shy of a mega-mansion. Like probably a thousand square feet off, give or take. As I corral Mikey toward the huge, double front doors, they immediately open and Jaden greets us with a big smile.

"Hey, Audrey!" He bends down to eye level with Mikey. "Hey, little man. Everyone is out back by the pool. Can I get y'all anything to drink?"

"Beer for me. Water for him." I can practically hear the whining starting, so I put a hand up. "You can have a soda when you eat dinner."

This placates the small demon, and he darts into the house, toward the flow of people through the backdoor.

I move to follow as Jaden shuts the door behind us. "Noah is out back, too."

I redden even as I try to act cool. I'm a little sick from the anger and anticipation fighting for space in my churning stomach. I mosey into the house, taking in the black metal banisters of the huge staircase and the giant windows in the family room. "Cool." I shrug, as if I'm not dying on the inside. "I'll grab a drink and head out there."

After the chaos of towels, goggles, drinks, chips, and sunscreen has been dealt with, I take a seat on a pool chair in the shade of a huge umbrella. I look over to the table to grab my beer and am startled when someone plops into the seat next to me. I whip my head around and see Noah. I suck in a breath because I haven't seen him in person since our kiss. Instead of having dinner to talk about his Seduxion deal, I've been sending emails. It's cowardly, but I haven't sorted everything out yet.

"Hey," he says.

"Hey."

We go quiet. This is painful. I feel so awkward after kissing him and leaving. We haven't talked about it at all. It's just lingering between us like so many other things. I know I'm giving mixed signals. If I wasn't still calming down from getting my ass chewed out by Sarah, I probably could make a better effort.

Noah, as always, takes it in stride. I know it's all on me. I'm the one who doesn't have the balls to say what needs to be said.

"I've missed you."

"Yeah," I shrug. "I've just been busy."

Noah's eyes drop to the bottle in his hands. "Don't do that." I frown at him. Why can't he keep things light while we're at his teammate's house? "Don't push me away because you're feeling bad about last week. You needed your space. I get that. Don't ice me out now that we're face to face. I can't take it. I want to talk." He takes a deep breath, and I can see the wheels turning in his mind. "I want to be with you. I said it that day we were in the coffee shop. I'll be anything you need me to be. You just have to let me."

I feel myself lean closer to him, hanging on his words.

"The need to respect your wishes, caring for you when you push me away, and doing what needs to be done on the field are heavy, but the need for this is harder to ignore. It screams at me louder than anything. Every day that goes by that you and I are not *more*…" he trails off. "It physically hurts."

Does anyone else want to take a turn fucking with my emotions today? This is too much to take in after arguing with Sarah. Shit is wound up and I can't bring it back down. He's saying the words I want to hear. That I don't have to do everything right all the time. That I don't have to make decisions that are in the best interest of everyone else except me. The control that I've been tight fisting since I left Hunter. More exhausting. I'm not even thirty and I'm tired.

My emotions were already buzzing just under the surface of my skin, and I find myself unable to hold them in. "I am not who you want to be with. I hurt you, rejected you, and for what? Money? My own comfort? You don't want someone who could do that to you." I laugh but it's empty and toneless. "I put work ahead of everything else. I'm not even the focal point of my own life. I'm too afraid to take what I want for fear of being hurt again. That doesn't sound like someone who is ready for a relationship."

"Then tell me. Tell me everything."

We're sitting so close together now. Our tone is heated and heavy compared to the summer fun going on around us. The other adults might not be entirely blind to what's going on over here, but they're keeping their distance, nonetheless.

In my silence he speaks again. "What happened today?" I look at him stone faced. "You were upset when you got here."

If Noah is going to continue this relentless, reckless pursuit of me, he needs to know the full reality. He has to have all the information before he can make a decision. I'm done holding back. I'm sick of protecting a sister who doesn't deserve it. I'm ready to light everything on fire and only keep whatever is strong enough to rise from the ashes.

"When Sarah dropped Mikey off at my house for us to come here today, she berated me about an answer I gave when he asked me a question. At his birthday dinner, he asked me why I didn't have any kids. I told him that some people find happiness from other things in life, so they don't have children. He must have said something to Sarah because she accused me of undermining her parenting and poisoning his thoughts of family." I pause, trying and failing to read Noah's face. When he just waits, listening, I continue. "And I just lost it. I'm fucking tired of the snide comments and the *you'll change your mind* declarations. I hate that my parents still think Hunter is a great guy whom I let get away because of my inadequacies." Anger burns my throat, choking me.

Finally, I explain the worst hurt. Arguably the worst thing I've ever done. "I started this whole thing with you in Common Bond weeks ago because she threatened me. She cornered me in the kitchen and told me that if I didn't help her financially with her custody case for Mikey, she was going to tell you that I didn't want kids."

"Why didn't you tell her to fuck off and tell me yourself?"

"I left Hunter because he thought I would change my mind. He was playing the long game, betting on the fact that I would change who I was. When I left him, my parents didn't understand why either because they also thought I would eventually come to my senses. No one in my life accepts me for me, except Nicole. No man has ever been okay with me not wanting to have kids. And here I had you. You were so kind and funny and charming and attractive. I was scared to let myself like you because I've been down that road before, and I've seen that the light at the end of the tunnel is actually a train about to run you over. If I'm going to end up alone eventually anyway, I may as well never get involved and save myself the trouble. That's what I thought I was doing." I look him in the eye for the first time since I started. "But you stayed. I couldn't shake you. Every time I pushed you away, you were right back when I turned around. Like my own buff boomerang. I told myself that this was working because I was helping Sarah, and I was able to be around you without making it serious. I couldn't help my feelings for you, and putting my emotions in a little box and locking them away every day is exhausting." I can feel myself running out of steam. The adrenaline from everything slowly ebbing. "I can't do it anymore. I don't care if you stay or if you go. I can't do this balancing act anymore. I can't wake up every day and put on the mask everyone wants to see."

I'm totally deflated. Everything that I've been running from for months now is out and nothing is holding me up anymore. It's scary as hell but also so damn liberating.

I prepare myself for the normal reaction—telling me that I just haven't thought about having kids with him yet, or that I will wake up one day in my thirties with baby fever. That women are meant to procreate... All the rest of the bullshit.

But Noah says simply, "Okay." My eyebrows reach for the sky.

"That's it?" I question. "You're not going to tell me I'll change my mind?"

"Why would I do that? I'm sure you've thought this through."

"I have. I've known since I was sixteen."

"I've never thought about it, though. I've always assumed that I would have them when the time came. I haven't thought much about what happens after football. What will my life be like when I retire? But you're right."

"I am?" I know I sound surprised, because I am.

"If I'm as serious as I say that I am, I should be thinking about these things."

I almost choke on my words. What kind of man says exactly what he's thinking? What kind of game is that?

Hope is on the very tip of my tongue. "So?"

"So, I don't think I can give you a fair answer right now. Like I said, I've never thought about it. I guess I thought that whatever woman I chose to spend my life with would just guide me with her decisions. I know that isn't right, and I'm going to take this into my own hands. I would never want to give you an answer without consideration, knowing that it could hurt you. Knowing you've been hurt before." He takes both my hands in his and kisses each individual knuckle. "I'm so glad you came tonight. I was worried that my actions last week ruined your trust."

"I was as much of a participant in that kiss as you were. If I wasn't at least partly willing, I would have never let you get close enough. And I certainly saw through the classic guy-teaches-girl-sports-thing. I knew what it was, and I allowed it." I glance down at his full lips. "I enjoyed it. Actually, I really liked it." His lips break into a warm smile.

The fog around us lifts. The upbeat pop music pumping over the speakers reaches my ears once again. I lean back on the pool chair and release the tension in my shoulders. Things are okay between us. This is not ruined.

I didn't ruin it.

I'm not ruined.

Sarah holds nothing over me now.

Chapter Twenty-Three

NOAH

I walk away from Audrey who is up off the chair, rounding up her nephew. I pull out my phone and shoot a quick text to my therapist.

> Hey, do you have any time for me this week?
> Not an emergency, just need to talk.

I put my phone back in my pocket and shift back into team player mode. Audrey has the kid out of the pool, plates in hand, ready to fill up on corn, potato salad, and hot dogs. I approach her and put a hand on her shoulder. "Need help?"

She slumps slightly in relief. "Yeah, can you get him a soda? The teeny ones if you can find them."

"Sure thing." I turn toward the covered patio where there are coolers iced down.

I'm bent over, digging through a fuck ton of ice when I spot Jaden's black Nikes coming up behind me. "What was that about? You looked super serious over there. Especially for two people who aren't together." I keep my head in the cooler because I don't one hundred percent know how I feel about what just transpired. I'm not completely put off from her because of what she shared, but it is making me realize that I was so focused on football that I failed to consider what I want my future to look like after.

"Audrey doesn't want kids."

"Right now?"

"Ever."

"Whoa." He takes it in, eyes wide. "That's not her kid?"

"No, dumbass. That's her nephew." I stare at the sodas in my hand.

Silence falls between us. Neither of us knows what to say. Jaden is the first to speak up. "Is that a deal breaker for you?"

"I don't think so." I shrug. "I haven't given it much thought, to be honest. My whole life has been about football. I never even considered..." I trail off, lost in my own mind.

"It's not crazy to opt out of kids these days. The world is burning, the oceans are acidic, and the cost of living is sky high. The NFL can be full of uncertainties."

I come up for air from the cooler, a small root beer in my hand. "All good points."

"No need to rush anything. The good news is y'all aren't even together. If this is a deal breaker, nothing is lost. Things between you stay the same, right?"

My stomach drops. "Right." Even though I know I'm falling in love with her. And just like falling off a cliff, the landing is going to hurt like a bitch.

On my way back to Audrey, I check my texts.

NINA

Of course. Is ten AM on Monday good?

I shoot her a quick text back telling her that it is. Then I put the swirling thoughts to the side. I can't figure out my future at a pool party. I have to be "right here, right now" as Nina says. Or the thoughts will overwhelm me, and I'll be an asshole to my friends and teammates. As Audrey cracks the soda for Mikey, I add "fatherhood" to my Therapy Topics notes list in my phone. That one-word bullet point is like a loaded gun. I feel the beginning tingle of anxiety at the base of my skull and take a couple deep breaths to bring myself back.

Later on, I end up in the kitchen with the other guys. I'm scooping ice cream on top of brownies in little bowls while Jaden does dishes. Others are putting things away, drying dishes, or just standing around drinking beer.

I can't stop thinking about my conversation with Audrey. There's going to be, like, fifty years to live after football, assuming I can play as long as some of the greats, but the average length of an NFL career is four years. Statistically, I'm in my twilight year.

I glance around me at the men in the room, all in the best shape of their lives, but brutalized on the daily. No one knows how long they have on this earth. No player knows how long they have on the field. The swirling of these thoughts prompts the words that tumble out of my mouth. "What are y'all gonna do after football?" Four sets of eyes snap to mine. I shake the can of whipped cream and squirt some right into my mouth just to have something to do while I wait for someone to say something.

Jaden is the first to speak up. "Like next spring when the season is over?"

I shake my head. "No, like when you retire."

"Why would I have thought about that already?"

"I don't know... because guys don't last in the league. You never know if this season could be your last."

Colin puts the pan he was drying away. "I'm going to

retire, then un-retire like Tom Brady. Go to some really shitty team and win another Super Bowl."

Wyatt leans over and punches his arm. "You have to win one Super Bowl first, dumbass." Colin fakes going at him, and Wyatt puffs his chest out in response.

A voice cuts through the noise. "I'm going to do porn." Wyatt and Colin immediately stop, arms falling at their sides. We all turn to face Mack. He gets a confused look on his face. "What? I'm serious."

"And what makes you think you'll be good at it?" asks Colin.

"I've got six-pack abs and a ten-inch dick." There's a quick beat of silence and then everyone bursts out laughing.

I'm spraying whipped cream on each dessert. "Okay, Mack. I think you've forgotten that we've all been in the locker room together, but okay. I meant more like family, marriage, where you'll live. That kind of thing."

Wyatt whispers, "I can never unhear that."

Mack asks, "Is this because of Audrey?" I cut a hard glance at Colin. *Blabbermouth.*

"It might be, but it's also an important thing to consider either way."

"I think it's futile to think about the future. You can make all the plans you want, then get hit by a bus tomorrow." He makes a little *poof* gesture with his fingers. "Then nothing matters."

"So, I should just go by how I feel right now?" Around me all the men nod. I nod back. "Okay. I'll start with that."

The rest of the BBQ passes without incident. I swim with Mikey, throwing weighted rings for the other kids to dive after. When the sun goes down, Jaden lights the fire pit and we all gather around to make s'mores. I sit in a lawn chair and take in the scene. The crickets are singing the final notes of their summer song, and I'm surrounded by teammates whom I consider family.

I glance at Audrey to my left. She's making sure the kids don't burn their hands trying to get their marshmallow off the roaster. Jaden tells a story about how when he was a kid his family went camping and his brother caught his marshmallow on fire. He panicked and started shaking the lit marshmallow around. It flung right off the poker and hit Jaden smack in the middle of his forehead. The kids around the fire dissolve into giggle fits and I chuckle too.

When I glance back at Audrey and see her smiling at me, I realize that this all feels an awful lot like home.

———

I walk through the front door of the building. Nina's in a tiny old house that was remodeled into a business. They're pretty common in the city where a lot of the general infrastructure was built around 1940. The office is cozy with a small waiting room. Fitted with a perfectly slouchy couch. I head back to her room since there's no front desk person. I knock lightly on the door. "Come in!" Nina replies from her office chair behind a big wooden desk. She rises as I walk and meets me at the super comfy chairs in front of her desk. She takes one and I take the other, closer to the door.

Nina has fashionable glasses that make her look younger than she really is. I've been seeing her since I graduated college to help with the whole professional athlete thing. In the beginning, we talked a lot about how to appreciate the hard work you put in once you finally hit your goal, not just looking forward to the next thing. Since then, we've had various issues to overcome. It's like once I get past one thing, something else pops up. Most recently, it was my injury. I was worried I would never physically be the same, or that I wouldn't be able to play as hard because mentally I would be afraid of getting injured again. I had nightmares about getting hurt. Ones where I broke my neck that would have me waking up with cold sweats. Nina's helped me through a lot.

She picks up her legal pad and pen. "Are you ready to get started?"

"Yeah, I am. Thanks for getting me in on such short notice."

"It's no problem, I had a cancellation for this morning anyway. What led you to texting me on Saturday?"

"I found out the woman I'm interested in doesn't want to have kids."

"She's your girlfriend?"

I sigh. "No, but I would like her to be…" I taper off. "It's complicated."

"I see." Nina leans back in her chair. She writes something down on her notepad. I bet her file for me is a foot thick.

"If we aren't on the same page, I don't want to waste her time. I know that there's no meeting in the middle when it comes to kids."

"And why do you think that is?"

"It's too much stress to have one just to please or keep another person."

"And what are your thoughts on children?"

"I've never thought about kids. I just assumed that eventually I'd meet a woman, and she'd know what she wanted, and it would all just shake out."

"That's a very male outlook on a huge life decision."

I lean forward and rest my forearms on my knees. "What do you mean?"

"I mean that as a young woman, she was probably told that being a mother was her whole purpose in life. If she's already made her decision, then she's likely been thinking about this since she was very young, maybe high school or college. Did you ask her?"

I had no idea what to say to Audrey when we talked poolside. I didn't have time to put my thoughts together. Hence, the extra therapy session. "She said she's known since she was sixteen, but the whole conversation kind of scrambled my brain, and when I came to, I realized it was something I had never taken seriously."

We're both quiet for a second. My thoughts churn so loudly in my head I swear Nina can hear me thinking. She's the first to speak. "If you decided you did want kids, would you be willing to move on from her so that you both could have the lifestyle you want?"

"Yes," I say, unthinking. It's not even a question. I will do anything to give Audrey the life she wants.

"Do you see having children as core to your life's purpose?" She looks at me over the thick rim of her statement glasses.

"No. How could I when I've barely thought about it?" I can't believe I've been living my life assuming something of that magnitude would just be taken care of for me. What kind of selfish asshole am I? No wonder Audrey didn't want to say anything.

"I know we've spent a lot of time talking about how to deal with the lifestyle and routine of football, but do you ever think about life after?" she asks.

"Not until this last weekend. I just was living in the moment, I guess."

"That's great, but sometimes we do have to look ahead to

make sure we're prepared. The longer you're in the league, the more sure you need to be of what comes next."

"I understand," I say and Nina gives me a second to think. "In a way, I can still let a woman influence what we do. Since it's not that important to me and I was planning on having kids if they wanted. I just happened to meet someone who doesn't want that."

"I have a couple other questions, but we're running out of time for today, so I'll email them to you and you can do some journal reflection before our next session. I'll also include the title of a book I think you should read. It might be easier to think about what you want when you're in your own space."

"Thanks, Nina. I think you're right. I just need some time." We both stand and I hand Nina her check for this session. She doesn't take insurance, so it's pricey, but well worth it.

I drive home robotically. *What do I want?* Am I good for Audrey? Why haven't I considered this before now? Has football been too much of a distraction in my life? What else have I been letting slide in favor of my career? If I did want kids, what does that look like when I travel at least nine weeks a year? I could wait until I'm done with the game to start a family, but what if I'm blessed with a long career? They won't see their dad six months of the year. Is that even fair? What if I get really hurt and I'm physically unable to care for them?

How did I overlook something so important? So life changing? It's a relief to walk into my bedroom, put on my workout clothes, and grab my gym bag. I have too much thinking going on and I need to quiet it with exercise. After I settle my mind and tire out my body, then I can come home and sit with the questions Nina sent.

I just hope that the answers lead me to a life with Audrey.

Chapter Twenty-Four

AUDREY

I wake up at six thirty, the sun barely lighting the sky, and my mind immediately starts racing.

Emails to return, meetings to schedule, Excel sheets to balance... I choke down the anxiety and get up to start work. There's no point in worrying, it just has to get done. If I take too long to get started, my mind will wander to Noah and the fact that it's been radio silence.

Luckily, I have piles of work to throw myself into. Often with no lunch break because I get too focused and forget to eat. If I'm not working, I'm not making any money. I'm sure there's a personal revelation in there somewhere, but today isn't the day for that.

Since I've mentally prepared myself to never hear from him again, I'm surprised when I see his name light up my phone.

NOAH

I'm sorry for clamming up on Saturday. I just needed to take a little time to think.

Is he thinking about the best way to let me down easily?

The best way to fire me? I steel myself immediately. Whatever he's thinking, there's about a sixty percent chance he's going to decide he does want kids, and tell me whatever is going on between us is over. I should be glad, right? I swore off men months ago, so this won't be any different.

I decide it's best to not give away too much so I just text back "Okay." Better play it close to the chest. If he's going to stop this insane campaign to win me over, it's smart to start ripping the bandage off now. By the time he sends the we-need-to-talk text, I'll only have a tiny bit left to rip.

Days go by like this.

I walk around in a haze of average.

My lattes taste just okay.

My savasana at the end of the sixty-minute powerful flow jam class doesn't hit as hard. My center is off. I can't find my balance in any tree or eagle poses.

Women are more educated and more successful than we've ever been before. We are dominating higher education attendance. There are very few things that our grandmothers couldn't do for themselves that women today still can't.

Except get a free, safe, legal abortion. Don't even get me started on that. I do not have time in my schedule today to lament about the loss of my rights, whether I wanted to have children or not.

Even my passion for the women's freedom movement seems further away now than it usually is. The feminist rage inside me is something that's always been there. Some people are driven by money or status, but for as long as I can remember, back to teenage me, I have been driven by the rage of being born a woman. Of having these expectations set upon me just because of the organs I was born with.

I shake my head. This tangent has gone on too long. It's distracting me from what needs to be done.

Today, I'm going to reach out to other professional athletes via their agent to see if they would be interested in my services. I'm anticipating Noah firing me. He has his pick of reasons. While I have him and things are good, I'm going to leverage his patronage to my advantage.

I know that Noah would never fire me over a failed relationship. He's too loyal. He would keep me around because he already made the commitment, and he would hate every second of it. I, on the other hand, would have to quit because I wouldn't be able to be around him. He's not a man who runs on pride. Noah does everything by the standard of his character.

Is a man of that character someone who can live a happy life without children if it means being with me?

Chapter Twenty-Five

NOAH

After cuts are made and the team is solidified, we are in Dallas to play the Outlaws for the last game of the preseason. Next week, the first week of September, is the beginning of the regular season. Since we both represent the same state and have very dedicated fans, things can get chippy. They like to call themselves "America's Team" but that's all advertising. Every season it's a battle for who's going to be Texas's team.

Every step I take away from Audrey feels like oxygen is thinning in the atmosphere, making it harder to breathe. If I lose Audrey, I'll suffocate. I'm not sure how to return to her life. Do I just show up like nothing happened? Text her to meet me for dinner and lay it all on the line?

In the hotel room, I try and stick to my normal pre-game night routine, but it doesn't seem to work. My hot shower/jerk-off combo leaves me feeling empty instead of sated. Laying out my arrival clothes doesn't excite me. Most of the time putting on the suit jacket makes me feel like my dreams have come true, but looking at them now, I almost feel like a kid playing dress up with his dad's clothes.

I lie in bed with the lights off for a long time, staring at the ceiling, waiting for sleep to come. It does, eventually, but not the good kind where you blink and it's been eight restful hours. More like the kind that feels like it goes on and on. Like every hour you're on the verge of being late for something.

The tone is terse and full of concentration on the bus on the way to the stadium. Stoic eyes everywhere you look. The new guys need to prove to the coaches that they made the right choice betting on them. I try to focus on myself and what I need to do.

The second I step foot on the field the electricity fills me and the hair on my arms stands at attention. The smell of the turf fills my nose. I walk over to the goal post and sit cross-legged underneath it. I pull my noise-canceling headphones over my ears and open up my meditation app. I close my eyes and let the voice of the narrator settle over me.

I've been doing this since my first season in the NFL. When I was having a hard time adjusting to the pressure of going pro, Nina recommended I try some guided meditation before games. I remember having my head in my hands on her couch and her telling me, "Some people's minds need more of a warmup than their body."

Today, like my whole week, I'm finding it harder to concentrate than usual. My breath isn't as easy to control as it usually is. Definitely has something to do with the fact that I'm just getting back into the rhythm of things. Getting hit like this takes some getting used to at the beginning of each new season.

When my meditation ends, I move through a series of slow stretches on the ground. I watch both teams as I move, noticing that their running back is slightly favoring his left leg. I tuck that nugget away for later. I get up, grab my water, and jog toward the bench to join the rest of the team with warmups. If there was any pushback about my quiet time before a game, they're long gone now.

Now it's time to focus on winning.

———

Everything is going to shit.

We aren't playing well as a whole. We aren't communicating. I ran the wrong route once and it almost resulted in a pick. Luckily, Colin was paying better attention than me and was able to throw the ball away. Things are looking dismal, including the score: three to twenty-one. Being two possessions behind is never good. We look like a team made up entirely of rookies, unable to find the end zone without an extremely detailed map.

The guy guarding me on the Outlaws is getting on my last fucking nerve. He bumps me every time I walk past, even after the whistle blows. I know he's just doing it to get under my skin. The constant shoving and shit talk would have me ready to throw hands on my best day.

It's not even close to my best day.

We break from the huddle and move to the line of scrimmage. Number forty-two and I have been going at it all night. Colin calls for the ball and we all slam into motion. I'm gripping this guy by the chest plate, blocking him. We struggle against each other until he pulls a swim move on me and lunges toward our running back carrying the ball. Jaden weaves through the gap, but number forty-two gets him by the shoestring because I blew my block. Two-yard gain on the play in a third-and-ten situation. Not converting on fourth and eight is a sure sign of a team slowly breaking down.

I can feel the anger burning in my chest. The outside of it is tinged with fear. Is this what our season is going to look like? If so, then my fears of possibly being traded from the Hurricanes and having to start over somewhere else in a city that doesn't feel like home is now full-on terrifying. Darkness swirls in my mind as I move back to the line. Which is why, when number forty-two starts his bumping shit again, I lose it.

"Back the fuck up, dude," I snarl.

He moves a step closer. "Or what?"

"Or I'll put you on your ass."

Referees blow their whistles like there's no tomorrow. Every one of my teammates on the field is taking hasty steps toward me, ready to tear me away from this guy or aid in the fight. "Gentlemen!" Whistles blow some more. "Back to your line."

My breath is heaving as I send a final glare his way and take my position again. I've got to keep my head on straight. This fourth down is too important. He knows it because as soon as I set my cleat on the line, he starts up again. "I heard your social media bitch fucks her clients. Think you can give me her number?"

"Fuck you."

"I bet she would. Never look back at your ugly ass after she gets a taste of this." He cups a hand over his junk and the movement is so lewd I black out completely. All I can feel is rage. I lunge at him with all my weight, throwing my whole body into his chest, mowing him down.

I stand over him and hold my arms open. "Let's go, bitch." He's quiet for a second. "Oh, that's all you've got to say?" Referees come rushing back up and a smile splits his smug face. I see the yellow flag on the ground next to him.

Fuck.

"Unsportsmanlike conduct. Offense number forty-nine. Fifteen-yard penalty. Still fourth down."

I killed the play. Ruined our chances at a first down. At fourth and twenty-three, we're forced to punt.

The punting team comes out on the field, and I jog off, defeated.

How weak of a man am I to get goaded into a fight? I'm just another testosterone-driven caveman who catches a ball for a living. As together as I've convinced myself I am, it's all fallen apart in minutes. I go right to the bench and sit down. Rip off my helmet and fume. I see Coach stomping toward me, steam practically coming out of his ears cartoon style. "What the fuck was that, Fox?" I only have the energy to look thoroughly embarrassed. I don't have an excuse for myself. "How am I supposed to trust you after this? Who am I supposed to lean on in fourth and long if not you?"

"I'm sorry."

"I'm sure you fucking are, but it doesn't fix a goddamn thing."

"I know."

"So how about you sit your ass on this bench for a while and get your shit together."

I hang my head, ashamed. "Yes, Coach."

For the rest of the game, all I can do is watch as we fall apart further. Our punt returner drops the ball after muffing a fair catch. Colin throws a ridiculous interception. Our lineman jumps early and gets called offsides. We're taking it from every direction right now and I'm sitting on this bench, wallowing in my own self-pity.

When the game ends, we file into the locker room like each of us are attending our own funeral.

"It's a long season, fellas, but it's going to be a helluva lot longer if we go out every week and play like that." He looks around the room, picking random guys to look in the eye. "I expected more, especially from the veterans on this team. There is no reason we can't be a playoff team this year except for the way we perform. You have to be hungry! Starving for a win! We lost tonight because the other team wanted it more than you."

After Coach finishes ripping us a new one, it's a quiet bus ride back to the hotel. I look around at my teammates, head down, AirPods in. Defeat is written across all of our faces. The bus reeks with it. A ten-minute bus ride feels more like ten hours. No claps on the back, no talking about crazy plays, no hyping ourselves up for the next game and replicating touchdown celebrations we saw. Just the deafening sound of defeat hanging heavy in the air.

The only break in the density is Jaden leaning across the aisle whispering, "At least you didn't throw a punch and get fined." I laugh and we fist bump.

"Hell, yeah," I say.

My dad must have some kind of sixth sense because the second I step into my hotel room, my phone rings. I look at his name flashing on the caller ID and take a deep breath. I know exactly why he's calling. May as well get this over with.

"Hello?"

"Noah," he starts.

"Yeah, Dad?" I ask like I don't already know where this is going. Like I didn't already get reamed by Coach and he's about to tap in for round two.

"Don't take that tone with me. I shouldn't be calling my grown son to scold him for the way he behaved in a professional football game, but here we are. What the hell is wrong with you?"

"I was just having an off night. Things were going bad and that guy was making them worse." I sit down on the bed and put my head in the hand not holding the phone to my ear.

"This kind of shit is unacceptable."

"I know."

"Don't let me find out that the reason for this is some girl." I suck in a breath and hope he doesn't hear it through the line. Of course that's exactly what it's about. What else pushes grown men to fighting more than comments about a man's woman or their momma?

"It's not," I lie. I don't exactly feel like taking his shit tonight. I've been feeling shitty enough going days without talking to Audrey, spending all my time wondering if she'll take me back—if there's even anything to get back.

"It better not be." *Or what?* He's going to come down to the practice field and kick my ass himself? He's going to go to Coach and tell him to bench me for a game to teach me a lesson? This isn't high school football anymore. He can talk all he wants, but at the end of the day there's nothing he can do but call and bitch.

"The first game of the season is next week. I'll have my act cleaned up by then."

"You'd better. I shouldn't have to remind you what's at stake here."

"You don't."

"Then start acting like it."

"I will, Dad." I glance at the clock. I only have thirty minutes to grab my stuff before the team is scheduled to travel back home. "I've got to go get packed up for the flight home."

"Okay. Maybe use that time to think about how you're going to change your attitude."

"Bye, Dad." I hang up before he can go on any longer. It's

been a while since he got to chew me out for something this stupid, I'm sure he had more pent up and ready to go, but I really do have to get going.

Getting talked to like a teenager again really makes me feel like I was right earlier when I thought my suit and tie made me feel like I was playing dress up in my dad's clothes. The truth is the size of his legacy might never fit me.

―――――

I don't usually get rowdy with the boys after a game, but tonight I'm making an exception. I've been trying to deal with my emotions all the right ways and none of that shit saved me. So, tonight I'm going to get blasted. I obviously didn't have enough time to feel sorry for myself during the game, so I'm extending it into the night. And then to the drive home tomorrow when I'm hungover beyond belief.

We're at a bar in downtown Dallas that Mack used to go to when he went to college here and it's packed to the fucking brim. You can barely walk without bumping into someone or getting a drink spilled on your shoes. The music is so loud I can barely hear Wyatt as he practically screams in my ear that he's ordering another beer. Colin, Jaden, Wyatt, Mack, and I are all in the upstairs VIP lounge that's roped off and overlooks the thrumming dance floor below.

When we pulled up to the red brick building nestled in downtown, we were quickly whisked into the bar and up the stairs. Four waitresses dressed in black immediately came up to us and spoke to Colin (our obvious leader), who apparently ordered bottle service. Not ten minutes later, two waitresses return with bottles of vodka in hand. The other two carry those cheesy indoor sparklers all clubs have. If people didn't know we were here before, they do now.

The problem with bottle service is you serve yourself and I have no bartending experience. I mean, I worked at a Wendy's in high school. I spent most of that time working the drive-thru eating stolen chicken nuggets. I have no idea what a shot should look like in a full-size glass. After two hours of mixing our own drinks, we're all three sheets to the wind. Jaden is missing his tie, and it's likely he will be on the plane home tomorrow without it.

Wyatt leans way too close to me, and I can smell the liquor on his breath. I'm sure mine smells the same. "What are you going to do about Audrey?"

I do not want to talk about this. Doesn't he realize I'm drinking all my emotions away, including the ones from that shitty game?

"What about her?" I shout back.

"To get her back!" He gives me a look like *duh*.

"I haven't lost her."

"Maybe not right this second, but any day now she could get swept off her feet by some other dude at yoga. And it's against your contract to do yoga during the season."

I shake my head. "She knows I'm serious about her."

"Does she?"

"Yes!"

"How? What have you done to prove it?" I'm thinking but he goes on. "Do you post about her online? Does she have your jersey? A game-worn one? Do you know her Chipotle order?"

"Really, Chipotle? Do you know Nash's?"

"A burrito with steak, brown rice, corn, medium salsa, lettuce, and shredded cheese."

"Fuck," I huff. It's a no to all those things.

Wyatt sees the defeat in my eyes and pats me gently on the back. "You still have time to show her."

I've done the readings and the work. I've had the time and space to make up my mind. I'm ready to get her back. I take my phone out of my pocket. "I can start right now."

"That's the winning answer, broski."

Chapter Twenty-Six

AUDREY

SEPTEMBER

I canceled my morning yoga class because I stayed up all night watching replays and breakdowns of Noah's scuffle. I probably watched it a thousand times trying to make out the words. Watching Noah push the other guy around. It was scary and hot at the same time. Made me want to let him throw me around a little.

My doorbell rings at eight on the dot.

Who could be here this early?

I put my pen down and head toward the door. My comfy slippers make a *wsh* sound as I cross the room.

I peek through the peephole and see a man I don't recognize. I'm not about to fling my door wide open for a stranger, so I angle my body to the side and barely open it.

"Good morning, miss," the man says. He's well dressed in a black suit jacket with a white button-down shirt and black tie. His black patent leather shoes shine in the morning sunlight.

"Good morning." I'm sure he can see the confusion marking my face.

He hurriedly explains, "I'm Davide. I work for the Foxes."

My eyebrows pop up. "Noah sent you?"

"Yes. He told me to pick these items up and deliver them to you." He bends over to pick something up, and that's when I notice all the boxes and bags at his feet. They're all different shapes and colors. Stores I've never dreamed of stepping in to. My face heats. Davide reads what appears to be a text off his phone. "He instructed me to ask you what your Chipotle order is."

"What for?"

Davide shrugs. "I couldn't begin to guess. Mr. Fox is a good man, but he is a mystery." Boxes in hand and bags hanging from his arms, he asks, "May I put these inside?"

I open the door wide and step back, letting him enter. I'm dying to know what's in all these boxes.

My dining room table is covered from top to bottom when Davide turns to me, pulling a card out of his pocket. "My card so you can reach me any time should you need further assistance." He heads toward the door, and I trail behind to walk him out. At the entrance he turns to me. "I'll be back at five o'clock sharp on Sunday to pick you up."

"Pick me up for what?"

"The game. Did he not mention it?"

"No." I cross my arms. "I'm out of the loop here."

"He has box seats for you and your friend Nicole at the Hurricanes home game against the Vultures Sunday evening."

"Oh."

He peers over me to the dining table. "I assume everything you'll need can be found in those." And with that he shuts the door behind him. Leaving me to the silence that has been all too present lately.

For a second, I debate if I should invite Nicole over to enjoy this with me. I've been pretty distant lately, and this will definitely make up for that, but I quickly decide that this is a message from Noah that I should see first. After two weeks of silence, this is him breaking the ice. Testing the waters.

The first box contains a beautiful bouquet. I take a second to put it in a vase and fill it with water before moving on. The next one contains one of Noah's game-worn jerseys. FOX is huge across the back, the number forty-nine in bright white. There's a handwritten note nestled among the tissue paper:

I need you.
- N

What does that mean?

I glance around, looking for more clues, and my eyes catch on a Good American bag. I snatch it and find a beautiful pair of jeans inside. *I see what's going on here.* The next has a pearl Tiffany bracelet. The next has a Prada mini bag. Lipstick. Earrings. Shoes. Perfume. Everything a girl getting ready could possibly need.

I sit cross-legged on the floor, surrounded by carcasses of discarded bags and ripped paper. There's one bag left. It's black with felt details. What could I be missing? I pull the paper out of the bag. I reach in and my fingers touch the smallest stitch of clothing. If you can even call it that.

The bralette is beautiful. With black floral lace, one sparkling gem where the cups connect in the middle. The black thong matches it. One single gem right below my belly button.

So things are good between us? He doesn't hate me? He's not disgusted by me? These gifts are his sign of affection, not just words, but his action. By having these delivered to my house, he's giving me an out. In case I change my mind.

It's a good thing he finally decided because I was almost at my wit's end without him. Haunting my own house. Moving from room to room in my robe and slippers. Not even wanting to get dressed to work. Ordering in food so I don't have to leave.

This has been the longest two weeks of my life. Even though I was at peace with ending a relationship over this, it's not the way I would have wanted it to go down. If I could do it all over again, I would have been more honest and forthcoming from the start—before feelings were involved.

I've had a lot of time to think. Laying it all out with Noah was the best thing I could have done, though. I took back power that Sarah was trying to take ownership of. I think it's time for me to have the hard conversations with my family too. They are all expecting something from me that they, themselves, wouldn't offer in return. I don't want things to continue on like this. I don't want bad feelings to keep us from missing out on each other, specifically with my mom. If there's something to be saved, it's time to do the saving.

———

Lying in savasana after a tough 9:00 AM yoga class at Big Power Yoga is definitely helping drown out the anxiety that woke me up. I try to remind myself that oftentimes anxiety and excitement feel similar in the body. The second my eyes opened, I knew that I couldn't just be at home all day. So I got up, made coffee, ate some yogurt, changed for yoga, and headed out the door.

Now that yoga is over and my body is tired, I have to find something to do with my mind for the next eight hours.

Excellent. I can still fit in a whole workday.

Nicole arrives at two with a huge backpack on her shoulder. "What's all that?" I ask. She's already dressed in her game-day outfit, so it's not her change of clothes.

"Makeup, duh. Your skin needs to look just as stunning as all those gifts you're wearing, babe."

The sleek black Town Car Noah sends arrives at five on the dot. I've been ready to go for about an hour. My hair is hot curled into big waves, my makeup is more than I normally wear, but not anywhere near full glam. I've got on my new jeans and strappy heels, but tonight it's topped off with Noah's jersey and everything else that he had delivered.

I tuck the purse Noah gifted me over my arm and look at Nicole. "Are we doing this?"

She throws her arms around me in a tight hug, and I breathe in her lavender scent. "You are." She pulls back and looks right at me. "And you deserve it. Everything." I smile back. My best friend who knows how I've struggled, doubted, and hurt. We're both ready for me to be happy.

I drop my hand to hers and grasp it hard as we step out of the door.

―――

The stadium is huge and looming as we pull up. I stare out the window like the main character in a rom-com, pulling up to her new destination for the first time. It's giving Lizzie

McGuire in Rome. Davide parks the car, and I unbuckle. He comes around to my side to open the door. "I'll be outside this same exit when your evening is over."

I smile. "Thank you, Davide."

I start off a little wobbly in my heels on the pocked concrete, but I quickly gain my balance, leaning on Nicole, just as I always have.

The passes on the lanyard Davide gave us make getting into the stadium easy. A young woman with tight curls walks right up to us and tells us to follow her. Her own lanyard says Lydia on it. We walk behind Lydia as she weaves through the crowd. I recognize a few people from the day I was here for preseason and from Jaden's house, so I assume this is the friends and family area of the stadium. My nerves grow as we walk, a tightness in my shoulders and stomach.

Rows of suites roll out in front of us. I peek into each one as we pass. One has walls covered in gold. Lydia sees me looking and says, "That's the owner's box. It was handed down to him by his parents. He grew up in Houston and went to college here as well."

"That's really cool. Like homegrown."

She leads us to a box filled with people. This must be a box that Noah and a couple other players pay for so their families can watch the game peacefully. When I step in it feels like a hundred eyes turn to me. There's a pause, but maybe only I can feel the tension. Might be all in my head. Smiles break out and I lower my shoulders back down from my ears. I'm glad Noah got me all this over-the-top stuff. I feel like I fit in better with the other women. Of course, Chrissy was so welcoming that first day, but I didn't know if that would last up to this point. Everyone is all smiles until the small talk inevitably turns to children, and when I don't have any of my own to coo over, I'm quickly left behind.

A smile breaks across my face when I finally spot Chrissy standing near the bar. I speed walk to her side, Nicole following me like a lost puppy. "Thank God you're here!"

She turns to me, and I get the full brunt of her sunshine demeanor. "Thank God *you're* here! I thought things didn't work out with Noah!"

I wince. "I haven't really spoken to him, but he sent flowers and tickets and this jersey." I motion with my hands to the huge forty-nine on my chest.

Chrissy tuts like only a southern woman can. "You poor thing. Men's heads can be thicker than the walls of this stadium."

I remember Nicole behind me. "This is my best friend, Nicole."

"Lovely to meet you! Come sit by me for the game. It should be a good one!"

Seeing the stadium full of cheering fans is a different vibe than when I was touring around the practice campus previously. Could that have been less than a month ago? It feels like years have passed since Noah had his arms around me; since we kissed on the practice field, the white lines spreading out from us in every direction.

When the announcer starts to bring in the home team, we get to our feet. The stadium lights dim, spotlights appear, and the announcer's voice booms over the speakers. In the home corner, the cheerleaders shake their pom-poms and smoke floats away from the tunnel.

"ANNDDD NOWWWWWW," the announcer begins. "YOUR HOUSTON HURRICANES STARTING LINEUP!"

Chrissy, Nicole, and I are full-on screaming. Polite, lady-like cheering is forgotten as the announcer calls Noah's name. "From Houston University, tight end, Noah Fox!" My heart soars. It's so light I almost can't take it. I have no idea what he will say when he sees me. I just know it can't be goodbye.

My feet hurt from stomping and my hands sting from clapping as the rest of the team comes out of the tunnel. Finally, Colin is announced and runs in carrying a Texas flag while classic rock blares through the speakers. We continue to scream at the top of our lungs as the guys meet on the field and do an extensive handshake.

The game holds my rapt attention. This is my first time at a professional football game and it's so much more hardcore in real life. I watched Noah's last game on TV and was shocked at the brutality of it all, but hearing the hits in person as they collide is a bit horrifying. Noah on the field is not the same man I know who cooks homemade dinners and has a crush on Lara Croft. He's aggressive. He seems sure-footed. The grit and power he displays when he blocks is overwhelming to watch. I know level-headed, thoughtful, careful, balanced, loyal Noah, but the Noah on the field is all athlete, all competition.

It's driving me wild.

I'm practically vibrating in my seat as the half comes to a close. It's tied twenty-two to twenty-two. I'm watching the team run into the locker room for halftime when I see a girl I've never met standing next to Chrissy. "Nash! Wyatt is doing great!" We all rise to let the new girl into our row, and I realize how freaking tall she is. She's easily six feet, built lithe and long.

She clasps her hands in front of her. "I know, I'm so glad! He was a bit nervous about this game. The Cleveland Vultures are nothing to joke about, even though we're favored by three-

and-a-half points in the spread." Her eyes fall on me (and it's a long way down to my height). "I don't think we've met." She sticks out her hand for me to shake. "I'm Nash."

I take her hand. It's warm and friendly, like her smile. "Audrey, nice to meet you. And this is my best friend Nicole."

"She's with Noah." Chrissy blurts out before I can say I'm a guest of Noah.

"Happy to have you! It's always more fun when the WAGs box is full."

I scrunch my nose. "WAGs?"

"Wives and girlfriends," Chrissy explains.

I turn to Nash. "Who's your boyfriend?"

She waves me off. "Not boyfriend. Wyatt and I have been best friends since college."

My brows shoot up my forehead. "I see." I look at Chrissy who has a certain gleam in her eyes.

My cheeks redden. "Oh, I'm not. I mean, we haven't talked about... we don't have a label really."

How do I explain my complicated relationship and my very real feelings for Noah in what's left of halftime? It seems too daunting to even try.

Chrissy is happy to step in.

"Oh, buckle up for this made-for-TV movie." Her eyes are alight. As much as Chrissy likes to talk and be in everyone's business, I can tell it comes from a place of genuine care. "He made her bleed, took her to dinner, and then she hit him up for money."

I balk and look at Nash. My mouth opens like a fish. "It's not what it sounds like!" Chrissy breaks into a giggle fit. "I can explain!" I'm exasperated but there's a smile on my face as I fill Nash in on what's actually happened between me and Noah.

Nash's back hits the stadium chair. "Wow, that's crazy. So you're up here right now hanging in the balance, not knowing what he will say when the game is over?"

My shoulders slump. "Basically. I'm shooting my shot. YOLO or whatever the kids are saying these days."

The music blasts once again, signaling the end of halftime. We all get to our feet to cheer on the men as they return to the field. I can see Noah's eyes taking in the stands, but I can't tell if he sees me or not. Maybe it's better that he doesn't. For him or for me, I'm not sure.

The game carries on, I know the basics thanks to *Friday Night Lights*, but Nash explains the rest to me. She plays on a recreational flag football team, so she really knows her stuff. Cleveland gets the ball back at the half, but can't convert on fourth down, so they punt. Noah runs back out with the offense, and we settle in to watch the possession.

The Hurricanes march down the field. They've got the Vultures defense on their heels and they aren't letting up.

On the twenty-yard line, they line up for a go at the end zone.

Nash leans over to me, knowing this is my first football game. "They're in the red zone now. If they don't score here, they will have to punt it away to the other team, giving them another chance to score before the quarter is over."

Noah is out wide. The ball is snapped, and Noah moves to block. Once the quarterback steps out of the pocket, he rolls off the block and out toward the sideline, wide open. Colin sees him and throws him a dart. Noah secures the catch and turns to run, toeing along the sideline toward the end zone. Nash, Chrissy, and I are all on our feet screaming. Just when I think Noah is going all the way, a safety comes out of the peripheral and gives chase. He's trying to stay in bounds for more yards but is on his way out.

A second Vultures player slams into him. The crack echoes through the stadium. My cheer is stuck in my throat along with the contents of my stomach.

Next to me, Nash is irate. "What the fuck was that? Fucking dirty hit! Throw the fucking flag, ref!" A millisecond later, the yellow flag hits the grass. "Finally!"

Nash got what she wanted, but Noah hasn't gotten up. He's on the ground, face down, knees tucked under him. The shape of him slumped on the ground reminds me of child's pose, and I can't help but think about how months ago he was a stranger in a yoga class.

And now he's everything.

He's holding his chest. The replay starts on the Jumbotron, and I see that Cleveland player's helmet hit him right at the bottom of the rib cage as Noah's foot touches the line. "That hit was late as fuck!" Nash finishes.

The referee steps on to the field, turns his mic on, and holds his arms straight out. "Unsportsmanlike conduct. Number thirty-seven. Defense. Fifteen-yard penalty. First down."

Noah still isn't on his feet. Trainers surround him, leaning down to hear what he's saying.

My eyes are wide as I look at Chrissy. She's already looking back, reading the panic in my eyes. I don't know what to do. Everything feels like too much. The lights are too bright, the music is too loud. I can't think. I can't focus. My heart is beating out of my chest, and tears sting my eyes. I'm not used to having someone I care about in danger like this. I've never seen the disparaging roughness of this game up close. I'm going to toss the literal cookies I ate before coming to the game. Chrissy puts her hand on my arm, and I suck in a breath.

We watch as Noah gets up on his own. The teams clap as he walks off. I watch as he's guided back through the tunnel by one of the training staff. I meet Chrissy's concerned gaze with my wild one. "Where are they taking him?"

"Probably to the X-ray room to make sure nothing's broken." I can't seem to get a full breath. My eyes are on Chrissy, but all I'm seeing is Noah lying on the ground. "Do you want to go to him?" I nod, not trusting my words. I can't find my voice. Seeing a man I thought was invincible taken down has rattled me to my core.

I have to put my hands on him and see with my own eyes that he's okay. I have to expel the minutiae of words beating the back of my skull. I've had enough tiptoeing and waiting. Being afraid and not taking my life into my own hands.

I know what I want.

Everything. I'm ready to fully trust him, say everything that's on my mind.

Chrissy grabs me by the hand, and tugs me toward the exit. The world blurs around me. It feels like it takes a million years to get down to field level. Thank God Chrissy is here; though who would have thought I'd be saying that when I first met her because Noah was just my client I was trying to tamp down feelings for, and now look where I am. I'm glad I don't have to think. I just have to let her lead me to him. Where I need to be. "Wait, what about Nicole?"

"She'll be fine here. I'll make sure she gets home safe," Chrissy says.

Chrissy stops short at the door to the training area and gestures to me that this is where I need to go. I drop her hand and take a deep breath. I was so sure two minutes ago, but now that only this door separates me from Noah, I'm losing my resolve. Chrissy takes me by the shoulders. "You want him?"

"Yes," I croak.

"You love him?"

I swallow hard. I wasn't ready to admit it yet. Not until everything had been sorted out. "Yes."

I mean, I didn't figure out I loved him in the high times when we were laughing and joking—I found it in the worst times. Like finding out how important breathing is when it's hard to inhale your next breath.

She shakes my shoulders once, clearing away the doubt. "Then go fucking get him."

She kisses my cheek, turns on her towering heels, and strides back the way we came.

Chapter Twenty-Seven

AUDREY

As I walk, I go over what to say in my mind. I have to steel myself for the possibility that this is all too much for him. That he was cool with hanging around, but has decided that he doesn't want to take it any further. That he needs to focus on football, and not getting injured again. Life is dangerous, but it's even more dangerous when you hit and get hit for a living.

If that's true and he wants to end things, why send gifts? Why send tickets? Why am I here?

I'm jogging now, peeking around doors, trying to figure out which of the overly lit rooms Noah is in. My heart pounds in my chest, breath coming in short bursts. I can't see the posters on the wall or the items lined up in the hallway. Just each room and its contents. The only noise in the hall is the clack of my heels on the tiled floor. The fluorescent lights burn my retinas, but still I search.

I whip into the last door on the right and stand completely still as dark green eyes meet mine.

Time stops.

I just look at him, taking him in. Sitting up on one of those training bench things, one arm around his middle holding an ice pack to his ribs. My heart hurts at the sight of him. He's shirtless in just football pants, and the sight of that makes my lady parts ache in time with my bruised heart.

After a tense beat, we both try to speak at once, but I can't wait another second.

The words tumble out. "I quit."

Chapter Twenty-Eight

NOAH

"You're fired," I say at the same time.

Audrey's eyebrows jump toward her hairline. Her eyes are wide. When she came bulldozing in here, she looked mad, panic in her eyes. But that's been replaced by fire. A flame I love to stoke.

"What?" Color rises in her face. "You can't fire me, asshole. I just quit. So fuck you." Her words are fierce, but there are tears in her eyes and her voice is watery.

She walks closer and I reach out and grab her wrists, keeping her from flailing around or storming out. I hold her still. "You can't work for me anymore because I know it wasn't your decision." I keep her eyes on me. "I want to start over, Audrey. But this time I want everything to be on your terms."

"I'm terrified."

"I know, baby."

"I *care* about you. I promised myself that I'd never trust a man again, but I've been lonely and I hate it. I figured if admitting that was going to scare you away, I'd rather just get it over with. I'll deal with Sarah later."

"But it didn't scare me away, did it?"

"No, it didn't. Today, seeing you on the ground, not knowing..." Tears are freely flowing over her cheeks now. "Made me realize I've been wasting time. Denying myself you is a waste of time. Not going for it and saying things plainly isn't working."

I reach out and grab her elbow, pulling her toward me to stand between my legs. "I know what I want now. I can't keep pretending to be polite at meetings when I want to bend you over and make you take me." Her breath hitches and I take that as a good sign. I hop down from the table. My ice pack hits the ground with a plop.

Worry flashes across her face. "Your ribs! You should sit."

I shake off her comment. "I'm fine. Nothing is broken. I'll be able to play next week."

"You scared the shit out of me!" she yells, batting at my chest.

I suck in a sharp breath. "Okay, that one did hurt a little."

Her hands fly to her mouth. I can tell she's about to lose it. Tears well up in her eyes again as emotions overwhelm her. I put my hands on either side of her face. "Hey. It's okay. Look at me." I take a deep breath, and she copies me. "I'm fine. Everything is fine." I pause, wanting to acknowledge the truth of her being here right now. Wearing the jersey I sent. Not wanting to pop this bubble of warmth we have. I'm not ready to lose the soft feeling of her presence. She's just looking at me, eyes wild, and I'm tired of thinking. I kiss one cheek. Then the other. Then her forehead. "I'm okay," I murmur. I kiss her nose and each eyebrow. I kiss her eyelids, reassuring her after each one.

Finally, I pull her lips to mine. I kiss her with the adrenaline I feel when I come off the field. The pressure in my chest that tells me this is everything I thought it could be. Our lips mingle perfectly, like brownies topped with ice cream. She kisses me back, and I can feel the answers to all the questions lingering between us on her lips. I invited her to come because I know what I want. She's here because she wants to be with me. We drag out this kiss as long as possible, and in my mind "She's Like Texas" by the Josh Abbott Band plays.

The knob turns and someone opens the door. We quickly jump back like two teenagers getting caught making out in the back of a truck. The trainer, Wendy, looks between us. "Noah, I need to wrap that ice pack to your ribs before I let you go."

I nod and look back at Audrey. "Everything is fine. I'll meet you right after."

Chapter Twenty-Nine

AUDREY

The Hurricanes miraculously pull out a win even after all the injury drama. Chrissy and I hold hands outside the arena where the players exit. I've filled her in on the whole thing and sent Nicole home with Davide. I'm not usually touchy feely like this with other ladies, but her hand is the only thing keeping me from bolting right now. I don't want to make a scene in front of all his teammates, but my fingers itch for his touch. I know there's so much to talk about. I know he and I are on the same page, but I need to figure out which paragraph.

I think I knew the second I got in the Town Car earlier today that he was going to take me back. The standard I had been holding myself to was choking me. I couldn't breathe through the pressure of keeping Noah at arm's length and my family happy. I couldn't think straight. My mind was a jumble of clients' Instagram posts and the lingering feeling of his mouth on mine. I was jumpy, wondering what my family would demand of me next. I cared so much about what they thought when they didn't think that much of me. So I'm finally putting myself first for once in my life.

Noah approaches us dressed in his slacks, carrying his bag. He gestures toward where his car is parked. "Shall we?" I nod and follow him like a little puppy. I turn to glance at Chrissy who is giving me an enthusiastic thumbs up. I shoot her a small smile.

The drive to Noah's house is contemplatively quiet. I'm chewing on the inside of my cheeks as he navigates us through the darkened Houston streets. He turns to me. "I can practically feel you overthinking."

I set my hands on my knees. "I know. I'm not trying to be like this. It's just a lot all at once."

He returns his eyes to the road as he drives through his neighborhood gate.

"What else do you want to know?"

"You sent me the ticket for today." It's not a question.

"Yes." He smirks at me, the streetlights coming and going over his face. "And the gifts. Don't forget those."

"Right." I blush, knowing I have many of those gifts on right now, including the black lace lingerie set. "Which means…?"

"That I want to be together. No matter what. I'm sorry for the way I left things after the BBQ. I was just surprised. Not by you, but by the timing of it. We weren't anything serious yet, and according to you we would never be, but you're giving me these pieces of you that I didn't deserve to have. I'm glad you gave me the time to figure out what I want. I work hard to keep myself level-headed, and I didn't want anything I said to hurt you, so I needed to take time to think."

We pull into his driveway, and he puts the car in park and turns in his seat to look at me fully.

"And what do you want?"

"I want you. Us. I want to give this a shot."

"And you're good with no kids?"

"I can say wholeheartedly that, right now, I am open to not having kids. I understand that as time moves on I might change my mind because I haven't thought about this as much as you have, but I'm willing to ride this wave with you now. I promise that if anything changes there will be an open and honest line of communication about it." I lean into his words that are breaking my heart free of its chains.

I put my hand in his upturned one. "I would never want you to be unhappy. Even if that means being with someone else."

"The book I read said we should pick a later date and revisit this then, but..." He squeezes my hand and continues. "We have a lot of missed time to make up for—and I want to start making up for all the hours I couldn't touch you over the last two weeks...starting right now."

In a blink, Noah's pupils blow wide with attraction. I move my hand to his thigh and let it rest. I tighten my fingers a little on either side to feel the strength hidden there under his dress slacks. Noah makes a strangled noise. "If you keep touching me like that, we aren't going to make it inside before I see if you are wearing that lingerie I sent over, babe."

Chapter Thirty

NOAH

Today has been a day about taking chances. Another injury right after coming back from last year's broken ankle rattled me. Every day we walk a precarious line between being okay and not. Today was another reminder of just how thin that line is.

The cliff you stand on playing professional football is steep and unforgiving. I know this is what I chose for myself, but the reminder hits hard anyway. There's more destruction at the bottom of that fall than most careers. It's high risk, high reward. That's what I was thinking about when Audrey burst into the room and back into my life. I was peering over the cliff waiting to see if I was going to fall when she appeared, filling all my senses with her clean scent. I knew I would regret not reaching for what I want. And right now, in this moment, her hand in mine, as I lead her up the stairs, I'm immensely glad that I did.

I shut the door behind us and push her up against it. I see the excitement and anticipation flash in her eyes as her back hits the wood. If it's a little rougher than I intend; she doesn't seem to mind. She seems eager. I put my hands on either side of her head and push my knee between her thighs. I can feel the heat radiating from her through the fabric of my slacks. It doesn't escape me that I'm fully dressed in my game-day suit and tie. I think it's working to my benefit right now—at least based on her reaction.

I put my mouth on hers, gently searching. Asking permission for more. She knows and nods just slightly. I slide my hands up under the jersey that has touched my own skin and has my last name on it. "You're driving me fucking wild with my name across your back. You know that?"

She reached down for the hem of the oversized jersey, practically swallowing her frame. I put a hand out to stop her. "No. It stays on."

I move my hands down to the buttons on her jeans. I pause and look at her. Her pupils are wide with want, and I'm sure mine echo the same. "Is this what you want?" She nods. I shake my head. "I need your words, baby." She tilts her head back to the door behind her.

"Take them off. I want everything. With you." She looks down at me as I get on my knees and slide the denim down her hips, her thighs, lower as I watch, taking in every inch of pale skin and black lace. She uses my shoulders for balance as she picks up one foot and then the other to let me slide them off.

Holy—fuck me. Her wearing the black lacy thing I sent her and the reality of it is one-hundred-thousand times better than what I imagined it would look like when I picked it out. The thin strip of dark lace against her creamy skin has my dick aching.

"I've been waiting a millennium for this. I've been dreaming about this pussy, wishing for it, and I'm not going to waste another second." I pull the thong to the side, raise her leg over my shoulder, and put my tongue on her center. No teasing, just tasting. She tastes like heaven, and I eat while she tries to squirm under me. I pin her hips down with a forearm so I can better devour her.

I'd rebreak my ankle a million times over if it that means I'd be right here, right fucking now, hearing her moan and calling my name.

Chapter Thirty-One

AUDREY

With Noah's mouth on me, I'm about to float right off the floor. It's levitation-level good. But I know that tonight I need everything. I told him so, but he seems A-OK with taking his sweet time. Meanwhile, I'm dying. If I don't get what I need from this man, I'm going to scream. And what I need is him inside of me.

"More. All of you," I whimper. He looks up at me, mouth still covering me fully. Our eyes meet over the swell of my breasts, and I can't believe this is real. He pushes me closer to the edge as I grip his hair and then stops.

I squeak when he wraps his arms around my hips and lifts me from the ground. I fold over his shoulder like a sexy sack of potatoes—if potatoes wore decadent black lace—and he carries me toward the bed. Noah sets me down so gently, like I'm the most precious, delicate thing. My heart is soaring from finally getting this intimacy with him. He pushes the jersey up and up until my breasts are exposed. My nipples pebble beneath the thin lace in response, or maybe in anticipation of his mouth. He settles his long body next to me, his arm stretched out over my belly. He kisses my mouth and nips at my bottom lip before kissing a trail down my neck to my chest. He kisses me once in the middle of my breast bone, and then gently takes one nipple into his mouth. His tongue is teasing but his mouth is warm. My back arches off the bed, encouraging him to continue. His hair is so soft when I thread my fingers through it again.

I reach my hand down between us on the bed and start pulling at his belt with one hand. My core is pulsing. I can feel the heat pooling low in me, the lust making my mind fuzzy. I'm so lost in my haze of desire that I can't get his belt undone.

I put my hand to his chest and push. "Roll over."

He lets me push him over even though he could easily withstand my meager strength. "I want you naked." *Who is saying those words? Me?*

I start at the buttons on his nice shirt. The color flatters his eyes. Makes the depth of them even greater. I don't care, though. It's got to come off.

Once I reach the final button, I slide my hands back up his stomach and push the shirt off his shoulders. He sits up and shrugs it off. He reaches down and pulls his undershirt over his head. I inhale. "Oh my God."

The toned skin is covered in purple and green bruising. It's concentrated on the right side, but snakes across his chest and around toward his back. I feel the tears well in my eyes before I can stop them.

Immediately, Noah notices. "Hey, hey. What's wrong?" He wipes at my tears as they fall.

I touch my fingertips to the bruise. "You're hurt."

"I'm going to be okay. It's just a bruise."

"What if it wasn't just a bruise? And I was there and I

hadn't told you how I felt yet? What if you had to go to the hospital and I didn't get to see you?"

"I would have brought you to me before they took me away. I would never leave you without you knowing."

All of the emotion I've been stifling comes through and I kiss his mouth, my tears wetting both our cheeks.

"What do you need, Audrey?" he whispers.

"Your cock." I'm panting. I cannot let this moment slip by. If I'm going to love a man who is at risk like this, I'm going to make every second count.

"Let me show you just how okay I am."

"You smug asshole," I tease, but I think: *Oh, hell yes.*

"Condoms?" he asks, as I take this time to leisurely peruse his body. Strong arms and broad shoulders, easily the hottest thing I've ever seen.

"I have an IUD, and I haven't been with anyone since I got tested after my last relationship. But can you pull out so we don't take any chances?"

I gasp as he pulls me closer to the edge of the bed by my ankles. "Does that mean you want this cock raw?"

I've still got his jersey wrapped around my chest, but I manage to say, "Yes."

I twitch when I feel the head of him slide along my slit. "You're so fucking wet. Are you ready for me? Tell me with words that you're ready to get fucked."

My body shivers at his filthy words. "I need you."

Noah needs no more encouragement. He pushes into me, not too slowly, but not too swiftly. "So fucking tight," he groans.

He leans over the bed onto his forearms and I'm just along for the ride, willing to take whatever he has to give. "You gonna take it all for me?"

In my lust-filled haze, it takes me a second to realize that wasn't rhetorical. "Yes," I whimper.

He pounds into me in a smooth rhythm. I'm completely wrapped up in the heat of the moment, but I need more to finish.

"Do you want to watch me fuck you?"

"Please, I'm so full." Noah reaches his hands behind my head and cradles me in his huge hands, titling my head until I see where his cock is easily sliding in and out of me. I'm so completely held and supported by his hands, his body moving over me, it's easy to find that first thread of release.

I want to keep my eyes open and see Noah's green ones watching me, but the pleasure rolling through me is too much.

"Fuck, Noah." My breath is coming fast. "Right there. Don't move." I pluck at the other strings of pleasure wafting around my consciousness. The fullness of his cock are too much. Noah stills over me, letting my orgasm rip through me. It feels like relief and release at the same time. Like the tightness in my body from the rigidity of my life has finally dissipated. I can feel it behind my eyes as I come apart underneath him.

When Noah feels me slowing down, coming back to reality, he picks up his pace. I'm so sensitive. It's like I can feel every little thing about him. His tip, his ridge, and even his thick veins. "Watching you come on my cock is going to send me over the edge."

With one last thrust he pulls out and I watch as he paints my stomach with his cum. A smile breaks out across his face, and I find mine reflected in his.

He disappears into the connecting master bathroom and returns with a warm washcloth to clean me off.

"Shower?"

"Yes, please." I realize that I didn't intend to come over, or sleep over. I look down at my naked lower half and around the room at our clothes strewn across the floor. "I might need to borrow some clothes."

He takes my hand and leads me into the bathroom. "No problem."

It's huge with one big shower head on the ceiling and smaller ones on the side walls behind a glass sliding door. The black tile gleams under the heated overhead lamps.

In the shower I soap up a washcloth and run the cologne-scented bubbles over Noah's strong body, careful of his bruised ribs. *I could really get used to this.*

After we finish in the shower, I step away from my towel and into the sweatpants Noah brought me. They're navy blue with a Hurricanes logo by the pocket and a drawstring. I have to roll them down three times to make them somewhat fit, but it's better than nothing.

"I'll be right back," Noah says as he heads towards the door while I finish getting dressed.

When I'm nice and cozy in his clothes, I walk out with a plume of steam around me to find Noah waiting for me on the bed. There's a spread of every snack you can think of laid out before him. My stomach growls at the sight of chips, candy, popcorn, and more. I realize I haven't eaten since halftime.

Noah pulls me to him, and he kisses my knuckles. I feel the kitty turn on again. *Down, girl.*

"How do you feel?"

"Like Jell-O."

He snorts. "I'll take that."

"I'm starving, though." He pats the space next to him and we get comfy on the pillows up against his huge leather headboard.

He picks up the TV remote. "What do you want to watch?"

"Mmm, I don't care."

"Have you seen the crime docu-series on a lawyer who's stealing money from his personal-injury clients?"

At the mention of white-collar crime, my ears perk up. "Oh my God, no! Put it on!"

He smirks. "You sound as excited for fraud as you did for my cock."

I laugh. "They're on a similar level for me."

Noah's eyes flash. "I'm going to have to do something about that... make sure that my cock ranks number one over a documentary." I feel myself blush. I'm still tingling a little from my orgasm.

We dive into our massive pile of snacks. I swear Noah kills a bag of popcorn and an entire bag of gummy worms by himself.

After I slam my body weight in salt and vinegar chips, I settle back and poke at Noah's arm until he lifts it so I can cuddle up against him.

Thoughts about what this will mean for my sister and Mikey are breathing through my post-coital bliss. How my happiness is dependent on my family's reliance on me. Noah seems to notice. "What are you thinking about?"

"What I'm going to say to my sister."

His rough hand plays with my fingers. "You know it was wrong of her to use you like that, right? Just because you're family doesn't mean she gets to treat you that way. If a stranger did that to you, we'd be calling it blackmail." I hate that he's right. "You need to decide what you're willing to do to help out and what you're not. They're allowing Sarah to treat you like this and she's taking full advantage of it. I mean, why can't your parents give her money? What does Audrey want? Does she want to babysit? Does she want to deliver checks? It's all optional because none of it's your responsibility. This is your life and it's your decision to live it the way you want."

I've convinced myself that my family was disappointed in me, but we've never talked about it openly. It's not normal to make your sister your babysitter on a family holiday. It's not normal to hold things over her head for money. It's not normal to feel like you have to earn your parents' affection back because you disappointed them with your life choices. Anyone besides myself would have seen it.

He places a soft kiss on my head. "Nothing has to be decided tonight." I rest my head back against him and watch the lawyer get his comeuppance. Eventually the steadiness of his breathing, the sureness of him next to me, and his oven-like warmth lulls me to sleep.

Chapter Thirty-Two

AUDREY

I wake up to sun streaming through the blinds and a hardness at my back. Noah's heavy arm is thrown over me, his breathing slow and even. The morning's escaped us. It's definitely closer to noon than anything. Ignoring the stiffness behind me, I allow myself one moment to soak everything in. I'm cozy in Noah's king-size bed with dark sheets and a gray comforter. The shirt I borrowed says 'Property of the Hurricanes' across it, which I find ironic.

Everything changed last night. Things I can't take back and don't want to. I feel lighter. Like an elephant has been lifted off my chest and I'm taking my first full breath in years. There's someone on my side and only my side. Who's looking out for the best for me and me alone. I feel like I can do anything with that support.

Said support stirs behind me, finally waking up.

"Good morning." His voice is rough with sleep.

"I think it's more like noon."

"Either way, I'm making you breakfast." My stomach growls in answer and we both smile.

We sit at his breakfast nook, pancakes stacked high between us, maple syrup glistening. The house smells like pancakes and coffee. I lick syrup off my thumb and momentarily enjoy the sight of Noah's face contorting, trying to hide his lust.

I chew slowly before asking, "Are we going to talk about it?"

"It's perfectly acceptable for a grown man to prefer chocolate chips in his pancakes. Just because I'm an adult doesn't mean I have to settle for fruit pancakes like you."

"You know that's not what I meant." I shoot him a look. Part of me is relieved that Noah is leveling the tension with a joke, making things feel normal. "I meant what we are now."

"Boyfriend and girlfriend." Like the answer is written on the walls, plain as day for anyone to read. He shoves a huge bite of pancake into his mouth.

"What does that look like, though?" What about my business? What about his travels?

"We spend all our time together when I'm home." He reaches across the table and takes my hand again. "You'll have a seat waiting for you at every home game, and I want you on the field before the game starts like the other WAGs. I'll buy you a plane ticket to any away game you want to go to. I'll make sure you stay in the same hotel as Chrissy."

"I'd like that."

His green eyes pour over our connected hands. We rest here for a second, soaking in each other. The whole world is starting a new week, but we're just here. Together.

"What are you going to say to Sarah?"

"Things I should have said years ago." I can tell Noah doesn't fully understand.

"Do you want me to be there?"

I shake my head. "No, this is something I have to do by myself." I pause, considering. "But if you want to drop me off and pick me up, just in case things go south, that would be nice."

Noah's smile is huge. "Even though this is your battle, I want to be there for you."

I push back from the table, picking up my plate. "That's for another day, though. Today I want to pretend like we never spent any time apart." Quieter, I say, "Like I never fucked this up."

He rounds the table toward me and wraps me in his arms. "That's the thing, Audrey, I was never really gone."

———

"Last chance if you want me to come in with you," Noah says, pressing a kiss to my forehead over the center console. "It sucks knowing you're about to go in there and argue and I'm supposed to sit out here and wait. I'm like one of those women in old war movies who say goodbye to their husband at the train station, wrap their jackets closer, and decide to just get on with their lives."

"I'm fine, Noah." I know he wants to be there for me, but this is something I have to do by myself.

I step out of the car with my tiny Prada bag clutched like a sword. The gifts might have been excessive, and I don't need labels, but the purse and jewelry feel like armor when I wear them, like a part of him is with me, giving me strength.

"Good luck. Not that you need it."

I nod, using his words to mentally reassure myself. "Thank you." And with that I shut the door, leaving Noah to watch me walk away.

I'm not sure why I picked Common Bond to do this. You would think I wouldn't want so many shitty moments marring my favorite coffee shop, but it feels like an advantage knowing the layout of the battlefield.

I take my seat at a small table near the window. The table where I met Noah is open, but I figured I should pick a different one. I made sure I would be here before Sarah because #*strategy*.

I look up to see Sarah removing her bag from her shoulder and sliding into the chair across from me. There's a terse silence between us, and the people-pleaser in me wants to smooth it over. I strangle that thought and hold out. I'm not going to be the one to break the silence. She's in the wrong, and if she feels uncomfortable in the quiet she created, so be it.

"You could just Venmo me the money, you know." I know she doesn't see me in the light I would want us to be as sisters, but how did we get here?

The beautiful silver glint of my bracelet from Noah catches her eye and I take the second to say, "There won't be any money." Just like every other time, she doesn't take me seriously at first.

She rolls her eyes. "Okay, sure."

"No, I'm serious, Sarah. I'm done."

Sarah leans forward as if daring me. "There will be if you want to keep gifts like that bracelet." I lean forward to match her, resting my arms on the table between us.

I hold my wrist out in front of me, examining the jewelry. "I think my boyfriend is quite fond of gift giving, actually." I look directly in her eyes. She looks different now. The youthful curve of her face is gone, replaced with one that's fully adult. When did that happen? Do I even know my sister anymore? Have I even tried?

But I'm trying now. "What happened between us?"

"I don't know what you mean."

"We were close as kids. I know we have different careers and lead different lives, but…" I trail off in thought, leaving her space to jump in. When she doesn't, I continue. "I don't want us to be like this forever. But I also won't be your ATM."

I see a flash of emotion in her eyes, but I can't fathom what it's from. She quickly looks down at her hands to hide it. When she looks back up, a hard exterior has replaced any chance of peeking through. "I didn't skirt the realities of life. I didn't shirk my responsibilities to society like you have."

"You don't think there's any way to be involved in society other than marriage and reproduction?"

"Not in as meaningful of a way."

"Did you ever consider that I know that I wouldn't be a good mom?" I can see this rattles her. She hadn't thought of this before. She assumed, like many do, that every woman is wired to be a caregiver. "It's responsible, when you think about it, to seriously consider if you want to or are capable of bringing a life into this world. Even if I was, I want my freedom. That's part of running my own business. You know I've never liked being told what to do." I smirk at her across the table.

"No man wants a woman who doesn't want—"

I'm not giving her a chance to finish that. I hold up my hand, smirk falling from my face. "Do you know how hurtful it is to say that? I could flip the script and go on to say that maybe men don't want someone who has another man's child. Is that hurtful for you to hear that? Once again, I'm being demonized for picking myself over society's expectations. You're my sister. Don't you want me to be happy? Even if that doesn't look like your happiness. Could I be a mother? Sure.

Would I enjoy it? No. Would I love a child the way they deserve their mother to love taking care of them? No, I wouldn't. So I'm opting out. For myself, yes, but also for my theoretical children. They deserve better. And so do I." I let that sink in. The silence isn't tense anymore but full of power. "It's not about undermining your parenting or influencing Mikey. It's actually not about you at all." I can feel the rightness of every decision I've made in the last forty-eight hours rushing through my veins. It's the same sense I get when I feel the universe pushing me in a certain direction. "Noah knows everything. He took some time to decide what he wanted, as is his right, and that time apart nearly broke me, but it meant that he could come back and stay with me without any doubts. I understand there's a chance that in the future he will change his mind, but even if that happens, I will never regret the time I have with him."

For her part, Sarah looks thoroughly doused. Like she was sitting front row for the log flume ride at Splashtown. Her words are nearly a whisper. "Don't you want me to have Mikey?"

I reach across the table and put my hand on top of hers. "Of course I do, but Tyler is his father, and if he wants time with Mikey, that's his right. Until he does something that deems it unsafe, he can fight for whatever he wants. It doesn't matter that he's still with the woman he cheated on you with. He can be a bad husband and still be a good father."

"What will Mom and Dad think about all of this?"

"They don't make my decisions for me." I stand to leave, sliding my bag over my arm again. "If you need me to babysit, feel free to text, but it will be if, and only if, it fits into my personal life. This doesn't mean I don't love you or my nephew. These are my boundaries. It was wrong of you to blackmail me. That's not what family does. But I love you, Sarah. We're sisters no matter what. But the guilt ends with this conversation."

I'm done letting other people drive for me. I've learned stick shift and I'm taking over the wheel of my own life.

With that I turn to leave, heart beating like I just finished a marathon. My strides taking me to the shelter of Noah's car are quick.

Telling your family off is hard. That's all I can think as I pick my way through the parking lot to find Noah exactly where I'd left him. Of course he hadn't moved an inch. Yet I feel like I just moved light years ahead with my life and it feels even better than my most recent orgasm.

Chapter Thirty-Three

NOAH

When I finally check my phone after Audrey heads into Common Bond I see three missed calls from my mom.

"Shit." I hit dial. It only rings once before my mom's voice comes through the phone.

"Noah?" Her voice is high pitched with worry.

"I'm sorry I didn't call you back. I came home and went right to bed and didn't see."

"I was so worried about you. When you weren't answering, I texted Colin who told me that you'd been released and were fine."

I'll have to send him a message thanking him. I'm sure Chrissy told him I took Audrey home with me last night. "I'm all right, Mom. Just a little bruised."

"I swear I've never gotten used to seeing my baby boy on that field. It's a heart attack every time you hit someone."

"Good thing I'm normally the one doling them out," I say, trying to inject some levity into my voice.

"I thought I was done with this stress when your father retired, and there you went right into it after him."

"I'm sorry, Mom."

"You didn't even do our sign to let me know you're okay. I can see it on the TV, you know. Just like I could from the bleachers." When I first started playing serious football, post peewee, Mom and I came up with a hand signal that I could do to show her I was fine. That way she would know if I had broken something, or just got the wind knocked out of me. With everything going on lately and the brutality of that hit, I forgot all about it.

"I promise I'm fine."

"Your father is worried too," she says in a way that suggests he hasn't actually *said* he was worried about me, she's just inferring it.

"I'm sure he is."

"All the football lessons are how he shows he cares."

"Mom, it's fine. I'm fine. You're fine. Everything is fine. No reason to keep rehashing it on the phone."

"I wish you two would have a more understanding relationship."

"We have the exact relationship that he wants us to have."

"What's that supposed to mean?"

"He called me the other week after my fight on the field to scold me about it, but I don't have any missed calls on my phone from *him* after getting hurt. Just you."

There's a long pause. "I'll say something to him."

"Thank you."

"You know that we both love you very much."

"I do. I love you, too, Mom. Talk to you later. Don't worry about me."

"Okay, I won't."

It's not long until Audrey gets in my car. She still hasn't said anything, and neither have I. I don't want to say something to steer her away from the conversation with her sister if she wants to talk about it. If she wants to sit in silence and soak it all in, we can do that too. I noticed she came out empty-handed and knew she wouldn't think to get a drink. I back the car out of the parking spot I've been in and circle us around to the drive-thru. May as well, we're already here.

Silence floats around us in the car like big, billowy clouds. I'm a little worried she didn't say anything to Sarah. That she went in there and couldn't find her courage. Maybe I should have insisted on going in with her. I reach over and take her hand because I think she needs the physical touch to bring her head out of the clouds.

"So…" she starts.

"So…" I echo.

"I told her there's no more money; there's no more secrets between me and you. I hope that also means no more secrets between me and her as well."

"What did she say?"

"I think she's still hurt by Tyler's infidelity. It's going to take some time for her to move on from that. I also think she's a little jealous of the freedom that I have now that she's a single mom, and wanted to trap me like she might feel trapped at times. Misery loves company and all that." Quiet falls over us again, blanketing like soft snow. "I also think she was surprised I spoke to her like that."

"Like what?"

"Like I come first and what I want is more important." A tear slips from her eye, and I can't help but wipe it away. She looks at me, eyes a soft liquid brown.

Relief floods through me, at least partially. I didn't need to worry about her. She had everything handled. I gently kiss her nose. "I'm proud of you, baby." And there's this moment of silence filled with overwhelming peace between us.

So when a voice comes through the drive-thru box, we both jump sky high. "What can I get started for you today?" Audrey puts her hand over her heart. We look at one another and burst into laughter.

Chapter Thirty-Four

AUDREY

OCTOBER

"Thanks, Davide!" I call as I step out of the black Town Car. I turn back to grab my purse off the bench. "I'm really glad your mom is feeling better." Two weeks ago, when Davide dropped me off at the game, she was battling bronchitis. "It's so wonderful that she's on the mend just in time for the holidays."

He tips his hat, which I don't think he sees as a cliché for a driver, but it definitely is. In his suit and his shiny shoes, he fits the classic driver look. "Thank you, Miss Audrey."

"How many times do I have to tell you that Audrey is fine?"

"I simply couldn't." He waves the suggestion away.

I wink at him. "We'll work on it!" I turn from the car and start heading toward the stadium with a wave. I'm not sure what he does while I'm at the game. Maybe he reads or even runs by his mom's. She apparently lives not far from here and he has easily four hours to kill. But you know what they say,

Houston is an hour away from Houston. Maybe he reclines the seat and takes a nap?

I turn the corner in the concrete and cinder block hallway and find Lydia in our usual spot. "Hey, Lydia!"

"Good to see you!"

"You too! Too many away games in a row."

She waves her hand. "Don't I know it."

"It's good to be back." We walk side by side toward the field to an area where I can see Noah before the game starts. I smile to myself thinking about how lost and overwhelmed I was the first time I came to a home game a few months ago. Crazy to think that I had no idea what it would be like, or how at ease I would come to feel. The first time I was here, I had to follow behind Lydia, not sure where I was going. Now, I walk in step with her, my cowboy boots clacking against the floor. It's surprisingly hard to find an outfit in theme for every game. Today, I'm wearing a jean skirt, my boots, and Noah's jersey tied up in the back. I'm really embracing my Texan side. Feels appropriate, all things considered. You'd think in October it would be too cold for skirts, but I remember Christmases where it was too hot for jeans.

I'm never prepared for the feeling that stepping on the field gives me. I think it's hard to tell how massive a stadium is on TV. The field seems to go on forever. If it were the horizon, you'd never find the end of it. The din of everyone moving and talking hums behind warm-up music blasting. I'm a little early, so Noah is still sitting under the goal post, cross-legged with headphones on. Press photos flash around us, and some of the WAGs who are more social media-minded have their phones out taking video. I'm sure I could do some of that and bring attention to my business, but I'm not there yet. It seems like we just got things ironed out. I want clients to come to me naturally, not because I'm attached to Noah.

My stomach flutters when Noah gets up and his eyes land on me. He jogs over, helmet in hand. His normal stature is inflated by his gear, making him tower over me more than usual. I'm sure the spikes on his cleats give him a few extra inches, too, but the pads on his shoulders make him as wide as a boulder. I'm a little dizzy being on the field, looking up at the height of the stadium ceiling. It feels like an ant wandering around under a magnifying glass.

"Hey, babe." He kisses me and I can feel the adrenaline buzzing through his lips. It soaks into me, and I embrace it like I can take some of it on for him.

"Hi, how are you?" I keep my hands thrown over his shoulders, holding him close. "Did you get all your warmups done?" I know he has a very detailed routine. Some of the other guys do too. Mack eats one singular sweet potato fry the night before. He said he did it one time in college, and they went on an eight-game winning streak, so he never stopped.

"Much better now that you're here. I'm afraid you're part of my pregame warmup now and I'll suck if I don't see you before every game."

I giggle like a schoolgirl, flattered. "Are you asking me to go to every away game?"

"If you want to? Or you could just FaceTime me before?"

"I think we can make something happen."

I fear something is already happening. So much so that I can't say no to anything he asks me for.

Chapter Thirty-Five

NOAH

The stadium is buzzing for the high-stakes game. I can feel the ground rumbling beneath my cleats in response. Today we're playing our AFC rivals, the Griffons. The season is already close to over. We are starting to back ourselves into a must-win position. The race for playoffs is on. We've been heating up, and tonight I think we might be on fire.

Sports broadcasters are already talking about the ways that the cookie has to crumble to get us in the playoffs. Right now, we're fighting for our lives to get a wildcard spot. We won't have any homefield advantage or playoff byes, but we don't need them. We just need a chance, and at seven and four we might have one.

The Griffons are one loss behind us and they're getting desperate. Everyone knows if they don't come home with something this year, their head coach is getting canned. That's the way it works in football. Each head coach has a couple years to make something happen (or have a good excuse why it didn't) and keep their job. Without a championship, Super

Bowl, or winning record to show, their ass is grass. Players aren't much different either.

We need this win to propel us into the off-season schedule.

So it's about to be a bloodbath.

Chapter Thirty-Six

AUDREY

When the door to the box opens, I'm hit by the sounds and smells. Family and friends of the team talking and laughing, music playing while the team finishes warming up on the field far below. My mouth waters a little at the smell of the food. Spinach and artichoke dip with crackers and bread sit next to big metal warmers filled with fried chicken and waffles. Looks like they've got a little brunch theme going on since this is a noon game. A huge, stainless-steel espresso machine sits behind the bar, and I make a beeline to it.

"Hi, Katie! One small hazelnut oat milk latte, please."

While she works on my coffee, I look around, seeing who's already here. Most people are carrying a drink already, a mix between coffees, waters, and mimosas. I look through the windows to the left side of the private stands where my now usual seat is located and spot my girlfriends already there. Having a "usual spot" here feels just as normal to me now as the one I have at Big Power Yoga.

I wrap my hands around the coffee cup, thankful for both its warmth and its comforting smell. I weave through everyone and smile at my friends who are already settled into the seats. I do the awkward dance of dodging feet and legs while sitting in a chair with your hands full of stuff. "Hey, guys!" Chrissy and Nash are balancing plates of food on their knees, chatting and eating. They turn their bright eyes and blinding smiles on me. "Good morning, Audrey!"

"How are y'all this morning?" I don't have an accent, despite living in Texas my entire life, but I do have use for all the southern slang. The girls nod their heads.

"Good," Nash says.

"Glad this is home and early. We need a break after all those away games. All that travel on top of the game really takes a toll on Colin," Chrissy laments.

"Thank God it's a bye week next week," Nash says, and we nod. "All the guys could use a break."

Chrissy perks up. "We should all go out and do something fun!"

Nash and I look at each other, then back at Chrissy. Her idea of fun is fancy dresses and espresso martinis, and that's not either of our vibes. Nash speaks up first, "We should go dancing!"

We all light up. "Yes!"

"Okay! Next Monday night, we'll all plan to meet at Whiskey River."

I give her a confused look. "Monday?"

"Monday is the boys' Saturday. And it will be easier for Colin to schedule." I nod, understanding. The team is used to a certain schedule, and just because it's finally their break doesn't mean they will lose that routine.

I turn to Nash. "Has Wyatt ever been two-stepping?"

She tilts her head, thinking. "I don't think so. They have country bars in Wisconsin, but they don't really two-step there." Wyatt is from Wisconsin and Nash met him when she went there to play college volleyball.

"Maybe he'll like two-stepping and fall in love with Texas." I try and reassure her.

The smile on Nash's face doesn't reach her eyes. "Maybe."

Chrissy claps her hands a few times in a quick burst. "This is going to be so fun!"

By the time plans are made and rides are settled, the boys are in the tunnel ready to run out onto the field. After they're announced, we made a quick run to the private restroom to be sure we are back and ready for kickoff.

I didn't think when I met Noah that he would come with all these wonderful people. I never disliked Hunter's friends, but we didn't click either. Somehow, even in the short time that I've known Chrissy, I know that if I ever needed anything, she would come to my aid no matter what. No questions asked. If I ever got in a fight, Nash would back me up in a second. If my car was ever stranded on the side of the highway, Colin would be there to give me a ride.

Sadly, I can't say the same for my own family.

I have no clue who here knows about my engagement. Noah could have told everyone or no one, but nobody has so much as whispered anything about me in earshot. That doesn't mean there's no gossip going on, but with the homey feeling I get from this group, I doubt it.

It's time to focus all my efforts and energy into people who put their effort into me.

———

Spirits are high Monday night as we all gather around the marble island with a waterfall edge in Colin and Chrissy's beautiful kitchen. After a huge win over Tennessee yesterday, everyone is in the mood to celebrate. With a week of rest in front of them, they have plenty of time to nurse their inevitable hangovers.

Jaden is playing pop music on the aux. Everyone has their drink of choice in hand. Chrissy even had a pitcher of margaritas prepped for us when we arrived. That's what I'm sipping on. I can easily go to vodka soda or vodka cranberry at the bar and not get too far into mixing my liquor. I look around at everyone, probably fifteen or twenty people altogether. Some of the guys brought women I've never met.

Nash, Chrissy, Wyatt, Colin, Noah, and I are all hanging around. I'm checking out Chrissy's cowgirl boots, which are sparkly, of course. Nash's look like she actually wears hers to work on a farm, and not just to dance in a couple times a year. Hers are perfect to pair with Wyatt, whose boots are in even rougher shape.

I appraise Noah over the top of my margarita glass. He usually has more of a casual city or athletic style, depending on what we're doing, but tonight he pulled out all the stops. My eyes rove from his black ostrich boots to his Wrangler jeans, and I snort a little laugh over the top of my drink at his overly large belt buckle. I have no idea where he got that from. I'll have to ask him in the Uber. I lick the salt off the rim of my glass to accompany my next sip as I continue my perusal, taking in the long-sleeve shirt he wears. It's more casual compared to Wyatt's actual pearl snap shirt, but the fabric hugs his biceps, and is thin enough to see the outline of his collarbone.

I must have lost track of Chrissy because she suddenly appears to my right carrying a black tray full of pink Starburst shots. Nash shakes her head. "No! No way!" Chrissy deftly ignores her, passing around the shots.

She looks Nash directly in the eye. "We're going to have a good fucking time tonight. So drink the fuck up."

Nash's eyes dart to me, then to Wyatt next to her before she shrugs and holds the drink out for the rest of us to cheers with. Our drinks meet hers in the air then and we all tap the bottoms on the table and shoot it back. The sweet, fruity flavor hides the bite of the liquor well, and I lick the excess off my lips. "These are so dangerous!" I laugh.

Noah catches my eye with a knowing look, and I give him an innocent smile back that says *I promise to behave*. I feel his smirk all the way to my toes.

I'm sure we're a sight to see. Four Uber XLs pull up to the local country bar, and six huge dudes climb out followed by six ladies in varying states of going-out attire. Everyone is shuffling, the ladies are throwing their bags over their shoulders, the men are clapping each other on the back as we make our way up the wooden ramp toward the entrance. It's completely empty. I guess that's what Chrissy meant by Colin's scheduling.

The bar is dark, but the accent lights are swirling. In the middle there's a huge dance floor with a wooden guardrail around it for people to sit on barstools. A few Hurricane couples are already spinning their way around the sawdust floor to the country song playing over the speakers. Noah and I are standing behind Wyatt and Nash while they order their drinks.

While they wait for the bartender to grab their beers, they turn to us and Wyatt says, "When I was in college there were only two bars in the whole town. Tuesdays they had quarter night where all well liquor was only twenty-five cents."

"I am so jealous. Houston has never seen drinks cheaper than five dollars, ever. How could you not get shit faced when it's that good of a deal?"

Nash laughs and swats Wyatt's shoulder. "Oh, he did."

Wyatt leans closer to us and talks loudly in our ears to be heard over the music. "I had a buddy, the kicker on the football team, who would show up with a Ziploc bag of coins to pay for his drinks. It would last him all night; I shit you not."

I blink once or twice. "Wow, Wisconsin sounds like another planet."

"It is," Nash adds quickly.

The bartender, a woman with dark hair and a tied-up checkered shirt, sets down their beer bottles and Wyatt whips his wallet out of his back pocket to pay. Noah steps in and puts his hand over Wyatt's, stopping him.

"Rookies!" Three young men quickly step up to the bar, already reaching for their pockets. Two I recognize from seeing them around, the other I don't know at all. I watch as the rookies decide who's going to pay. The one with dark hair and tan skin pays, then slips his wallet back in his pocket and saunters off. The other two seem to be deciding who will pay for my and Noah's drinks, and the third wanders off in the same direction as the first.

I look at Noah. "What is that about?"

He shrugs. "Everyone knows the rookies get stuck with the bill."

"You haze them?!" They look so young and sweet!

He holds his hands out in a *pump the brakes* motion. "This is not hazing. Trust me. I had some friends in college who were in frats, and they could tell you some horror stories. You'd never look at a stick of butter the same way again."

Nash grabs a napkin to wrap around her beer, but Wyatt whips a koozie out from his other pocket and hands it to her. He grabs a second one and shoves the navy Hurricanes koozie over his own beer bottle. I raise my brows at Noah. That's some boyfriend shit. But in all the conversations we've had, Nash insists they are just best friends. I personally think that's bullshit, but I'm not one to push, so I leave it where she obviously wants it. Let them have their secrets. I'll be the first one to say "I told you so" when they end up together. Actually, maybe second because I don't think I'll be able to beat Chrissy.

Speaking of, I look around for her. She won't be hard to find. I saw her sporting a light-up, white sequined cowboy hat about five minutes ago. Looked like something the DJ hands out at a wedding to get the crowd going after the grandparents have left for the night. I spot her, martini glass in hand, dragging Colin toward the dance floor.

Noah and I step up to the bartender. "What are you drinking?" she asks.

I scan the beer on tap and the liquor bottles on the shelf and decide I better stick to what I started with. "I'll have a margarita." Noah turns to the bartender and orders two. I like that he asks what I want, but speaks up for me to order. I don't often feel taken care and I'm soaking it in. The combination of his ass in those jeans, the blatant heat in his eyes, the alcohol in our systems, and how close I know we'll be when we dance... *Is it hot in here?*

I pick up my margarita after the brunette sets it down, thanking her. Noah leans toward me. "Sorry, no margarita-specific koozie."

"Would you have had one for me if I'd ordered a beer?"

"Nope." He pops the 'p' at the end. I glance over my

shoulder where Nash and Wyatt went off to. "What's up with them anyway? Nash says they're just friends."

"Oh, he's in love with her. He's just too afraid to do anything about it, and she's gone so much playing international volleyball." I nod. *That I knew.* "I assume they will eventually see what they've been missing out on."

"I get it, though. It's scary to put yourself out there. And at the risk of ruining a friendship? No way."

Noah's eyes train on me, pinning me in place. "It's worth it." I'm taken by his sincerity and the desperation in his tone. He's not convincing himself though. That extra effort is for me.

I'm amazed by Noah on the dance floor. He leads me so effortlessly; we look like the couples you see who've been dancing together for decades. He keeps the perfect pace and never steps on my toes. We're a few drinks in but that doesn't seem to have an effect on Noah's sure-footedness.

He's aware of the others dancing around us as we move in a circular motion, keeping us from running into anyone. Which is great because I am totally lost to the moment. Lost in the heat of his arms and the smell of his cologne and the feeling of his body pressed against mine. The way he leans over me slightly to meet my hands. He spins me out, around, and back as the last song ends, but when I hear the beginning notes of "The Kind of Love We Make" by Luke Combs I melt right back into his arms. We are definitely staying on the floor for this one.

Chapter Thirty-Seven

NOAH

As I guide Audrey around the dance floor, I notice how much it's filled up since we got here a half hour ago. I recognize all the dudes and nearly all the ladies. It's nice to get out of the routine of eating lunches together in our respective position rooms and let loose a little. Teams are supposed to work together *and* have fun together. Damn if I'm not having fun tonight. Audrey is so easy to lead, so eager to lean into me during a slow song. Always ready to be spun around. I keep spinning her because I love how the little dress she has on under a jean jacket twirls around her toned legs.

I keep our pace as we circle the floor, and when Luke Combs croons about turning the lights down low, I turn Audrey in my arms so I can dip her real slow. She brings her knee up, exposing more of her lush thighs, like she's been dipped a million times. I pull her back to me and our foreheads meet. We're standing still as other couples continue to swirl around us, but I couldn't breathe in this moment even if I wanted to. We don't speak because we don't need to. Her body has spent the whole song talking to mine. If I didn't know Audrey was sleeping at my house tonight and that I'd get what I desperately need, I would be dragging her out of this bar caveman style.

The song fades out and the next one starts. I haven't heard it in a million years, but you could place the beginning notes of it anywhere. Audrey pulls away from me and looks over to the girls who are doing the little tippy-toe dance girls do when they're excited. The bunch of them move swiftly toward us. I lean back, confused as to what I'm missing. It's just a Ke$ha song from 2013. I don't see what the big deal is. I realize just how wrong I am when every lady in this bar swarms on to the dance floor in mere seconds. I think some of these women could run a forty in four-and-a-half seconds.

It's like a flash mob. Audrey puts a manicured hand on my chest, puts her drink in my hand, and pushes me backward off the dance floor. "Looks like it's just the ladies!" she calls as she turns and leaves me behind. She shimmies as she speed-walks back over to the girls. I look next to me and see all the dudes lined up to watch. The women are all grouped together, stomping their feet. When Ke$ha starts singing, they start dancing.

I have never in my life seen a line dance to this song, but I'm not at all surprised it exists. They step up in little shimmy steps, then almost skate backward. Moving in one huge group like lionesses hunting together—and we are the lions watching hungrily. My eyes are transfixed on the way Audrey's hips rock, and judging by the stillness beside me, I can tell that Colin, Wyatt, and Jaden are in the same trance as me. Then all the women simultaneously drop it low when she sings "It's going down" in the last chorus. I feel my cock stiffen behind these hella starched jeans.

Colin elbows me in the ribs. "Are you seeing this?"

I nod. "Yeah, I'm seeing it."

I'm pretty sure every dude in here could die and go to heaven right now. It's like watching the *Birth of Venus* in real life. I catch a pair of eyes standing a head above everyone else. It's Mack, of course. Out there dancing his ass off with all the ladies and fucking killing it.

They repeat the same moves, facing a different direction, turning with every sequence. When they're at one-eighty, I'm treated to the whole routine again with a perfect view of Audrey's ass in that dress.

When the song ends and the girls all pile off the dance floor to find their dudes, I'm working on calming myself. It's not cool to be horned up in a bar filled with your teammates. Audrey strolls right up to me, takes her drink out of my hand, and downs it. I must look as dumbstruck as I feel because she looks at me and says, "What?"

"You *all* know that dance?"

She shrugs. "Yeah, every girl in Texas knows 'Timber'." Like the goddess flash-dance we just witnessed was no big deal. She grabs me by the hand and drags me back to the bar. I follow like a lovesick penguin. I'll bring her as many pebbles as she wants. I see Colin talking to Chrissy, trying to keep his tongue in his mouth like a cartoon dog. That dance single-handedly turned every man in this room into an animal.

I want to see Audrey this happy all the time.

We belly up to the bar. The same brunette comes up to get our drink order. These margs are hitting the spot and I don't plan on switching. Audrey is leaning over the bar to talk to the bartender. "Where do you get your nails done? They look so good!"

A linebacker walks up to us, and we greet each other with

the dude hand grab/back slap combo. "Hey, man, what's up? Having a good time?" He rubs his hands together. "Yeah, I am. There's not many single chicks here, though." I shake my head at him. "Just enjoy the time with your teammates then."

"A player's gotta play."

I laugh as he salutes me and walks off in search of someone else to greet.

I turn back to Audrey and I immediately sense something is wrong. Her previously languid body is ramrod straight. Her eyes are downcast instead of confident. I immediately hate anyone or anything that could make her look like that. I glance from her to the people behind the bar. The same girl as before, her hair bouncing around her face as she works, and a dude I've never seen before.

I tuck a piece of Audrey's hair behind her ear, hoping to bring her back to me with my touch. "Hey…" She looks up and her eyes are uneasy. Unsettled. Her mouth makes a little O like she wants to speak up but can't find the words.

"Are you going to introduce me to your friend?" The voice cuts through our bubble like nails on a fucking chalkboard. One sentence and I know exactly who this fucker is.

I stand back up to my full height. My focus solely on the pale, puny guy across the bar from me, currently wearing a shit-eating grin. He looks like the cat who caught the canary. His hair is so gelled it looks like a helmet.

I'm keeping my cool and my manners in check right now, so I stick my hand out across the bar for him to shake. "Noah Fox. Nice to meet you." I could let myself get all wound up by his insinuation that Audrey and I are just friends, but I'm secure enough in this relationship and my dick size that I'm not worried about the opinion of rats. His hand is soft as it connects with mine. I have the feeling that he's trying to squeeze hard to intimidate me, but he's not strong enough to faze me.

"Hunter Inglish." He's speaking to me, but his eyes are on Audrey. "I didn't realize NFL players had to settle for leftovers." He shakes his head in mock disbelief.

I smirk. "And Audrey didn't mention how small you are." His eyes heat. He's the kind of guy who has six feet listed on his dating profile when he's definitely closer to five-foot ten. I'm sure there's *other things* he botches the measuring on as well. He's a liar, after all. What kind of asshole can look their future wife in the eyes every day for years and tell her you're okay with something when you're not?

"If you and your meathead friends want to stay and enjoy my bar, I suggest you not speak to me like that." My fists clench at my sides. I don't want to get my team thrown out, ending our fun night, but I can't stand having Audrey around him another minute.

"You're the manager, Hunter. Don't act like this is your bar." Audrey speaks up and pride soars in my chest.

I open my mouth to reply, but I'm interrupted by Colin. "We don't need to stay." The authority in his voice is commanding. "I'm sure there are plenty of empty bars on a Monday night eager to serve an entire NFL team."

I chime in. "We're happy to spend our rookies' money elsewhere."

Colin adds, "We can easily get out of your hair."

Hunter is still for a second before he speaks. Surely waging an internal war between his job and his pride. He holds up his hands in surrender. "There's no beef here. I'm a huge Hurricanes fan." His eyes dart to Audrey. "I just didn't realize you were too."

That's it.

I put my palms flat on the wooden bar with a loud *smack*, leaning my torso over it with the intent of grabbing this dickwad by the collar. Before I can snatch it, there are three pairs of hands on my shoulders, hauling me back.

Colin leans in. "Not worth it."

I tap my hand on the bar twice and walk backward, not taking my eyes off the fucker. I can't believe after getting his ring handed back, he's still talking to her like that. Got some balls on him, that one.

I turn to look at Audrey for the first time since shit went sideways. Her brown eyes are wide and full of conflicting emotion. Our night out turned into a confrontation with her ex. Being called used in front of her new friends has to sting. The boys make sure Hunter walks away, likely crawling back into the hole he came from. I wrap my arms around Audrey, breathing in her beachy scent. Letting it settle my racing heart and the rage bubbling in my chest. I whisper through her hair, "Are you okay?" She's using her auburn curls to hide her face from Colin and the gang. Tough to have your dirty laundry aired out on a bar night, but she's not the first. I tuck her in to my side and maneuver us away from the bar top and the crowd, back toward the restrooms.

I tilt her chin up. "I'm so sorry, Audrey. Please look at me." Her eyes meet mine and I try my best to read the emotion written there. "I'm sorry. I didn't mean to lose it like that." I close my eyes against the thought. "Just—the way he was talking about you, I couldn't take it." She's still quiet and that makes me start rambling. "I will control myself. I didn't mean to embarrass you in front of all our friends. You know I'm not normally like that. I was pushed past my limit. I'll do anything to make up for it. I know you don't want any drama with him but—" I'm not even close to done with my word vomiting, but I'm stopped by her grabbing onto my shirt and hauling me to her, ending with the press of her lips on mine.

That was not the reaction I was expecting, but certainly is the reaction I live for.

Chapter Thirty-Eight

AUDREY

I swipe my tongue across Noah's lips, my tongue plundering his mouth. I can't remember the last time I was in control like this, but I'm absolutely burning from the inside out. Our tongues tangle and retreat in a hypnotic rhythm.

I pull back just enough to break the kiss. "That was the hottest thing I've ever seen in my entire fucking life." I throw my arms around his neck and go back to kissing him with fervor.

He pulls me back by a fistful of my hair. "You liked that?" He shakes his head. "That was completely unacceptable. They could have thrown us out!"

I take him by the hand and start dragging him toward the ladies' room. *More stalls. Cleaner than the men's.*

I talk to him over my shoulder as I move. "No one has ever stood up for me like that."

I pull open the door and feel it rattle on its hinges. The two girls standing at the sinks checking their makeup must see the feral look in my eyes because they make a hasty exit.

When we're finally alone, I whip around on him. "When I

left Hunter, people pitied me, but I'm glad it fell apart. I tried to do the same thing to you by not being forward, but I'm never doing that again. It's worth having the hard conversations with the people you care about." I put my hands on his chest. "But you stuck up for me, no questions asked, and I've never been so seen or so turned on in my life."

I make a beeline for the lock on the bathroom door and flip it. I love how he follows. He's so much bigger than me, but there's no resistance. It's like tonight there's only my strength.

I push him up against the door and try not to think about what might be on it. My hands immediately start to work on his belt with the giant buckle. "Whoa." He grabs my wrist. "What are you doing?"

I look him right in the eye. "You." I return to his belt. "Right here, right now." I get the belt undone. "Where did you even get this monstrosity?"

"Wyatt got us all one for Christmas. They're custom." I've got my hands on the button of his jeans. His hands cover mine, stopping my undressing. "Give me a chance to catch up! Two seconds ago I was ready to start a bar fight. I thought you were going to burst into tears, and now you're all over me?" I move up his chest to his neck and lick from his collarbone to his ear in one smooth motion. His eyes are molten when he looks down at me. "That'll do it."

He slips out of my arms to the side and pins me face first to the door. I turn my head to the side to breathe.

Noah slides his hands up the back of my legs from the top of my boots to the fringe of my dress. He presses his body against me as he moves his hands to the front and runs his pointer finger over my pussy lips. "If I pull these panties aside, would you be soaked for me?"

I'm still feeling fiery, so I grit back, "Why don't you find out?" He bites my ear while simultaneously tearing my panties to the side. The lace never stood a chance. With one swift movement, he has two fingers in me. The other hand comes up to my neckline and dips under the dress into the cups of my bra to play with my nipples.

"I need it," I pant.

"You need what?" Noah says. "Say it."

I gulp. "Your cock. I need your cock. Fuck me right now." I hear his egregious belt buckle clank as his jeans slide down his hips along with his black boxers. He pulls my thong down around my boots and flips my dress up over my ass. I feel the breeze of the strong AC, but I honestly need the icy touch. I'm burning up inside. The dancing, the rage in Noah's eyes when he almost hit Hunter, and now having sex in a public place where anyone could walk in... well, the door is locked but anyone could hear us.

At the last second, he turns us to his right to face the mirror over the sink, and with one quick thrust, Noah's in as far as he can go. He pushes me down with one hand between my shoulder blades. I put my hands out to support myself on the sink and he wastes no time starting to move. He fills that empty spot in me. I couldn't wait to have him. To show him I love him with my body. Even though what we're doing right now is not lovemaking; it's fucking. In the filthy bathroom of a bar. I haven't thought about Hunter in so long, I didn't make the connection that this is the bar he manages. Plus, Colin and Chrissy organized the whole thing, and I didn't want to be the contrary one. I knew that with Noah by my side I could handle it if I did have to see Hunter.

The new sensations overwhelm all my heightened emotions, and I'm so close. I just need—"More," I beg, and he wastes no time. He reaches around my waist, one hand holding my hip, my toes barely touching the floor, and he fits me to his perfect angle. He's so deep I can feel him in my stomach, and it's the perfect spot to intensify the circling of my clit. Stroking me higher and higher.

"That's it, baby," he croons. "Come for me."

The wave that starts in the pit of my stomach races up through my body until it hits just right, and I shatter on him. I gasp and moan, trying to keep myself from getting too close to the sink in front of me, but unable to hold myself upright on my own.

I'm still riding my high when he demands, "Look at me." I bring my eyes to the rectangular mirror in front of me and meet his electric gaze. That's all it takes to push him over the edge with me. He pulls out, and I feel the warmth of his release over my thighs.

I stay still as he tucks his cock away and turns to grab some paper towels from the dispenser. He cleans me and it feels far more intimate than what we were just doing. He throws the dirty paper towels in the trash, and in a second, he's back, his warmth enveloping me. He rests his chin on my shoulder, soaking in the moment. The two of us are locked in here while the world turns outside. "Feel better?" I nod because I do. A smile plays on his lips. "Damn, babe, that was fucking incredible. I should almost start a fight more often." He's obviously very self-satisfied.

"Maybe let's not."

He slaps my ass, kisses my mouth harshly and swiftly, then steps by me to unlock the door. "Let's get the fuck out of here."

When we get back to his place, he makes me come a few more times without the threat of a fight just to test that it's possible.

And it most certainly is.

Chapter Thirty-Nine

NOAH

"Thanks so much for coming with me. I'm sure there's tons of cooler things you could be doing on Halloween than accompanying me while I take Mikey trick-or-treating."

I lean down and peck Audrey on the cheek. "I'd do anything you wanted to do. Adult Halloween is usually just getting drunk anyway. It'll be nice to enjoy Halloween the way we did as kids."

With that we get out of Noah's car and walk to my parents' front door. Sarah lives in an apartment, so she always brings Mikey to Mom and Dad's to trick-or-treat.

Before we let ourselves in, I ask, "Where did you say Sarah was again?" Why wouldn't she want to be the one to take Mikey around?

"She's got a community college class on Thursday nights now. I guess after our fight over money, she decided to use the time she was working extra hours to go back to school for a degree that will allow her to make more money and be a more stable home for Mikey."

"What is she going for?"

"Accounting, I think. But she has a lot of basics to take since her bachelor's is in education." She opens the front door and calls out, "Mom, Dad, we're here!"

A bright blue streak of lightning comes flying out from the side hall, appearing in front of us. Mikey is wearing a football player costume. He's got shoulder pads on and a helmet that's two sizes too big, so he keeps having to push it back from covering his eyes.

Her mom rounds the other corner at the same time gazing lovingly at her grandson. "He's had that costume on since the second he got up this morning." Her eyes turn to us and land on Noah. She holds out her hand for him to shake. "You must be Noah. I'm Sally."

I reach my hand out for hers. "Nice to meet you, Mrs. Dupree."

"Oh, please. Call me Mrs. Sally at least. I'm not old enough yet to be Mrs. Dupree."

I chuckle politely. "That I can do."

Audrey turns to Mikey, hands on her thighs to get down to his height. "Did you pick this costume out yourself?"

"I did," he basically shouts, too excited to use his inside voice. Then turns instantaneously shy. "I wanted to be like Noah."

My heart melts a little at his words. I don't think I've ever been someone kids look up to. I've always been busy looking up to my dad, making sure I was doing the right things for him.

I pat my hand on his oversized helmet. "That's super cool, little man."

"Are you about ready to go?" Audrey asks and Mikey nods. "Go get your Jack-o-lantern bucket to carry your candy and we'll head out." He shoots off in the direction I'm assuming the bucket is in.

Her mom takes this chance to turn her eyes back on me. "Doesn't he look so precious in that get-up?"

I nod. "He definitely does. Maybe he'll be in the league one day and you'll have photos of him from tonight to show off at his draft party."

"Wouldn't that be something? I'm sure you're great with kids."

Audrey clears her throat next to me. I can tell she's getting uncomfortable. Is this the kind of thing she gets all the time? I can see why it's annoying.

"I'm not sure, I haven't spent that much time around them."

"Oh, well, you'll enjoy getting to know Mikey then."

"He's been fun so far. We had a great time at Jaden's pool party." Mikey had a great time. Audrey and I? Not so much. But it's what finally broke through Audrey's barriers and got us here, so it's hard to be ungrateful for it.

"You're a natural, I can tell." She pats my shoulder. "Full of fatherly instinct."

We're saved by Mikey coming back around the corner, Jack-o-lantern bucket bouncing on his wrist.

Audrey seems all too happy to have a reason to leave. "Okay, buddy, let's get going. It's already getting late."

We go right back through the front door, waving as we go. We get to the sidewalk and start walking to the left. "We'll start with this neighbor because they always have full-size candy bars," Audrey says as she walks.

We follow Mikey most of the way up the path while he makes his way to the door. We stop a few feet from the front door as Mikey goes up and rings the doorbell.

I take the time we're out of earshot to ask Audrey about her mom's comments. "Is she always like that?"

Audrey waves to the woman who opens the door. "Who? My mom?"

"Yeah."

"Pretty much." We watch as Mikey gets his first piece of candy. The bar so long it almost sticks up out of the pumpkin bucket. "Say thank you," she calls to Mikey as he turns to come back toward us.

"Even after everything from your ex? She still lays it on like that?"

She shrugs as she guides a hyper Mikey down the walkway and back on to the sidewalk. The next house has their porch light on, too, so we go up toward the door with him. We stop a few feet from the front porch as Mikey goes up again. "I don't know if it's because I've never spoken up enough, or because she doesn't know when to quit."

"I guess only time will tell on that."

We continue to walk, enjoying the cooler temperatures and the crisp feeling in the air. Mikey runs into a friend from school and his parents, so we walk together for a block. When they split off, Audrey checks the time on her phone. "We'd better start getting back, Mikey."

"I don't wanna," he whines back at her.

"You can hit the houses on the other side of this street on the way."

This consoles him for the moment, but no less than five houses later, he's in front of Audrey asking to be carried because he's too tired to walk more. "I can't carry you anymore. You're a big boy now. You'll knock me over."

I speak before I even realize it. "I'll carry you. Give Aunt Audrey your helmet and candy to carry."

He hands over the goodies to Audrey, and I bend down to let him climb on my shoulders. We walk the rest of the way home, rating the other costumes we see go by. I ranked a bunch of teenagers dressed as the apostles highest, Audrey rated a little girl dressed like Tour Guide Barbie her highest. Mikey was just looking for other football players to form a team.

We delivered Mikey right to his grandma to get him ready for Sarah to pick him up after her class.

If seeing Mikey in his adorable Halloween costumes for five years hasn't changed Audrey's mind on having kids, I'm certain nothing will. I'm still on the same page: we let it rest for a few years and check in later on. If we want different things, we move on because that's what you do when you care about someone. You want them to have what they want in life, even if it's not with you.

But I'm damn sure that for me, it's her.

Chapter Forty

AUDREY

DECEMBER

The leaves in Houston don't change colors until December. Places that have a real fall and winter are on a way different schedule. Nash told me the leaves start changing at the end of September in Wisconsin. Still, this is one of the best times to be in Texas, when there's that beautiful break between the hellscape of summer and the detrimental freezes of late winter.

Things have been so good between me and Noah. I go to all his home games and sit with Nash and Chrissy, who have become some of my closest friends. I learn all about Nash's overseas volleyball career and promise to go to her games during the upcoming inaugural season of the Women's US Pro Volleyball Federation. When Nicole isn't working, she tags along, and I think she wishes she could get an introduction to a few players.

When the Hurricanes are away, I either go and share a hotel suite with Chrissy, or I stay home and work. Noah has decided to stay a client even though I gave him a stern talking to about business ethics. He said, and I quote, "I don't give a flying fuck." Now that I know a bit more about his career, I realize that he actually owns the commercial strip The Lush is in. He's more than just a supporter, he's an investor. When I asked him why, he told me that real estate is a good investment, and that he is able to keep the rent low for Pia by owning the building. His kindness for someone he considers family makes my heart swell, and that particular "business meeting" ended with me on my knees for him in the dining room.

"Happy New Year's Eve!" Chrissy exclaims as she opens her front door for us. "Come in, don't let the heat out." It's only fifty degrees, but for Houston, that's cold. I remember when I was a kid there was a New Year's that was like eighty degrees and it was miserable shooting fireworks when it wasn't even a little chilly.

Noah, Nicole, and I step into the house chock full of Christmas decorations. I can see three different trees just standing in the entryway. I'm a little surprised Chrissy isn't the type of person to take them down the day after Christmas, but then again, I can see her enjoying the ambiance until January second. The house smells like she's been cooking and baking all day. Of course, she refused to let anyone else bring anything. You'd think with all their money they would just cater, but Chrissy loves hosting.

The days between Christmas and New Year's that are usually an unaccounted for blur are not that way when you're dating a professional football player. The Hurricanes played the last scheduled game before the break for the end of the year, so Chrissy and I packed our heaviest jackets and went with the men to Denver for the weekend. We spent the Saturday living our winter dreams with cute snow outfits and oodles of hot chocolate. We topped it off with a win on Sunday.

I worked all the days between that game and New Year's because Noah was at practice, so what else did I have to do? I could have spent more time with Mom and Dad, but they are only closed on Christmas Day and New Year's Day, so they were working too.

I'd been taking turns between sleeping at Noah's place and mine. As much as I loved waking up next to him, I couldn't leave the girls alone too long. One morning he suggested I just bring them with me, but moving my pets into his house seemed a little too serious to me.

When we walk into the living room/kitchen combo area, we're loudly greeted by the rest of the gang. Jaden is sitting on the arm of one couch looking over Wyatt's shoulder at a video on his phone. Nash sits next to them, a mug of what smells like Wassail in hand. Mack is here, too, fiddling with the remote control, flipping through the channels. He whips around quickly when he hears me say, "You guys remember my best friend, Nicole?" Nash gets to us first, giving us all hugs in turn.

"Good to see you, girl," Nash says to Nicole, who in turn points at her mug and asks, "Can I have one of those?" Nash takes her by the hand and brings her to the stovetop where a pot is bubbling away.

"Do you guys want anything to drink?" Chrissy calls from near the enormous fridge.

"We're good for now," I call back as Noah and I take a seat on the couch.

I lean over to Wyatt. "How was your first Texas Christmas?"

"I couldn't get on that flight to Wisconsin fast enough."

"You got to see your family?"

"Yeah, I left the day after we got back from Denver and flew back last night. It didn't even feel like Christmas until I saw the snow-covered trees through my parents' big living room windows."

I sat back against the couch. "Huh, I never thought about that. I don't think we've ever had a white Christmas here. At least not in my memory. There's been years where it's too hot to wear jeans on Christmas Day."

Wyatt visibly frowns. "Ugh, that sounds disgusting."

"I think over time you get used to it. It's the same as the saying about home being where the heart is. Christmas is about the people you're with, not the weather." He only grunts in response, saved from a reply by Nash sitting back down with her steaming mug clutched in her hands.

"I didn't know if we'd see you tonight or not," I say to her.

"I'm so glad I got to come home for the holidays. There really was no reason to stay in Rome since the season is over, and when next season starts in January, I'll be playing here."

"I'm so excited for you. I'm going to be at every home game."

She barks a self-deprecating laugh. "You'll be the only one in the stadium."

"Nonsense," says Noah. "It will be her, me, Wyatt, Jaden, and Mack, and no one else."

Mack turns up the volume so loud we have to end our conversation. He points to the TV. "The game is on."

I look sideways at Nash. "Because what else would football players do on their time off if not watch college football?"

She shakes her head. "They can't go one minute without it."

At halftime when I get up to use the restroom, I spot

Nicole and Mack standing close and talking over what remains of the amazing Zuppa Toscana soup Chrissy made. Nicole is quite literally batting her eyelashes; something I've never seen her do for any man, but I don't interrupt. I just slink by.

When the game ends after three overtimes, with whatever confusing rules college football has for overtime, the girls gang up to choose the next activity.

We all stand, arms crossed in front of the TV. Chrissy is—obviously—our leader. "*When Harry Met Sally* has the ultimate New Year's Eve scene."

The men acquiesce knowing that in two hours they're going to be able to go outside and blow things up. But when I look over at them, while Billy Crystal runs through the streets of New York to get to Meg Ryan, they're all enraptured.

Finally, it's fifteen til midnight and it's time to go out into the cul-de-sac and get ready to blast in the New Year with my friends—new and old. We all bundle up, except Wyatt, who walks out in his jeans and T-shirt.

We carry folding chairs out to the front lawn so those of us who don't want to shoot fireworks can sit and watch. Before all the fun begins, Chrissy comes out of the house with a huge bowl.

She motions for us all to gather around. "In Latin America, a New Year's tradition is to eat twelve grapes to bring good luck, so I went and got exactly ninety-six grapes for us." She walks around us and hands each of us our grapes. I sit in the lawn chair next to Nicole and eat mine. We watch all the guys eat half their grapes at one time.

I put another grape in my mouth. "So I saw you chatting with Mack during the game."

"Chatting?" Nicole says. "What is this, *Love Island*? We

weren't *having a chat*, we were just talking." Her fake British accent is horrible.

"I was just curious." I laugh.

"Nothing honestly, he's not exactly my type." I open my mouth to ask her exactly what her type is because she never had many dates in school, but I'm interrupted by the start of the countdown.

"Ten!"

I get up and make my way over to where Noah stands.

"Nine!"

Part of me wishes we were having a cozy night on our own at Noah's house, but I think this is a memory I'll look back on lovingly in the future when things look so different.

"Eight!"

I touch Noah's arm, "Hey."

"Seven!"

He turns those green eyes on me, lit up by people shooting their fireworks off early. "Fancy seeing you here."

"Six!"

"Funny, I was just about to say the same thing."

"Five!"

He leans down and kisses me. "You literally have five more seconds until midnight."

"Four!"

"I'm sorry, I couldn't wait. You look so beautiful."

"Three!"

I can feel my cheeks flush under his gaze.

"Two!"

Finally, we both join in on the count. "One!"

Fireworks burst in the sky, so many of them it almost drowns out the cheers cropping up all around the neighborhood. Noah takes my face in his hands and brings his mouth to mine. The kiss is slow and easy, exactly how it feels to have the entirety of a new year ahead of you. No rush to do anything or go anywhere, there's still 365 days left for that. Right now is just for savoring the feeling of his lips on mine and the burnt smell of sulfur in the air.

I look up at him after we pull back. "Happy New Year," I say.

He just smiles and kisses me again, and for the first time in five years, I truly do feel like this year will be a good one.

Chapter Forty-One

NOAH

JANUARY

"Big Cats win!!!" We all jump up and down, screaming and hugging. Grabbing each other and our girls as we celebrate another NFL team's win in Chrissy and Colin's living room.

With that victory, and a loss for the Cyclops, the Hurricanes are headed to the playoffs!

For the first time in what feels like forever, I can taste the greatness coming. All that's left is to reach out and grab it.

Sure, wildcard means we don't get a break this week like some of the better-ranked teams. Yes, we have to go to California and play the Goldrush in their home stadium, but what matters is that we have a chance. One we just have to step up to.

The week of practice flies by. Every second of my day is about cramming for this game. I never even studied this hard in college. Never took classes as seriously as I'm taking this. I'm studying film like I'm a teenager trying to get a perfect score on the SAT. I only come up for food and for one episode of a TV show per night with Audrey.

Thankfully, she's understanding of what's at stake, and is grateful for any time I can give her right now with the hectic practice schedule we have.

Because she has the drive to make her own business a success, she understands the focus I have for this game. She hasn't been pouty or needy about my not sleeping over or inviting her to stay the night with me. I need to be focused. This is the most perfect I've ever had to be in my life, and I can't have anything start to unravel before the referees even flip the coin.

She's coming to California, of course. Seeing her on the field before a game has become a key part of my pregame routine. I can't be without her. Her absence would be bad luck.

I walk down the sideline now, stopping and checking on guys. I tap their helmets with my gloved hand as I go. "Let's fucking go, boys!"

Colin pats me right back. "This is it!"

"Your time to shine, baby! Let 'em know!"

I stand and watch as Colin and Dakota, the Goldrush captain, go to the refs and do the coin toss. It's announced over the loudspeaker. "It's heads. Would you like to kick or receive?"

"Kick," Colin says. Smart man. That means we'll get the ball back at the beginning of the second half.

Now I wait for the defense to do their job.

They come through. Holding the Goldrush to only a three-point field goal. They can score some points, but holding them from a touchdown is big. You want to bend, not break. Offense wins games, but defense wins championships.

All those clichés. But they're clichés for a reason.

I jog on to the field. I shouldn't, but I look up to where Audrey is sitting anyway. There's no team suite for us at an away game, so she's tucked into the stands like every other fan. *That's the only time I'm allowed to look for her tonight. No distractions.* My eyes travel a few rows above her and my eyes widen in surprise when I spot my parents. They called to tell me they were coming, but since I didn't buy their seats, I had no idea until right now where they were sitting. They're leaning close together talking so they don't spot me looking at them. My parents and the love of my life, separated by less than seven rows of stadium chairs.

My stomach drops when it hits me—they're going to meet each other for the first time. Right here.

Today.

We have to win this game. I don't even want to know what form of disappointed my dad will take if we don't come out of this with a win. I don't want that to be Audrey's first impression of him.

We run it on the first play, so I block the guy across from me to give Jaden some space to slip through. He does and goes for a couple more yards, making it third and five.

We continue to move the ball. The defense is wary of our shotgun downfield plays, so they're giving us some slack. They've also taken to a bend-don't-break style of defense. We've got patience, so we don't have a problem moving the ball slowly. The longer the offense is on the field, the more time the defense has to catch their breath.

Things are close until Nixon, our punt returner, flubs his punt return. It slips through his hands and rolls across the ground. The Goldrush recover it on our five-yard line and are in position to score before the end of the quarter. The crowd is going wild. This is the turnover of a lifetime for the home team.

"Let's go, D!" we scream from the sidelines.

It's fucking awful being on offense. Watching the defense take their stand in game-winning scenarios while I just sit on the side like an idiot, unable to do anything but cheer them on and cross my fingers. If I could play both sides of the ball and be in on every snap, I would. I've actually heard there's a kid in college doing that exact thing this season, which is wild.

Wyatt makes the stop. He's been up in the quarterbacks's face all day, not giving them any time in the pocket, and you can tell he's getting mad. He slams his helmet down when he runs off the field, frustrated that they couldn't convert in the red zone. But that's exactly what we needed.

When the first half ends, we're down 19-13. We're not out of this yet. The defense has actually saved us from this game being 29-13.

Defense continues to make stop after stop in the second half. Forcing the Goldrush to punt on their next two drives. They're the only thing keeping this game close, even as we edge toward the fourth quarter.

I line up to receive on a basic out route. When Colin calls "Blue forty-two. Set. Hut!" I burst into motion. My defenseman is all over me, but I beat him to the edge. I turn to look for the ball from Colin and see him scrambling toward me. I turn in his direction and circle back his way, giving him someone to dish to. He sees me and throws it just out of my natural reach. I dive for it and make the catch. They move the sticks, and we settle in for the next play.

Jaden is a shifty son of a bitch as he flies through the defensive line a couple plays later. We line up again at the seven-yard line.

This is it. If we don't get a touchdown here, they get a chance at one on their next possession. If they do that, we might be out of this game completely.

Colin snaps the ball, and I run the cross route behind the defensive line and toward the end zone. Colin zips it to me and I push my way with all my weight to the end zone...

TOUCHDOWN.

The stadium is horribly quiet as we get together in the end zone to celebrate. Lineman pat my helmet and bash me on the shoulders. Colin and I knock our helmets together. "Let's finish this!"

When we kick off to the Goldrush, it's the beginning of the fourth quarter. We're up by one point. A horrible amount to be up by because the only thing worth one point in football is an extra point, which you can only get after you score a touchdown or a safety. If they march down and score a touchdown, and go for two instead of the field goal, we are fucked.

Just as they have throughout this entire game, the defense holds. They're an immovable wall in the backfield. They strike fast as lightning on the blitz. The quarterback's frustration over his lack of time in the pocket has made him unfocused. They're only able to get to our twenty-yard line and are unable to find the end zone. So they have to settle for a field goal, which they make.

We take the field again, the score at twenty-two to twenty. We need a touchdown or a field goal to win. And we need to make sure we don't move down the field so fast we give the Goldrush the ball back with enough time to score again. This is when you have to lean on your offensive coordinator to know the game within the game well enough to lead you to victory.

Their defense finds their balls and makes a good final

stand. Everyone is running out of gas, but this is the time to dig deep.

Do or die.

I block for the run. I sweep out for the pass and watch as Colin throws the ball toward Jaden and it tips off his fingers and falls toward the ground. The safety is on him like glue, diving for the ball as it falls. All I can do is hold my breath as it plays out in front of me. An interception at this point will kill us. This is our last possession of the game, and it has to end in points.

I watch, not breathing, as the ball pops in and out of their hands. When it hits the turf and the refs call the play dead, I sigh with relief. It does waste a down, but it isn't a dagger to the heart.

I have no idea where the defense mustered the moxie to make this stand, but they did, and they do. We aren't able to get in the end zone. The coverage is too tight, and we are running out of attainable first downs.

We're going to have to settle for a field goal.

Our kicker is pretty new. Booker is a rookie out of Kansas State. He's not been super reliable this season, and it's been frustrating to watch him miss time and time again. He's had a lackluster year, and now we have to put this game in his hands.

I stand on the sidelines, again, as the special teams line up for the kick.

It's snapped.

Held.

Booted.

And…

It's not good.

The *doink* reverberates off the goal post and straight

through my fucking heart as our chances at the Super Bowl die right here.

The home crowd goes wild. They just witnessed their team duke it out in a super close game and come out on top.

I look at my feet. The cleats on the turf. I won't see this view for another eight months. Some might be proud of what we did this season, making it farther in the playoffs than any other Hurricanes team in the last five years, but it's not enough for me to come all this way and lose. All my individual achievements mean nothing when the team isn't winning.

I move out toward the field with my teammates and coaches to shake the other team's hands and congratulate them on moving forward. It fucking hurts to do, but it's important to be sportsmanlike. Everything feels too heavy. The pads on my chest, the muscles in my legs. Everything weighs one-hundred pounds more than it should.

I try not to literally hang my head as I approach the stands. Most of the fans have filed out of the stadium already, leaving just a few lingering. Audrey is scrolling through her phone, likely checking her email, while she waits for me. I glance up over her and see my parents collecting their things. All three of them see me at the same time. The difference in emotions on their faces are stark. Audrey is beaming at me like I hung the moon even though, if anything, I definitely just tore it down and let it all go to hell. My mom looks ready to wrap me in one of her everything-will-be-okay hugs that she saves specifically for after losses. My dad... he looks like someone spit in his ice cream sundae. They all move in unison, sliding out of their respective rows and coming down the cement steps to meet me. They're standing nearly shoulder to shoulder, all wearing my jersey, none of them realizing who the other is.

I know I have to be the one to break the ice first. "Hey,

Mom and Dad." I turn to Audrey. "Hey, babe." Their eyes immediately whip to one another and then back to me.

"Well, this is unexpected," my mom breathes.

I probably could have done that a better way. I clear my throat. "Mom, Dad, meet my girlfriend Audrey. Audrey, these are my parents, James and Nora."

Audrey stretches out a polite hand for them to shake, but my mom pushes right past it, pulling her in for a hug. She holds Audrey's shoulders in place as she leans back to take in her face. "You're so beautiful. It's so nice to meet you. I'm so glad you were here to support Noah."

I aim my thoughts at my dad, as if I could control his actions with my mind: *Do not be an asshole to her because you're mad at my performance.* To my relief he just holds his hand out to Audrey and accepts her handshake.

It seems the shock of Audrey meeting my parents at an away game of all places has worn off because she turns to me and throws her hands around my neck, her arms resting heavily on my shoulder pads. "I'm so sorry, Noah. You played really well." She pulls back to look at me. "You'll get them next year."

"If you're still on a team in their division," my dad says. And here we go.

"I'll still be here. We went to the playoffs."

"Losing the wildcard game is barely making the playoffs." He waves casually at someone behind me. Probably some offensive coordinator who was in the league when he was years ago. Everyone loved him. I just disappoint him. He looks back at us, Audrey still standing close to my side. "Now I can see why."

"What's that supposed to mean?" Audrey asks, then looks at me like she didn't mean to be so forward with my dad. I can imagine she thinks it's a bad look for her, but I love that she did it anyway.

"I warned him before this season even started that he needed to keep his head in the game. And what did he do? Go off and find a cheap distraction."

"James," Mom warns.

"No, Nora. This is his career, and he's got goo-goo eyes on a girl in the stands instead of on this make-or-break game."

"He's just one player. He doesn't make or break a game for the entire Hurricanes team. *He* didn't throw an interception. *He* didn't fumble the punt return. The *team* lost this game," Audrey spits, and it might be the hottest thing I've ever seen. "What's the point of coming here if you were just going to be a dick to Noah's face when I'm sure he's already being hard on himself for this loss?"

My dad opens his mouth and nothing comes out for a second. I see it, exactly when it crosses his mind that now is not the time or place to rip me a new one. Not just in front of my girlfriend he's meeting for the first time, but right after losing a game that I already knew the stakes of. Audrey is right. I'm going to spend the flight home berating myself over every mistake I made. I don't need him to do it here. I haven't needed that in a long time. Dad looks at me, eyes softer than I've seen them in years. "I'm... sorry, son. I just wanted you to be better than me, but I think I've been putting football before our relationship." After twenty years of lectures and lessons, I didn't expect this to happen today. He looks at Audrey, still beside me like a guard dog ready to strike. "I'm sorry that I couldn't keep my act together long enough to properly meet you. You're obviously very important to Noah."

Audrey smiles back at him, sticking out her hand. "We can start over. I'm Audrey." This time it's my dad who bypasses her outstretched hand and goes in for the hug. My mom and I stand by as onlookers as the love of my life embraces my father. I'm struck by a feeling that even though we lost this game, I haven't lost everything that's important.

When my tunnel vision recedes, I realize how long I've been out here doing family drama time while everyone else is back in the locker room. "I've got to go." I say it to Audrey, but I mean it for everyone. I kiss her and hug my parents goodbye, then back away toward the entrance to the visitor locker room. I barely make it twenty feet before the cheery little TV reporter approaches me and I groan internally.

She motions me over and I walk reluctantly into the lights in front of the camera.

She raises her microphone, but it's so loud in here I have to lean down to her so I can hear. "Noah, congratulations on making it the furthest any Hurricanes team has in the last five years. How does it feel?"

I lean in to the microphone. "Awful. We wanted to go all the way. This is the team that could do it. It sucks that we got cut out at the wildcard game, but we'll be back next year with a vengeance."

"You've had an outstanding season, especially for a player returning from injury. You received one-hundred five passes for over a thousand yards and eleven touchdowns this season. What do you attribute that success to after having such a hard time last year?"

I scan the crowd behind the camera, looking past the blinding lights the crew holds. There's not a lot of navy in the crowd, but one jersey stands out from them all. Audrey talks to Chrissy, who is obviously trying to stay cheery for the team, as she walks. I look back at the reporter; Erin I think is her name? "Her. It's her."

The reporter glances toward the stands, but if she doesn't already know who I'm referring to, she won't be able to pick her out in the undulating crowd. She smiles at me sweetly, eating up my romantic answer. "Thank you, Noah. Good luck next year."

I smile and thank her before walking swiftly away.

We may be out of the playoffs this year, but I definitely won at life with Audrey by my side.

Chapter Forty-Two

AUDREY

FEBRUARY

Postseason bliss looks good on us.

I am absolutely glowing over all the time Noah has on his hands, which he's been using to shower me with attention. He still has off-season workouts and podcast appearances to keep him busy, but besides that, I have his full attention. It feels like being carried everywhere I go.

My house is almost like an office at this point. I go there during the day to get as much work done as fast as possible. I let the girls run around and chill on the couch with me while I eat lunch, and then I run back to Noah's house after.

Earlier I got a text from Noah:

NOAH
Be ready to go out tonight.

Where?

It's a surprise. Wear your favorite yoga gear.

Oooooh 😌

It does ruin the surprise a little that I need my yoga clothes. It's obviously a class. Maybe it's private? That would be amazing. A chance to perfect my chaturanga under the eye of a knowledgeable teacher with me as their only pupil. It could be a psych out? Maybe a couple's massage? I know Noah is fond of them and goes often during the season. A hike? The weather is decent since it's February, but all the trees are dead.

Either way, I'm ready for him to come get me. Wearing my favorite set—navy leggings with a white long-sleeve top that fits tight as a second skin, I shoulder my mat right as the doorbell rings. I'm aware that I don't know that this is, in fact, yoga, but one should always be prepared. I'd be less comfortable and unable to focus if I had to borrow a mat.

"Hey, baby!" Noah calls as he strides into my house. He has those delicious man leggings under his athletic shorts. *Just the way I like it.* He greets me with a searing kiss.

When we pull away, I say, "Getting a little ahead of yourself there."

"Am I?" he mocks, thinking. "I thought we could hit a quickie before we go?" His smile is sly.

I roll my eyes even though my cheeks are bright pink, giving me away. I smack him on the chest and push him backward, out the door. "Let's go. You promised me a surprise —and don't even say you have a surprise for me in your pants or I'll smack you."

You can't give this man an inch, or he'll take you to bed.

"Babe, you ruin all my fun, but fine, let's go. The surprise in my pants will still be here later."

Chapter Forty-Three

NOAH

We pull up to a little storefront in Montrose. The front windows boast huge mandalas. I see hanging pathos just behind the windows. Their cheery green leaves cascading toward the floor. I've never been here before, but one of the trainers swears by the chakra cleansing they do.

Audrey beams at me. "What is this?"

"This," I pause for effect, "is a private tantric yoga class." She lights up. Her happiness cranks up to a ten. She claps her hands together in front of her.

"I've always wanted to do this!"

I smile back at her, my heart beating loud in my chest. I couldn't frown at this moment if I tried. I would be lying if I said this wasn't a gift for me too. I just started doing yoga, but ever since I've wanted to try something like this.

We hold hands as we walk into the studio. The smell of incense is strong, even in the front. A young woman with long, black hair stands behind the counter clicking away at the screen. She looks up when the chimes above the door jingle. "Good afternoon! Welcome to Twisted Bliss Yoga! I'm Lotus. Is this your first time here?" We both nod. She clasps her hands together. "Amazingggg." And the *amazing* sounds so feathery I wonder if she's totally here with us.

Whatever this lady is smoking, I hope she'll share.

Just kidding. I get drug tested all the time.

Audrey jumps in without missing a beat. "I'm Audrey, and this is my boyfriend Noah." My already flying heart soars higher hearing the word boyfriend on her lips. My chest puffs a little with pride.

"Nice to meet you both, have you done couples tantric yoga before?" We both shake our heads. "Do you have a regular yoga practice?"

"We're both members at Big Power Yoga on Waugh," Audrey explains. If it's possible, Lotus looks even more elated.

"Oh, great! You guys are basically pros. This will be so fun!" She steps out from behind the counter and starts walking toward the back. "If you'll follow me, I'll take you to the studio we'll be using." As she walks, she explains, "This studio has been here for twenty years. We offer everything from regular yoga, hot yoga, tantric yoga, yoga teacher certification classes, and more. This space is only fifteen-hundred square feet, so it naturally lends itself to smaller, more intimate classes. Today, we'll be in the back room." She dims the light in the small space with soft floors and a mirror along the front wall. It's mildly heated and cozy. In the center of the room there are two mats, two blocks, and two bolsters.

Lotus walks in and spreads her arms open like a dancer. "Come in, please get settled, and we'll begin."

Audrey and I put our stuff down in front of the wall right by the door. I brought us two water bottles, not knowing how heated it would be. Audrey brought her mat, which doesn't surprise me at all, but the mat Lotus provided is huge. Way bigger than a single mat.

Lotus hits play on her phone, and slow spa music starts up over the speakers. "The most important thing," Lotus begins, "is paying attention to your partner's body and listening to what they need. Don't be afraid to ask for more or less. This is meant to be enjoyable and amorous." She gestures for us to sit before her.

I've never had this much attention from an instructor before, and I feel a little watched. When my ass hits the mat, though, I feel the comfort of the familiar rubber rush over me. I look at Audrey for a split second before we get started, and I see brown eyes full of excitement. Her radiance envelops me, and her sunshine scent fills my nose. In those skintight leggings and that high pony, she looks like a yoga goddess. I might have put myself in a world of hurt planning this little surprise.

Chapter Forty-Four

AUDREY

"Make sure your backs and entire spines are touching," Lotus instructs us as we sit cross-legged, back to back on the mat. I feel Noah move closer to me and the heat of his bare back envelops me. I wish I hadn't worn my long sleeves so that I could feel more of his skin on mine. Yoga is all about being connected to your body and the feeling of being in it, but including another person as part of that is incredibly intimate. Usually, you focus on the feeling of your feet on the floor or your forehead on the mat, but with Noah pressed against me— it's him grounding me.

"Now close your eyes and take a deep breath in." Lotus brings her arms in an arch above her head. Noah and I follow. "Fill all the emptiness in your chest with breath. Inflate the ribs to their maximum capacity. Feel your partner behind you." I focus on Noah's ribcage pressed against the back of mine as he takes in air. She pauses at the top of the breath and then continues. "Now, breathe out through your nose. As long as possible. We want a longer exhale than inhale for ujjayi breath. Picture your partner's face in your mind's eye. The color of their eyes and the shape of their smile. Let that warm feeling spread through your body."

She walks a circle around us, making sure we're perfectly placed to start whatever sequence she has planned. "Great. You guys are pros. Real yogis. Breathe in. Both arms back over your head. Now you're going to twist to your right, both of you. Place your right hand on the other's thigh and your left hand on your own knee." We settle into the twist. "Breathe in to lengthen, breathe out to deepen your twist." The sensation of the stretch coupled with the feel of Noah against me is surreal. It would be overwhelming if it wasn't so comforting, so stabilizing. I twist farther and my pressure moves my hand along Noah's thigh. I press my finger into the taut muscle there. *God, that's so hot.*

Lotus walks us through coming out of the twist and switching to the left side. After that, we move on to deeper heart and hip-opening poses. "Both of you move a little to your left, so your right hips align." She watches us as we scoot a bit awkwardly. "Great. Now tuck your right leg in and straighten the left. Place your bolster parallel to your extended leg. It should be close to the shin of your tucked leg." I adjust the pillow in front of me. I'm not super open in my hip flexors, so I'm going to need the support. "Breathe in. Right arms up. Now fall gently onto the bolster in front of you." She supervises our movements. Assisting when necessary.

Once we're on the ground, laid partially over one another, I breathe in to the stretch. It's made more intense by the assistance of Noah's heavy torso over my thigh. I cactus my arms to open my chest and breathe. I melt a little when I feel Noah's hand wrap around my foot. His thumb reverently strokes my arch as we lie entangled on the mat. I have an overwhelming need to touch him that I have to satisfy. I move one arm over my head and let the one closer to him roam over his ribs. I can feel each individual rib covered by a layer of muscle. My fingertips dance along his body, delighting in every sensation.

Too soon, Lotus instructs us to move to the other side. This time I put my hands above my head and Noah allows his fingers to dance along my stomach, finding the small patch of bare skin between my leggings and shirt. The rough pads of his fingers trail along the cinch in my natural waistline. His long arms give him an advantage for grazing anything he wants. My whole body shivers at the touch, and I know he can feel every movement of it in our jumble of limbs.

After what feels like two, but in reality, was probably closer to five breaths, Lotus asks us to return to sitting cross-legged. Over the next thirty minutes she takes us through another series of hip and heart openers.

"Before we begin cooling the body down with stretching, we're going to maneuver to our peak pose." She moves around us again. "Noah, lie down on the mat. Audrey, please stand at his feet." She clasps her hands together. Standing over Noah while he lies on his back staring up at me has butterflies swooping in my stomach.

"You two are now physically and emotionally in sync, and it's time for you to allow Audrey to fly." I glance at Noah skeptically and he looks back at me with a glimmer of something in his eyes. I can't tell if it's humor or determination. Lotus is unbothered as she continues. "Noah, lift your knees. Audrey, step up to meet him. Yes, like that. Audrey, take his feet and settle them on your hips. Make sure they're on the bones, and not the stomach. They're going to support you in this soaring position."

My eyes bulge. "In the what now?" I'm not sure I'm strong

enough to not just flop around like a ragdoll over his feet. This could all come crashing down on Noah, literally.

"Okay, grasp his hands and start to lean forward slowly." I start to tip my upper body, putting my weight against Noah's legs.

He's sound under me, and when I look at him, he mouths "I've got you."

In mere seconds my feet are floating off the ground, and Noah has my full weight. My eyes are wide as I get used to the feeling of flying. I quickly remember myself and pull my shoulders back, lifting myself with my back muscles. Lotus chimes in, "Keep lifting, keep lifting!"

A smile splits across my face. "Holy shit."

This is straight up the yoga version of that scene in *Dirty Dancing*. I look down at Noah and I can see a mix of pride and desire on his face. He smiles at me, and I truly feel like nothing can stop us now.

Chapter Forty-Five

NOAH

Seeing Audrey beaming at me from above was an out-of-body experience. I knew I had the physical strength to hold her up in the flying dove partner pose, and I know I have the emotional strength to hold her up in life. What I'm not sure of is if I have the strength to hold in the "I love you" that's been trying to burst out of my mouth.

It hit me like a truck when Audrey was flying over me. Something about the symbolism of our position on the mat in relation to our position in life knocked the thought into my brain, and now I can't unthink it.

I don't know how long I'll make it without blurting it out. Knowing me, it will be at the worst possible time.

———

The next day, as I'm still thinking about what we did, I shove another crumpled piece of paper in the trash bag in my hand. Because today we're cleaning out our lockers. Even though I plan to be back next season, we do this every year. I suspect it's to allow the custodians to get them clean. Six months of heavy, sweaty use has made them pretty gnarly. Other guys are around me doing the same thing. Sorting their stuff into different bags to keep or toss. Even though we went further than we have since before my time here, there's still a bit of sadness lingering in the air. We weren't ready to be done. You never really are. And now next year, no matter how far we make it in the playoffs, it won't be the same. Teams change every year. There are never two seasons where every single man on the roster is identical to the last year. The turnover rate is too high. Trades and injuries make it an ever-swinging door.

I might be packing my stuff up, but mentally I'm choosing a locker for next year. I think Colin and I are going to try and get one next to each other. I'm friendly with the equipment manager, so I might be able to swing it.

"Noah! Coach's ready for you!" Jalenski yells.

"I'm coming." I shoulder the bag I brought to get my stuff home. The guys around me bump knuckles or slap hands as I move toward the door. One even salutes me. "Give 'em hell."

I plan to. I had a breakout season for someone coming back from injury. Especially with dealing with a new relationship and everything that came with that. I never lost focus, no matter what was going on in my home life, and the stats show it.

I sit in the chair across from Coach's huge walnut credenza. I fold my hands in my lap and wait for whatever barter he has for me. I've never renewed a contract before, so I don't know if we negotiate now, or if we video Arie in. There is a slight shadow of doubt in the back of my mind. My stats were great, and we made it to the wildcard game, but I did get into a scuffle this year, which I never have before. When reporters asked me questions, I didn't necessarily stick to the team script. After the last game, I also made impromptu comments meant for Audrey.

"Fox," he starts. "You've had a great season, but not without any blights. Fighting on the field, for example, but your numbers speak for themselves. In fact, they more than speak for themselves. You're about to get a big new contract." He pauses. "I just don't know if it's from the Hurricanes."

My stomach drops to my ass.

He continues on, "You're worth a lot. Much more than when we signed you as a rookie. But there's a salary cap to compete with, and other guys who need to get paid too." Coach never pulls any punches; he just tells you what's up. "You should go out to the market and see what you can get. You owe it to the other tight ends to up the cost of a player of your caliber."

"Okay, Coach."

I should be elated. We're talking about millions more dollars guaranteed. I'm at the peak of my value, and Coach is right to tell me I should go see what I can get. Being an NFL player isn't all sunshine and rainbows. It's not all discount double-checks and tossing the Super Bowl trophy to someone from your private yacht. The time on the road is brutal, and at the end of the season, you're at the mercy of the market and the front office. That doesn't even include the wear and tear on your body. They can offer to see if anyone is willing to pay, but if no one is, I'll be a free agent.

"Chicago has made their interest in you clear. I would suggest going to meet with them. If anyone else comes out of the woodwork, your agent will let you know."

I rise and thank him, moving in a daze from his office.

Walking down the hallway knowing I'm leaving makes everything look brand new. I'm seeing the framed photos on the walls with fresh eyes. I've taken my time at the Hurricanes for granted, thinking there's no way they would let me leave. I never realized how special it was to play in my hometown. Most are not that lucky. Wyatt had his whole world taken away from him when he got traded to Houston.

Chicago hasn't been good since its glory days in the eighties, but they're primed to get a new hotshot quarterback in the draft in April. I think he'll breathe life into the team with his painted nails and TikTok dances. Hopefully, he can stand up to the pressure of being more than an NFL athlete and become the franchise quarterback Chicago needs.

I wander, lost in my thoughts, all the way to my car. When I turn the key in the ignition, it hits me that I'm leaving Houston.

I drive aimlessly until I realize that I'm actually headed to Colin's house. If there's anyone who would have sage advice, it's him.

I know he's home; he was already leaving when I got called to the office. I park in his driveway and let myself in through his back gate. His back door is unlocked and Colin's in the kitchen, standing shirtless in front of the fridge. Likely looking for a pre-dinner snack or adult beverage depending on how his day went. The end of the season is tough. I know Colin feels like that loss is on his back. If you had a Super Bowl ring on your finger, you'd probably be looking forward to whatever tropical vacation you have planned for the off-season. Not only did we not win anything, but I didn't do good enough to keep my roster spot. Or did I do so well, I sold myself out of it? Who knows.

Colin turns, whipped cream can in hand. One look at my face and he's spraying a huge mouthful and swallowing it. He silently hands me the can and I do the same. He places it back in the fridge and starts pulling ingredients out of the freezer. We still haven't said a word.

Sighing, he turns from the fridge, arms full of sauces, a vegetable, chicken stock, and more. "You're being traded." It's not a question.

"I was encouraged to see my"—I make air quotes—"market value."

"Ah."

I stare at my feet. It takes everything in me to get one word out. "Chicago."

He nods solemnly. "That blows."

"Any advice?" I gesture around the kitchen. "That's what I came for."

"Don't wait to tell Audrey." I'm already kind of procrastinating by being here and not heading directly home. "You owe it to yourself and every tight end in the league to see what you're worth on the market." He shrugs. "The managers are going to do whatever they want to do. Ain't shit you can do about it."

"It's times like this when I hate being a puppet with shoulder pads. At the beck and call of some old asshole with billions," I spit. "Like I don't have family here. A home. A life! Like it's so easy to pick all that up, say goodbye to my teammates, and fuck off to some other city to start over again?" Colin nods in understanding. This is his third team. He was a talented quarterback in the Big 10, but not as impressive as everyone thought he would be in the league. He's not worried about getting traded yet, but any year a great rookie comes through the draft, he could be looking at QB2. Things are still better here than his last team. The crowd booed him in their own stadium.

"Audrey isn't going to want to leave Houston."

"Did you ask her?"

I'm quiet for a beat. "No."

"Maybe you should let her decide for herself."

"Her whole life is here." I cover my face with my hands. "I'm not worth giving that up for."

"Again. You should probably ask her."

"It will kill me to leave her here, and it will kill me seeing her sad if I take her away."

His back is turned to me as he sets everything down on the counter. "If she agrees to go with you, then you're not taking anything from her." He pauses. "Did you consider she just needs a reason to go? Someone to start over with knowing she'll be taken care of?"

I feel everything at once. Rage builds in my chest at the Hurricanes for offing me. Tears sting my eyes at the thought of Audrey leaving me.

"I love her," I choke.

Colin turns toward me, and with two big steps he's pulling me into a hug. Not a side arm bro hug, but the real deal. This team has been my family, the players, my brothers. Their brotherhood is something I wish I had growing up. Losing them is crushing me from one side, losing Audrey is crushing me from the other. I'm suffocating.

Colin pats my back and then pulls away. "Everything is going to be okay. Don't worry about things that haven't happened yet. Just because we won't be teammates anymore doesn't mean we won't be best friends. You won't lose me. The chances of us being on the same team for the rest of our careers was always a long shot. We'll adapt."

I take a deep breath. "I needed to hear that."

"I know."

I check the clock hanging over his kitchen sink. "I'd better get going. Audrey is waiting for me. I didn't tell her I was headed here first. To be honest, I didn't know I was coming."

He nods, understanding. We clap hands and embrace. "Go on."

Without another word, he heads off toward the primary bedroom. Maybe he's upset about me leaving and doesn't want to talk about it anymore. Or maybe he's a man who's been in a long-term relationship and knows that I'll stay here all night procrastinating going home and breaking the bad news to Audrey.

Either way, I get the hint.

I head out their back door, calling goodbye as I go, as I head to the only place I can think to go before facing Audrey.

———

The flower shop door chimes as I walk through. The man behind the counter has dark hair and a large mustache. "Can I help you, son?" The whole place smells like a bomb of expensive perfume went off.

"Yes, sir. I need some flowers."

He gives me a look that calls me an idiot. I see his name tag says Jerry. "Celebration flowers? Anniversary flowers? Apology flowers?" He's drying out a clear glass vase with a towel and it's giving bartender-hearing-you-spill-your-guts vibes.

"Bad news flowers." I remember my dad bringing home flowers for my mom as a kid. I think he did it for her birthday, but also when he had to disappoint her. One year a game got rescheduled to her birthday after they had planned a short trip, and he brought home damn near a hundred roses. They're still married, so it must have worked.

Jerry sets the vase down and moves toward the big refrigerator bursting with flowers. "Ah. I see." He reaches for a prearranged bouquet in a vase. It's overflowing with creamy pink roses and greenery. It's double the size of my head. He sets it back on the checkout counter next to the register. I step up as I grab my wallet. "That'll do it."

My heart is in my stomach as I pull my Audi out of the parking lot and head home.

I push open the front door, head still spinning.

Should I sell this house or keep it?

Keep it. For when I visit Mom and Dad.

All I want is a long hot shower and some time to journal my thoughts, but Audrey is already here waiting for me. She has a code to the door, which is great because she can be here when I get home, but it's not that great when I'd rather have time to process things before I see her. If I could get a plan together, then I could present her with both the news and answers to her questions at the same time. Unfortunately, all I have is a city and a team name.

I step out of my shoes and Audrey must hear me because she calls to me. "In here!"

I head toward the sound of her voice in the living room. My steps are hesitant, like walking slower will push away the inevitable. Things have been so good between us, and I'm about to throw a wrench in it. Maybe it's better this happens now before we're too deep in this. She was going to see the reality of the life I lead eventually. At least I haven't told her I love her yet. That will make it easy to untangle herself from me. Though, I might never be able to untangle myself from her.

My heart calms a little when I see her tucked into the couch scrolling through her phone. She's got all the low lighting on, and a throw blanket wrapped around her knees. She looks so at ease here and I feel a swell of pride that she looks like she belongs in my house.

Her eyes go wide when she sees me holding the gigantic bouquet. "Noah! They're beautiful!"

When she looks past the flowers and sees the look on my face, her face drops. "What's wrong?"

I plop down on the couch beside her and pull her, blanket and all, into my lap. She lets out a small squeak but quickly wraps her arms around my neck. My mom always told me that it's important to be physically connected to each other when you have to have big conversations.

I wear my emotions on my sleeve, so it's impossible for me to hide that anything is wrong. I can never get away with it, especially saying I like something when I don't because my face always shows my dislike.

Quickly, I decide if I want to have a preamble for this or just go for it.

I decide to rip the bandage off. "I'm being traded."

Audrey gasps, her hands flying to her mouth. "No! That's horrible!"

"Well, it's not exactly a trade. They just think I should go to the market. See what other teams are willing to pay me."

"And who's interested?"

My chin hits my chest in defeat. "Chicago." Her small hand softly touches my cheek. That simple touch brings a tear to my eye. Like when you're already on the edge and all it takes is one person to ask if you're okay.

It's not just football. Yeah, it stings getting out in the first round of the playoffs, but most of all this is my home. Where I'm from.

There's so much to do. Moving, learning a new offense,

getting to know a new group of guys. My heart starts pounding at the idea of it all. Audrey notices and says, "Hey. Whoa now. It's okay. We don't know enough to panic yet. Everything is going to be fine."

"Everything is decidedly not fine."

Her other hand comes up and makes me meet her eyes. They're full of love and that hurts even more.

There's a time limit on us now. When I leave for Chicago, this will be over. No grown woman will want to do long distance with a man she's known less than a year.

I realize she's been talking this entire time while I was lost in my own thoughts. I finally tune back in as she's saying, "We just need to make a plan. We can start with a list of everything that needs to be done." She taps around on her phone, bringing up an organizational app. She starts typing, adding checkboxes as she goes. I watch over her shoulder as the list multiplies.

- Tell parents
- Tell teammates
- Go to Chicago and scope out housing
- Plan going-away party
- Research Illinois LLC laws
- Sublet rental house
- Line up long-term care for Noah's house

I blink twice in quick succession; not sure I'm reading right. "Audrey, why are you subletting your rental?"

She looks at me like I'm the dumbest person she's ever met. "Because we're moving?"

My brain does not compute. "What?"

Her face twists in confusion. "Were you not asking me to go with you?" She barks a laugh. "Wow, that's embarrassing."

"I can't ask that of you, Audrey. We haven't even been together that long. Your whole life is here." I gesture broadly at the city sprawling out around us.

She shakes her head. "I think you know me better than anyone. I think you see me more than I've ever been seen. You practically have X-ray vision." She runs her hands down the length of my arms to reach for my hands. "There's nothing keeping me here, Noah. My parents are disappointed in me no matter what I do. I've barely seen my sister since I told her I'm done taking her shit and won't give her any more money. My business is online and can be run from anywhere." She pauses. "The only thing I'm tethered to is you. You were there for me when I needed you. Now it's my turn to return the favor." She squeezes my hands to make me look her in the eyes. "This is what I want, Noah."

I take my hands from hers and cup her face. She instinctively turns into warmth. "Right now, all I have to give you is my words and my promises, but when we get to Chicago, if that's where we both land, then you'll see my love in action."

Chapter Forty-Six

AUDREY

I knew in an instant I was going with him. The split-second thought of living here without Noah would throw me into a tailspin. I'd follow him anywhere, even if I did have something anchoring me to Houston. This is where I started, so it's kind of where I stayed. I never actively chose it. If I made a pros and cons list (which I won't), the only things under the "pro" column for Houston would be good food and Noah. And if Noah leaves…

For years I've had my nose to the ground, doing everything that was expected of me. I was a good little fiancée, and the responsible, helpful daughter. The one you didn't need to worry about. What did all of that get me? A life that seemed full, but felt like a hamster wheel, and gave me nothing but a deep-seated distrust in men. I was so suspicious of them I almost blew things with Noah because I couldn't fathom a man who's honest and forthcoming with his feelings instead of manipulating me and everything around me.

Part of the reason I don't want kids is because I can make

decisions like this without taking anyone else's future into consideration. I'll have no problem subletting my house, packing up, and heading out. I'm not tied down to anything. Reba and Dolly are easygoing and don't get a say in life-changing decisions. I don't have to find them a house in a good school district. The only thing I'm responsible for is me. That makes this an easy decision because the only other person I have to care for is Noah.

We eat dinner side by side, our thighs touching. I think we just need the physical comfort of the other being there while we quietly eat our meatloaf and think to ourselves. The TV plays a restaurant renovation show in the background, but I know neither of us are watching.

I'm not sure what's going through Noah's mind, but I can't help but think about how my parents will react to my leaving. Will they pretend to be torn up? Would it actually be true? They're losing their most helpful child. The emotional support of the whole family. That doesn't mean they'll miss me as a person. Just what I can do for them. That thought stings a little, but I'm done ignoring reality.

My to-do list for today is a mile long. There's some easy stuff on there like my usual five-fifteen yoga class, but there are some huge tasks as well. Like telling Mom, Dad, Sarah, Mikey, and Lane that I'm leaving. Not just leaving, but moving to be with Noah. That's more than getting a new job and moving cross country for it. This is committing to a relationship on top of that. Saying "Yeah, we've only known each other less than a year, but my feelings are strong enough that I'm going to a different state to be with him." That's crazy to think, even for me, and I'm the one doing it.

I decide the best way to break it to them is to stop by the

shop during lunch. Noah wanted to come, but I told him this is something I had to do myself, and he understood.

I park my car around back and walk through the employee entrance. The shop itself is bright, lit up with fluorescent lights. The walls are beige, and the floor is white-ish. It smells like oil and rust with an undercurrent of the cleaner Mom uses on the floor. I know she's at the White Pine location on Thursdays, and I know she takes lunch at exactly twelve-thirty every day. I glance at the clock outside her office. Perfect timing.

I knock twice on the slightly ajar office door. "Mom?"

"Come in, Audrey!" She puts down the pen she was holding. "What a surprise! I didn't know you were stopping by today."

I pull the chair out across from her and sit. The leather is worn and soft under my legs. "I was on my way back from the post office and thought I would stop by." I cross my legs and then uncross them. I can't seem to get comfortable. "I have some news," I finally manage. Mom raises her eyebrows at me and waits for me to keep going. I continue, "Noah might be playing for Chicago and if he is, I'm going with him."

"This seems like a huge decision."

"It's not one I took lightly."

She nods slowly, processing. Her eyes meet mine, and for the first time in a long time I feel like I'm seeing her anew. "You're happy?"

"I am." I'm in love.

"You haven't been." She rearranges the pens on the desk in front of her. "Since you and Hunter broke up, you've been different."

"That's what happens when you find out your entire relationship was built on lies."

"No, I mean you've been working your tail off. You run yourself ragged with your business, then you go and beat yourself into a sweaty pulp at those yoga classes. All so when your head hits the pillow at night, you don't have to be alone with your own thoughts for one second."

I bite my lip, pulling it between my teeth. Is that what I've been doing? Making myself a hamster in a wheel that never stops spinning?

"I love my work."

"There's other things in life besides work, Audrey."

I bark a laugh. "Yeah. I know exactly what you think those other things are."

"Enlighten me." She sets the pen she was fiddling with down and leans back in her chair.

"Children. Motherhood." We both go silent. My words hang in the air around us. We've never broached this subject before. Not truly. Not honestly. "That's what you want for me."

"I just want you to be happy."

"But you'd prefer if that came with grandchildren." I choke a little on the emotions smothering my throat. "It feels like just me will never be enough for you."

"I think maybe it's hard for you to see, from where you sit and how society makes you feel, but let me tell you. I love you kids and Mikey so much, I'm literally unable to contain it. I want everyone to feel as elated as I do to be around my children, who've grown into wonderful adults, or have their heart want to burst when they hold their baby's baby for the first time. I never meant to make you feel like that's what we expect from you."

Have I been so defensive this whole time that I took everything as a direct critique about my life when really she's just so overjoyed she can't help but be enthusiastic? I was so insecure I was willing to see my own mother's words as an attack on me. A woman who has loved me since before I was born, and the only woman in the world who could truly want what's best for me. I've put us at odds when we didn't need to be because of my own insecurities.

I take a gasping breath, tears stinging my eyes, making my vision blurry. "I'm so sorry, Mom."

She reaches across the desk to take my hand. "There's no need to apologize. You needed to figure things out on your own. Heal from the hurt Hunter caused and see things for yourself. If I tried to tell you a year ago that I didn't care one way or another, you wouldn't have believed me."

"You're right. I was so angry. But now I know that if it wasn't that it would have been another thing with Hunter. It wasn't a healthy relationship. I don't want to dance around important topics anymore. I want to say what I mean and be heard." She gives my hand a comforting squeeze. I look at her again. "I'm going with Noah."

"If it doesn't work out—and I'm not saying it won't—but if it doesn't, we'll always be here."

A smile splits my lips for the first time since we started, and I can feel the negativity being torn from my spirit like a reckoning. Things between us aren't perfect, but this is a huge step in the right direction. I'm more than relieved that I will be in a different state and not confined by our rocky relationship.

"You'd better go get packing." She rises from behind her desk, looking like the matriarch she is and wraps her arms around me.

I'm flooded with warmth in her embrace, a sense of being exactly where I need to be.

A feeling that I haven't felt around my family in so long, and it's glorious.

She keeps her arm around my shoulder as she steers us out of her office and out into the shop. Dad, Lane, and Sarah are all standing behind the counter chatting about the game that was on last night.

Mom clears her throat to get their attention. "Audrey has some big news."

I take a deep breath. This is my family and they want to support me. I need to remind myself of that instead of taking the defensive. "Noah is getting traded to Chicago and I'm going with him."

Lane is the first to speak. "How exciting for him!"

Sarah gasps, out of shock or support I can't tell. My dad stands completely still for a second, taking it in. We've never lived farther than an hour from each other. I'm the first one in our immediate family to leave the city, much less the state.

They break out of the reverie and all collapse around me for hugs and well wishes.

"When do you leave?" Dad asks.

"I'm not sure yet. Next week we're flying to Chicago so Noah can meet with the team and we can look at houses."

"Let me know what time your flight is and I'll take you to the airport." I know we have Davide, but my dad is so busy with the shop usually that this is a big deal for him to offer. I'm sure Noah will understand the importance.

"That sounds great, Dad. I'll text you the flight info."

The bell above the door chimes as a customer walks in, effectively ending our family pow-wow. My mom squeezes my hand as she lets me go to greet the patron at the front door, Dad ambling after her.

Lane wraps his arm around me in that side hug all brothers

give. "Excited for you guys." He heads off to the stacks to restock the shelves. Then it's just me and Sarah. There's a beat of silence between us. We've not been so nice to each other in the last couple months. I kind of feel like it's on her to break the ice, so I wait her out. A small smile cracks her lips when she asks, "Chicago?"

"Chicago," I reply, quoting our family favorite movie from the '90s, *Tommy Boy* starring Chris Farley.

She completes the scene. "Ugh." We break out into giggles. We both have that entire movie memorized. And it feels like it fits my life right now.

"You'll come visit me, right? Bring Mikey to see a game?"

She reaches for my hand and I let her take it. "Of course."

It's not a lot, but I think it might be the foundation of a new era between me and my sister.

———

I hurry home to meet Nicole for the season premiere of *Survivor*. The thought of this possibly being our last in-person *Survivor* night for who knows how long makes my throat tight.

When I open the door for Nicole, she immediately says, "What's wrong?" I guess I don't do a good job of hiding the look on my face.

"Noah is getting traded to Chicago and I'm going with him." Saying it for the second or third time has really pounded into my head how real this actually is. It's one thing to agree to go, it's another to tell your closest friend you're leaving her, and it's another to pack up and dip entirely.

"That's great. Right?" Her voice wobbles a bit, moving between sadness and forced enthusiasm.

Tears prick my eyes too. "Right. A new adventure." But it

comes out quiet, not like someone who is ready to set off on a new quest.

We hug and hold each other for a long time. My best friend of more than twenty years, who's dedicated her life to helping others. How effective will I be telling her that she needs to do things for herself over the phone? I'll be way easier to ignore than in person.

We finally break apart when the sounds of the episode start pouring from the TV.

"We'll do video call *Survivor* nights, right?"

"Every Wednesday they're on. Unless you're working, then we can watch them later. I'll always save them to watch with you." Sadness drifts over me again. "I won't know anyone else there, so it'll be even more important to me."

"Join a yoga studio and I'm sure you'll make fast friends."

Tears sting my eyes again. It didn't even hurt this much to tell my family I was leaving. "I don't want new friends."

We watch *Survivor*, but I know I'm going to have to rewatch it later on because I take in nothing of the story. I don't know any of the competitor's names or backstory. I don't know which one is a lawyer lying about being a teacher for game strategy. I'll be so lost in a few weeks if I don't circle back.

I guess I'll have plenty of time to rewatch while Noah is with his new team and I'm alone in Chicago.

————

"I found someone to sublet my house way faster than I thought I would, so I'm packing up now and it will all just hang out in storage until we're ready to go. Before that, I'll live with Noah." Chrissy raises her eyes at me while she washes strawberries in the sink. "I know, living together already.

That's crazy, but I think it's Noah's plan for Chicago. This is good practice. I'll know if he hangs up his bath towel before we go to a brand-new city where I don't know anyone."

"That's important to know before seriously committing. You can train it out of them, but it takes years."

I take the clean strawberries and dry them gently with a paper towel. "I think we'll just get a housekeeper and then I won't worry about it," I say with a smirk. Noah has a cleaner now, but I didn't grow up with one. That was too frivolous for my parents. I can't say I'll put up much of a fight when Noah insists we get one in Chicago though.

Chrissy dries her hands on the kitchen towel and says, "When do you leave?"

"Our flight is Thursday and we'll be there all weekend." I take the knife and start hulling strawberries. Noah and I came early to help get stuff set up for yet another team get-together at Chrissy and Colin's. He might be the quarterback on the field, but in this house, Chrissy is QB1.

"And how did the parents take it?"

I sigh and focus on the berries in hand. "Noah's parents took it well. They're used to football life. They might even move to Chicago. My parents... I feel like I just found my footing in my relationship with my mom. I hope moving doesn't break that."

"It won't." She puts her hand over mine, still holding a strawberry. "I know you love him." I startle at her words. Of course, I said them to my mom just days ago, but I thought no one else knew. I haven't even told Noah.

I meet her eyes. "I do. I haven't told him yet."

"Why not?"

"Everything's been so crazy. He's sad to leave his team. I wouldn't want him to think I'm just trying to make him feel better about Chicago, or that I felt like I had to say it because I'm going with him."

"Don't wait too long. I think he loves you too." She turns back to chopping.

I think he does too. I saw it in his eyes at our partner yoga practice. I'm not going to pressure him into saying anything before he's ready, of course. So I guess we are both just waiting for the right time.

"It's going to be lonely around here without you two."

"I'm really going to miss you. You were my first friend in the Hurricane world."

"Are you breaking up with me?"

I laugh. "No! But we are going to be long distance now."

"True. That's a harsh reality. For the boys too." We look through the kitchen to the living room where the boys are roughhousing.

"Especially for Colin." She looks at me and I can tell she's about to say something serious. I set down what I'm doing and give her my full attention. "We've been trying to get pregnant for a year now and it hasn't been working. I know he's holding everyone up, but he's stressed out about it. I'm sure I'm not helping with fertility and ovulation tracking. Jumping his bones during my fertile window whether he's in the mood or not. At first we were trying to keep it lighthearted and just kind of making love when we felt like it and crossing our fingers, but now I've had to get scientific about it. We aren't making any calls yet, but it sucks."

I knew they were going through something. Noah told me about hearing phone calls between them when they shared a hotel room, but I didn't think it was this. Even though I don't want children for myself, that was my choice. My heart breaks for Chrissy, who obviously wants it more than anything. "I'm so sorry to hear that. I know you want a family more than anything. I hope the science works for you."

She puts her hand on my arm. "Thank you. That means a lot." She starts scooping the fruit she was cutting off the board to put in its spot on the tray. "So, are you and Noah thinking about starting a family in Chicago?"

I continue cutting the last few pieces of strawberry in front of me. Since ambushing me at Noah's scrimmage during preseason, I've come to consider Chrissy a close friend. I don't think she will care that I don't want kids, but I don't want to put a bad taste in her mouth after we just talked about her trouble conceiving. But if I've learned anything from the last couple months, it's to speak your truth.

"Actually, I don't want kids." There. Not so hard. My heartbeat quickens and I feel the need to try and smooth the admission over. "I know you do and that's super cool. I love motherhood for you and hate that it's been so hard. Don't think that you can't confide in me if you want to just because I don't have a similar dream as you."

She smiles at me and I can feel my shoulders relaxing. "I'm glad you told me. I've always said if it's not one hundred percent yes, then it's a no."

I breathe a quick sigh of relief. "Exactly."

We gather the rest of the fruit we've been chopping and pile them onto a serving platter with sweetened yogurt dip in the middle. This was the last thing to put out before everyone arrived. Everything else is either in the oven or on the grill.

When we walk out the back door, with a fruit platter in hand, I notice that lots more people have shown up in the last twenty minutes. People parked and went in through the back gate, so we never saw them.

They descend upon us like vultures. I barely put the dish

on the table before hands were everywhere. The cheese plate Chrissy has takes a similar beating. That's why they BBQ so much. It takes an unimaginable amount of sheer protein to fill these guys up.

I crack a beer and take a seat on the swinging bench. I watch Noah stand next to Colin as they man the grill, and I laugh a little on the inside about how stereotypical this all is.

When did I get so comfortable with these people? I remember showing up that first day. I had been planning to sit by myself and be as quiet as possible, but Chrissy pulled me in with her dazzling smile. Once she decided we were friends, there was no going back. I was in. All in with the team, then Noah. Now I consider them family, too.

That must be why leaving hurts so bad I can barely breathe.

———

Later that night, I pull back the covers and slide into bed as Noah is saying, "I told Jaden that's crazy. You can't freeze beer into ice cubes and make it a slushy."

I shoot him a sarcastic glance. "I'm glad someone is the voice of wisdom."

Noah's head hits the pillow. "It's a tough job, but someone's gotta do it." He's quiet for a second and I can feel the sadness in it. "Who will do it when I'm gone?"

"I don't know... Probably Colin. Seems like he's the next man up." Noah rolls to his side to turn the light off and I watch the way his muscles stretch. He's got nothing on but boxers, and as much as I enjoy the view, I'm not feeling very sexy tonight. Honestly, the vibe is more lulled and diffused. The camaraderie in the air at Colin and Chrissy's dissipated on our drive home when we realized the next thing we'd be doing is flying into O'Hare to check out what could be our new city —if they offer him a position on the team.

I'm not sure if it's the cover of darkness or the comfort of the king bed, maybe a combination of the two, but my throat tightens and tears threaten my eyes.

Finally, the heartbreak of saying goodbye to the only city I've ever known hits me. I'm leaving *everything*. Nicole and I will only get to watch *Survivor* on FaceTime. I'm leaving my blood family and chosen family. No more Rice Box – my favorite Chinese takeout – on nights I'm feeling sorry for myself. No more Big Power Yoga. My breath comes unnaturally, and I try to be quieter so I don't disturb Noah.

Tears stream across my cheeks, past my ears, and wets my hair. I take a shuddering breath.

"Hey," Noah says quietly like he's shushing a fussing baby. "What's wrong?" He moves toward me, wrapping his arms around me. We lay, spooning. His words whisper over my ear. "Why are you crying?"

"I'm scared."

"Of flying?"

"Of leaving Houston." My words come out in a whisper. It feels wrong to speak at regular volume with the only other sound in the room the ceiling fan spinning on high.

His arms tighten around me. "It's okay to be sad. This is a big change." He pauses. "You can change your mind. You don't have to go with me."

I sit up so I can turn over and see his face. "I've made up my mind. I'm going with you. I can be excited to go and sad that I can't stay."

"If it's any consolation, my contract will probably only be a year or two, so if we don't like it there, it won't last that long."

"Then we would go somewhere else?"

"That's the way the NFL operates. At least next time we might be able to choose where I go together. If there are options." He rubs calming circles on the back of my hand with his thumb. "Promise me you want to go."

"I promise I'll go anywhere with you."

Chapter Forty-Seven

NOAH

I'm used to flying, living out of a suitcase, sleeping in a hotel, and eating out for every meal. I'm not used to walking up to a training facility I'm unfamiliar with. I'm also not used to this cold. February in Chicago is gray and freezing.

I welcome the warmth of the building and greet the young woman waiting for me at the door. "Welcome to Chicago, Noah!"

I smile at her, but I'm not sure it meets my eyes. "Good morning. It's nice to be here."

"My name is Amanda and I'm going to take you on a quick tour of the grounds, then we'll head up to the coach's office."

"That sounds great."

I follow Amanda through the indoor field facility (nice since it's fucking freezing), the weight room, and the meeting rooms. I can't help but look closer at the wall of trophies. When they were good, they were really good. I wonder what it was like to play on this team during the glory days. I wonder if this is my chance to be a part of something like that.

"These facilities were rebuilt in early 2000. The designer

wanted everything laid out north to south. That's also the year heating was installed under the field so the snow could be melted away."

I nod. "You really need that here. It's freezing."

She smiles brightly. "You get used to it."

I'm not sure I will.

An hour later I'm face to face with Coach Higgins. He's a taller man in his late fifties with a comically large mustache. "I think Houston is crazy for letting you go, but we are thrilled to have you here."

"Thanks, Coach."

"Of course, we will eventually have to get down to the nitty gritty, but let me start by telling you what we see in store for you in Chicago." He leans his forearms on his desk. He has a friendly smile and a welcoming demeanor. "You put up great numbers this year. Of course we love that. You maybe let things get to your head once or twice, but what I like to see in a player is passion. Especially passion that can be molded and used. We have Tanner, a great receiving tight end, but I need a blocker. That's where you come in."

"That all sounds great, sir." There's a smile on my face, but my stomach is in knots. My skin feels too tight. It feels so wrong here. We have plans to see houses tomorrow with an agent recommended by the team, but I just want to get back on a plane and be in Houston as soon as possible.

The second that Coach says he'll reach out to my manager Arie and be in contact with me later, I shake his hand and speed walk to my car.

I need to get to Arie first. He knew I would be here today, so I'm not surprised when he answers in one ring. I don't give him one second to speak.

"I can't do it."

"What the hell are you talking about?"

"I don't want to go to Chicago. Find me a way out of it."

"What if the way out is not playing?"

"There's got to be something else. I'm open to anything. Tell the Hurricanes that they weren't willing to give me the price I wanted. Something!"

"Geez, Noah, okay, I'll see what I can do."

We hang up. I'm floating, untethered to the earth.

I might be ruining my career, but all I know is that Chicago is not my future.

Chapter Forty-Eight

AUDREY

The sky is overcast in the late afternoon when our plane lands back in Houston. Chicago was nice. We did all the touristy stuff including The Bean. We met our real estate agent and saw houses in a few popular areas. The agent, a woman named Sam, held back her laugh well enough when I was confused by the air vents being on the floor instead of the ceiling. Apparently, it has to do with the cold weather.

On the day Noah went to the training facility to meet the manager and coaches, I wandered around the city on my own. I found a cozy coffee shop to set up my laptop and work on a few things. I didn't need to. Everyone knew I was out of the office, but with Noah busy and me alone in a new city, I was craving the comforting smell and ambient noises of a coffee shop. It was easier to stick to a routine than it would have been to truly explore the city and think about what my life would look like here.

A quick Google search for "yoga studios near me" returned at least ten results in various parts of the city. One particularly nice looking one wasn't too far from the last house we'd seen with Sam. *See? Everything you need is here.*

Except Nicole.

And Chrissy.

True, this coffee shop is no Common Bond. But I've done harder things than uproot my life before—like leaving Hunter—and I survived. So this will be easy-peasy.

Noah was quiet on the flight home. Normally he talks about anything that crosses his mind. I think he just has a lot to think about. I'm sure meeting the team made everything real. Maybe it helped him get excited? Maybe they told him what an asset he would be to the team, or the kind of offense they run... but I don't know because we didn't really talk about it. I feel like he isn't excited about it yet. Like he was just going through the motions, and I didn't want to cause him to worry any more than he already might be.

But as we walk into Noah's house, I'm struck with the realization that somewhere between the butterfly exhibit and this moment, it started smelling like home, and I don't like the thought of losing that feeling.

Chapter Forty-Nine

NOAH

I'm supposed to be working out at Iron Man gym, a small place that most of the Hurricanes prefer to use in the off-season, but I'm having trouble concentrating. I haven't heard from Arie yet. Every time my phone rings I dive for it. I'm shocked Audrey hasn't accused me of cheating yet. That's how cagey I've been about my phone. I've been sidestepping questions about Chicago, saying nothing is concrete yet. Which *is true*.

I try and knock all that aside and focus on my form. I could have called Colin or Wyatt to come spot me, but I felt like being alone. I can't lie to them, so I'm just not talking. I watch in the mirror as I pull the dumbbell up for a bicep curl. Sometimes it feels nice to go back to the basics.

I startle when my ringtone blasts through my headphones. Siri asks if I want to answer it, and I answer "Yes."

"Arie?"

"Noah!" Arie exclaims. He's a salesman at heart, so he's always overly cheerful. He's also great at putting lipstick on a pig. Which might be why I'm his client now that I think about it. He might be calling me to tell me there's nothing he can do, but his tone doesn't sound like he has bad news. A little bit of hope creeps into my voice. "Whatcha got, Arie?"

"Great news!" I hold my breath. "You're staying a Hurricane!"

"How? Did they change their mind?"

"I told them you'd be willing to be tagged for the franchise. This is a traditional franchise tag, so you'll get the average of the top five tight ends in the league. It gets you one more year with guaranteed money as a Hurricane. Chicago wasn't coming in higher than fifteen million anyway."

"I'll do it."

"Are you positive you don't want to talk to some other teams? We could easily get you sixteen million if you stayed on the market. Chicago just isn't going to have the cap space for that when they draft the first-round quarterback in April."

"I'm sure. I don't care about the money. I just want to stay a Hurricane." The franchise tag leaves a bitter taste in some people's mouths because it's pro-owner. They get to keep their top talent at a lower rate than market price, and I generally agree with that. The exception is if the player wants to stay. Then it's a win-win.

"Then it's decided. I'll call over to the front office and let them know. This will be pretty straightforward; there isn't any negotiation to do. The price is set by the NFL."

"Thanks, Arie."

"No problem, kid."

We hang up and I go into full-on panic mode. So much needs to be done—*undone.*

I grab a wipe and start disinfecting my seat and weights. I grab my water and keys and jog out the door.

I have to get to Audrey before she turns her keys in. I

should just call her and tell her to stop packing, but I want this to be a romantic gesture. I was there the other day helping her pack, but she insisted I not skip my workout for her today. Plans change, and ours just changed in a big way.

I'm going to ask her to move in with me.

Chapter Fifty

AUDREY

A hand lands on my shoulder and I about jump out of my skin. I swear the top of my head almost hits the ceiling of my kitchen. I rip my headphone out and spin around, ready to beat some ass. I meet green eyes that are full of excitement. "You scared the shit out of me!" He was supposed to be working out while I finish cleaning up my house for the new tenant.

Noah scoops me up, arms just under my butt cheeks so we're face to face. "We're staying." My eyes go wide. "The Hurricanes are tagging me!"

"Wait, what? Oh my God!" I scream. "That's amazing!" I wrap my wrists around his neck, careful with my dirty latex gloves, and pull his face to mine. Our kiss has an undercurrent of relief without me acknowledging that. I pull back. "How? Tell me everything. Tell me what tagging means." Noah looks slowly around at how little I have left to clean, and it suddenly clicks. "Hold up. I have nowhere to live." I look at him, lost.

This little house that I have so many memories in isn't mine anymore. "I got here as soon as I could. Hopefully before you hand your keys over."

"It doesn't matter; I already signed the papers for the sublet." I pause, considering. "Wait. When did you know you were staying?"

"Literally fifteen minutes ago. I got the call from Arie."

"But when did you tell Arie you wanted to stay?"

His voice is quiet. "In Chicago..."

It's longer than I would have liked him to go without telling me something as big as this, but it was after I already signed my house away anyway. Home is where your person is, and I was willing to follow mine to Chicago.

"It shouldn't take me long to find an apartment..." I start, making plans in my head. Writing and rewriting my to-do list.

"Move in with me."

I push back from our embrace. "What?"

"Permanently," Noah clarifies. "Move in with me."

"It's okay. I chose to put my house up. I'll find a new place."

"I don't want you to."

"This is awful fast, isn't it?"

He gives me a quizzical look. "And leaving Houston with me wasn't? Where were you going to live in Chicago?" I purse my lips. He's got a point there. "I want you to stay. I love having you in my house. I love the way the bathroom smells like your body wash after you shower. I love the way your feet feel in my lap when you're trying to get me to rub them. I love the way your hand feels in mine when you hold it to fall asleep. I'm going to love hearing the happy squeaks of the girls every morning when they get breakfast." His gaze sears mine, overflowing with emotion. "I love you, Audrey, all of you."

I think I'd be lying if I said that I was shocked to hear it. You don't invite your girlfriend to move to another state with you if you're just infatuated with her, but I didn't think the universe would throw us this bone. To be here, in Houston, where we both grew up, with our families—however dysfunctional they may be. Together.

"I love you too." I pull him back to me. The physical need to express my love is taking over my mind. A slow, emotional kiss, slowly burns, needing.

Noah reaches behind me and swipes a big hand across the kitchen island, knocking the glove box and paper towels aside. He grabs me by the hips and lifts me on to the counter. I peel off my cleaning gloves with a quick snap. Noah kisses me, guiding me back to lie flat. I flinch against the cold of the granite. We look into each other's eyes as we make love on the counter. This feels like the final solidification of us. Cementing our admissions of love with the combination of our bodies.

While it feels like goodbye to this house.

It feels more like hello to our future.

Epilogue

AUDREY

SIX MONTHS LATER

I slash an imaginary tick mark in the air. "That's number ten on the gelato counter."

"Is coffee still your favorite flavor?" Noah licks his pistachio one. He's gotten so tan in the six days we've been in Italy. The sun barely kisses his skin and it darkens. It's so unfair.

"I haven't tried any other ones, and I don't plan on it."

"Of course you don't. You like what you like."

"Exactly. No need to fix what's not broken."

We settle into the tiny bistro chairs outside of the gelato shop. Every single part of Tuscany has been nothing short of amazing. When we first walked out the back door of our private villa and saw the hills rolling over the horizon, I couldn't help but think how ugly it makes Texas look in comparison.

Who was I to say no to Noah when he suggested a spontaneous vacation? We had a couple weeks left in his off-season, and I had a light client load, so off we went. I'm sure the girls are very happy with Nicole for a week.

"I can't believe it's our last night already. I feel like I blinked and it's time to go home." I watch as people pass by us. A steady mix of tourists and locals.

"I can't say I'm not ready for American air conditioning again. I'll sleep so much better."

I sigh. "One more dinner. Saved the best for last with pasta making."

"For sure." Noah's hair is wind swept from a day of walking the cobblestone streets. "Colin recommended this chef to me, so I'm sure he's good."

I lick the last of my gelato off the tiny spoon and stack my cup in his. "Ready?"

This time he takes a deep breath. "I guess." I laugh at his reluctance to walking back up the steep hill that our villa rests on.

I punch his arm. "Come on, football player. You should be in better shape than that."

He holds his hands up in surrender. "Whoa, whoa. Excuse me for being on break."

I stand, straightening my pale pink summer dress, and collect the trash. When I come back, Noah takes my hand in his and we start the trek. We take it slowly. Stopping to look at the flowers blooming on a trellis outside of the local bakery. The warm breeze flows through my hair and cools my neck in the heat. "Do you think we have time for a dip in the pool before dinner?"

Noah gives me a knowing look, his eyes sultry. "Not with what we've been doing in the pool."

I playfully smack him again. "Noah, stop," I protest, but my stomach does a little flip as I remember Noah's lips trailing down my bathing suit on the way to my bikini bottoms damp with more than just pool water. We both wordlessly pick up the pace.

When we finally make it back to our villa with it's dark gold stone walls with a barrel clay tile roof set into the side of a hill, I see a car parked out front. "I guess the chef is already here." The caretaker of the house said he would let the chef in so he could get set up.

"What's his name again?" Noah asks.

"I'm not sure how to pronounce it, but it looks like Pippo."

We open the wooden side door and step into the main room. The kitchen and dining area are huge and open. The windows are always open since the house was designed to catch the cross breeze. An Italian man in his late forties or early fifties stands at the sink, washing produce. When he sees us come in, a smile splits his face. "Ah, my friends have arrived for the evening. Are you ready to make pasta?"

I smile back, charmed by his enthusiasm and his heavy Italian accent. I immediately get fun uncle vibes from him. "We are." I look at the kitchen table, already laid out with the necessities, a rolling pin, a pasta machine attached to the edge of the wood.

"Okay, okay. Come wash up, and we'll get started."

I stand next to Pippo as he builds a perfect flour nest for the eggs I'm about to crack.

"Now, use your hand to mix the eggs into the flour and then knead the dough. I'll keep track of the time, just keep going."

He wasn't joking when he said he'd keep track of the time. It's been at least five minutes of kneading already, and Pippo is helping himself to another glass of wine. "My arms are tired." I whine to Noah.

"Let me have a go." He steps in and takes over. I watch as Noah's forearms flex as he moves the dough rhythmically under his hands. He sees me staring. "You're drooling."

My eyes snap up. "I am not."

"It's okay, I like it." He winks.

"We have to make it through this pasta class," I whisper.

"Make it through? I'm having a great time."

Pippo comes back, wine glass in hand, and announces, "Time is done for the pasta. Now, we roll it out."

He splits the dough in two so Noah and I both have a piece to work with.

"The dough is like a lady. She must be massaged to relax her and lengthen her so that we can fill her."

I freeze and look at Noah, my eyes wide. *Did I hear that right?*

Noah must have heard the same thing as me because he's barely containing his chuckle. He attempts to cover it with a cough, and I think it would have been more obvious, but Pippo is sipping his wine again.

Once we have two pretty flat pasta flaps in front of us, Pippo comes to show us how to properly cut them. "When you fill it, don't put too much or it will come out of the sides while it cooks. Make sure to seal the edges tightly so the water doesn't get in."

Noah attempts to seal his first ravioli, but somehow, it's crooked. "Is this right?"

Pippo leans in, his eyes a little glassy. "*Perfecto.*" Pippo's glass is magically empty again. "Now, Pippo must get a glass of water because he is a little drunk."

Now it's my turn to look intently at my ravioli, trying to hide my smile.

Pippo goes to the other side of the kitchen to dig up a glass of water, and I say to Noah, "Do you think he's going to be too drunk to serve dessert?"

"I hope not. I've been looking forward to the tiramisu."

"Good thing fresh pasta isn't very hard to cook."

"Too bad it's not fried, cause then the ravioli would be toasted—like him." This time I can't hide my laugh. Hopefully Pippo thinks it's just jokes between a couple. He seems focused on getting that glass of water down.

Pippo comes back, glass of water in hand. He takes my tray of pasta—pesto and ricotta ravioli—back to the stove with him and gestures for us to come over.

"Here we have very, very salty water. Salty like the ocean." He takes a few of the pasta and drops them in. "While these cook, I will tell you a story." I lean against the counter, settling in for whatever ride I'm about to be taken on. "Are you two married?"

Oh, great start.

I smile politely. "No, we're not."

Noah pipes up. "Maybe one day."

"Women are," Pippo begins, and I internally scream, "looking for the prince arriving with a white horse to grab them and kiss them, and they go away and get married. This is what they dream." I glance at Noah and he's working very hard to look intrigued and not entertained. Pippo takes a big breath that I can tell comes from years of women drama, then he continues, "The problem is after a while, they fall in love with the pirate." He puts a hand over one eye like a patch for emphasis. This time I do chuckle and so does Noah. We're loose from a day of standing in the sun and the evening's wine.

Not as loose as Pippo, though. "And making some

children, and then the pirate remembers that he's a pirate. And he runs away.

"The lady starts to think 'ah, but Phillipo, he was loving me so much, let me try to call him'. But Pippo now," he pauses to slap one hand on his arm and wave his fingers in a wide arch. "No way. I'm sorry. Too late. So, now you understood."

Noah and I are both stunned silent for a second. He gathers his wits first. "Wow. That's… a story."

I nod in agreement. "For sure."

He scoops the pasta out of the water with a flick of his wrist. We watch as he skillfully mixes them with olive oil and tops them with grated parmesan. Say what you want about his womanizing or his drinking, but Pippo knows his way around a pasta dish.

Noah and I head to the formal dining room to enjoy the fruits of our labor while Pippo cleans up and preps the dessert.

As soon as we sit down, I say, "What a character."

"I can't think of a better person to send us off from our Italian vacation."

I take a bite and flavors of fresh basil and quality olive oil burst in my mouth. "Oh my God."

"The man knows what he's doing," Noah agrees.

"Can you imagine this life? Every day of the week going to someone's private villa, cooking food you grew up eating while getting drunk with tourists? This is his literal job."

"I thought I had the dream job, but between us, I don't think I do." I take another bite; it's so good I nearly stuff an entire ravioli in my mouth at once. "It would be nice to not get hit for money."

"That's true, but then would we have ever met?"

Noah's eyes sparkle in the candlelight between us, and I can't help but think about that first night, our dinner at The

Lush. I think I knew when Pia told me he never brought dates there that this was going to be something amazing. I just hadn't been ready to admit it yet. "I believe that if someone is meant for you, they will always find you. It might have been later on, but we were destined to find each other in this life."

I reach across the stone dining table for his hand, and we hold each other while we eat. The breeze ruffles the trees outside and I breathe in the freshness of the Tuscan countryside. After everything, I feel blessed to be here with Noah, to have this time with him away from my family and his team, and before the next season starts and football becomes the third person in this relationship.

It's all worth it. Just for moments like this.

Want to see more of Noah and Audrey? Sign up for my newsletter to get their bonus epilogue and see what they're up to a year later.

Enjoyed Red Zone Realizations? Please leave a review on Amazon and/or Goodreads!

About The Author

Emily Rex is an author living in Houston, Texas with her dog and husband. She wrote a chapter book around age twelve about guinea pigs saving the world, but *Red Zone Realizations* is her first full length novel. In high school, she used to stay up late at night writing poetry in iambic pentameter for funsies. She thinks there's nothing better than a book that makes you feel the emotion in the back of your throat.

When she's not writing, you can find her reading voraciously, spending time with her family, walking the dog, beating Elden Ring, or diamond painting.

You can find her website here or through the QR code below:

instagram.com/authoremilyrex
tiktok.com/@authoremilyrex

Acknowledgments

First and foremost, I would like to thank my husband, mom and father-in-law. This would not have been possible without their encouragement and support. I cherish all the time I spend with them, but especially this time of my life where I'm living my dream of being an author.

Thank you to my editor, Elaine, who has had to talk me off a cliff more than once. I appreciate your experience and your guidance as I navigate first time book publishing. Your kind words have given me confidence when I was sorely lacking.

To Sam at Ink and Laurel, thank you for bringing my cover to life. I'm sorry I'm so particular, but you nailed it front to back. It's truly exceeded all my expectations.

To my writer friends who have helped me along the way with problem solving, encouragement, input, critique and company— thank you.

Today I hold a physical copy of this book in my hands only because of the support of these people.

Can't wait to do it all again ☺